Penguin Luck

Penguin Luck

Kay Mupetson

iUniverse, Inc.
New York   Bloomington

Penguin Luck

This is a work of fiction. All of the characters, names, incidents, organizations, and dialogue in this novel are either the products of the author's imagination or are used fictitiously.

iUniverse books may be ordered through booksellers or by contacting:

iUniverse
1663 Liberty Drive
Bloomington, IN 47403
www.iuniverse.com
1-800-Authors (1-800-288-4677)

Because of the dynamic nature of the Internet, any Web addresses or links contained in this book may have changed since publication and may no longer be valid. The views expressed in this work are solely those of the author and do not necessarily reflect the views of the publisher, and the publisher hereby disclaims any responsibility for them.

ISBN: 978-1-4401-6058-5 (sc)
ISBN: 978-1-4401-6056-1 (dj)
ISBN: 978-1-4401-6057-8 (ebk)

Printed in the United States of America

iUniverse rev. date: 09/25/2009

For Dana

PART I

I GLANCED AT MY WATCH AS the subway screeched to a halt in the tunnel. It was past three o'clock in the afternoon. I knew that my boss would be frantic by now, glancing at his watch every minute wondering what was keeping me. I had been expected to join a lunchtime meeting at our offices with the leading investment bankers of Goldfarb, Magillan & Company. This was the first time ever that bankers of such stature were bestowing their presence upon our pedestrian conference room.

I had been delayed filing motions at the New York Supreme Court. Annoyance was rising like bile in my system, as I thought of the one court clerk in particular who had raised inefficiency to a new art form earlier that morning. I realized that in general I spent far too many days not only dealing with stone-faced court bureaucrats, but also photostating piles of superfluous material or pleading with receptionists who were blocking me from delivering documents to their bosses. And soon, on top of having a miserable morning and now being stuck in a subway, I was headed to a meeting that required my acting skills much more than any legal expertise.

I reminded myself that these tasks were innate to an associate position at a firm like mine. Pellier & Spielman was not the kind of firm most of my law school colleagues desired or chose. But, in truth, I had never aspired to the French-cuff league anyway. Working at P&S, a seven-attorney firm primarily serving the lower echelons of society, enabled me to see friends, play poker, have a romantic life, and see Max, my father. In short, for 1989, a "controllable lifestyle"—even an enviable one.

The electricity was out, and it was getting stickier in the subway car. It was a blistering hot summer day, and the temperature underground felt like it was in the triple digits. Two passengers facing me were in various stages of dozing. A burly man next to them set down his newspaper for lack of light. Getting woozy myself, I closed my eyes. My tranquility was abruptly shattered by something poking into my ribs. Three tiny silhouettes, all dressed in tattered rags, were bunched together, with the oldest one, Tania, up against my hip, her sharp elbow jabbing me.

"We won't make it," Tania said in her childish voice.

Tania was the only girl and the only one of my spirits who routinely spoke to me. She would spurt out sentences, often verbalizing the emotions and thoughts of her mute counterparts, Yankel and Aaron.

"It's already been two days; Yankel is getting weak," she added as she stroked his granite-colored hair. His head was in her lap; he looked up at me teary-eyed.

"But this is the New York City subway," I protested, in a quiet voice, even though I knew it was in vain. "We're stalled. It's a power outage. It will be over in a few moments."

"We haven't eaten in days. There's no air here. He will die by nightfall," she said.

I felt my throat constricting, sweat dripping from my hairline.

I knew what she meant. We were in a sealed cattle car steaming toward the gates of Auschwitz.

"Even if we survive the journey, what awaits us?" I whispered, exasperated. I didn't feel like dealing with the three of them right now. "Maybe it's best this way."

"No, we will not surrender," she said, her eyes blazing. "What's wrong with you?"

"Stop," I blurted aloud. "How much control do you honestly believe we have over anything?"

I saw the burly man look at me in surprise.

Suddenly, the subway car jerked, its engines purring back to life. The ghosts instantly vanished. I caught my breath, relieved, and wiped my forehead. The train moved at a spastic pace at first, picking up speed as it chugged uptown. Ten minutes later, I exited, hurrying along the four blocks. On Fifth Avenue at Forty-third Street, I turned into the narrow corner building and headed to the elevator at the end of the gray lobby.

Getting off at the sixth floor, I strode past the receptionists, down the narrow hallway, and past the windowed offices, before I readied myself to swing into the conference room. Mumbling a lame apology, I slid into an empty chair. No one looked up.

For a moment, I thought I had come to the wrong place.

The conference table was set with elegant china cups. The coffee urn, usually sequestered in the metal front cabinet, was on the sideboard bubbling up pungent French roast. Assorted cookies and leftover sandwiches graced large, silvery platters. Katherine van de Vrande was planted to the left of our boss, Lenny Spielman. Her long legs, wrapped in black fishnet stockings, swayed as she scribbled notes on her trademark pink pad. She was Lenny's assistant, but she might as well have been managing partner of P&S. Despite her lack of a law degree, through the sheer force of her beauty and wit—not to mention Lenny's unrequited desires—she made many of the office decisions.

Lenny had combed his hair down and greased it with some type of gel. Three starched white shirts sat across from him. They had gathered at the behest of one of Lenny's more colorful clients, Dick Dorf. Three weeks earlier, Dick Dorf had decided that it was time to move from the world of used automotive parts to the burgeoning field of telecom, by way of prepaid calling cards. In a miraculous feat, he had convinced his cousin, a young investment banker at Goldfarb, Magillan & Company, to consider his proposed telecommunications venture. Today, Dorf's cousin was accompanied by his renowned department head and another much younger banker, whose name I didn't know.

I doodled on some paper as I listened to the interchange of ideas on technology, telecommunications, financing, competition, and the virtues of Wall Street. Finally, I sensed by the middle-aged banker's tone of voice that the bantering was about to become more focused. I perked up.

"The financing will be lukewarm at best," the dapper William Rodes said. "But if we can ultimately roll this into a deal where one of the big boys picks it up, we may have a sweetmeat," he continued. "What do you say, Winston?" He turned to Dick Dorf's cousin.

The twenty-something-year-old sat up in his chair. "Entry into these markets may actually become attractive for the telecom giants. There may be something to this idea. But we still need to work all the numbers, Mr. Rodes," answered Winston, with deference. He sounded so professional now in contrast to his earlier conversations with Lenny in our offices the previous week.

The third starched shirt, the youngest banker, added, "Certainly a fast-growing sector of the telecom industry."

Something about his firm yet calm voice made me take a closer look at him: his angular features and suntan reminded me of a rugged cowboy.

"Where are the initial breakdowns of the markets, the spreadsheets?" Rodes asked as he looked at my boss, Lenny.

"Oh God," I said. My first comment.

All heads turned to me. Lenny fidgeted in his seat; his jacket drooped on the back of the chair framing his body. His armpits were beginning to show signs of moisture. Katherine van de Vrande kept her gaze focused on her pink pad. At that moment, our receptionist breezed in with a platter of fruits, dried and fresh. Lenny did not even give her a glance.

"This is my associate, Doreen Lowe ..." Lenny nodded toward me.

"Lenny, the reports are all done. The numbers look attractive," I interrupted.

"Very good," Lenny said, nodding.

"There's only one slight problem—they're at home," I said as we had planned. "My apologies. I forgot to bring them this morning."

"Okay. Well, then, can you fax them to our offices later?" Rodes asked.

"Too much material, particularly with the tables and research material," Lenny said. "And the clippings—those are impossible to fax."

"That much?" Rodes asked.

"Tons," Lenny responded. "How about by messenger tomorrow?"

"Would really like to start on this today," Rodes said as he reached for a dried fig and peered at it for a few seconds before addressing Lenny again. "I think Ty should go with your associate and pick up the work." He indicated the youngest banker, the one who reminded me of a cowboy.

Lenny glanced at me.

Rodes turned to Ty and continued, "Go over the documents with Doreen, get a feel for the initial calculations, and then come around to the offices. The boys can crunch the numbers later. After all, it's early."

Lenny's plan was unraveling, and I could tell he was upset. Lenny and Katherine had reasoned that we would wait until we learned of the bankers' views on the proposed venture and then knead our business plan in accordance. We had prepared three skeletal business plans, all at my home now. But the scheme was failing due to the designation of Ty as personal messenger right now.

This is going to be fun, I thought. I had planned to go to the movies with my friend, Regina Astor. Instead, I would be wading through telecom material with a workaholic investment banker.

At least one thing had been accomplished: I now knew the youngest banker's name.

"Nice going on your part," Ty said to me in the cab. "Hope you have a different day job ready." He obviously thought I was going to be handed a pink slip.

His eyes cruised Sixth Avenue while he removed a file folder from his suede briefcase. I noticed that his eyes were gray with blue specks.

Ty didn't speak again during the entire twenty-minute ride.

"This looks a little steep for a junior associate's pay stub," he said as we pulled up in front of my apartment building at the corner of Eighty-first Street and Central Park West. The Museum of Natural History dominated the opposite side of the street.

"I live with Max," I said in explanation—maybe apology—once my feet were planted on the curb.

"How long have you two been together?"

"Twenty-seven years," I said as we rode up together in the wood-carved elevator.

"Really? Interesting," he said dryly, seemingly bored with the topic.

"He's my father."

Our apartment was cool and quiet. The high ceilings, egg cream walls, and flowing floor-to-ceiling drapes intensified the stillness. Light flickered on the Persian rugs and scattered antiques. I dropped my bag on the antique front foyer desk, solid mahogany.

"Someone likes antiques," Ty said, scanning the wide space.

"My mother," I said, removing my shoes and parking them close to the desk. The rare French Charles X desk was from the early 1800s, one of her favorite finds.

My mother, Hala, had died five years earlier, right after my college graduation, but I wasn't about to be sucked into a protracted conversation about her with Ty, so I headed for the Dorf reports in my bedroom. I looked through the reports and chose the one that best reflected today's discussions. Opening the drawer, I removed a folder stuffed with newspaper and magazine clippings and grabbed the binder of industry analysis we had obtained from an AT&T executive. I picked up some unfinished graphs stacked on my desk, surrounded by invitations to parties and scraps of paper scribbled with phone numbers. I strutted back to the living room.

"Here you go; take a look. I think you can do most of it tomorrow," I said, handing it to Ty.

"Doreen, Doreen, is it? You've got to be kidding. Tomorrow is way too late. Rodes expects the first draft done with at least some attachments, by the time he comes in for his double espresso at 8:00 AM," Ty said.

I really wasn't in the mood to spend the rest of the evening working. My workday usually ended at six, and that was the way I liked it—one of the pluses of employment at P&S.

I heard the key turn in the door. Max entered after stomping his shoes on the doormat. Surprised to see a stranger in the living room, he eased over and introduced himself.

"Ty? Is that a name or a piece of clothing?" Max said, looking up at the young man who was towering over him. My father's strengths lay elsewhere than in his height: he barely cleared five feet six inches, two inches taller than I was. Once upon a time, according to him, a full head of thick, dark, wavy hair added a "good few inches."

"Max, it's probably a nickname," I said in quick interception, trying to avoid a retort from the young banker.

"Tyler Rockwell," Ty said.

As I stepped toward the kitchen, I said, "I tell you what— we can work on some of it here. I'll walk you through my calculations. But before that, we should have some dinner. Can't work hungry," I explained. "Drink?"

"I'll take a beer," Ty answered. "I need to use the phone."

Handing him the lonely Budweiser from the back of the refrigerator, I said, "Use the first line, hallway desk. I'm just going to heat up some food."

Max stared at Ty, whose lips were wrapped around the glass bottle top. "A glass too much to ask?" he mumbled.

The second line rang. Regina, my oldest childhood friend, was calling from her office. She was an account executive at a cosmetics company.

"How goes?" she yelled into the phone. "Are we on for the movie?"

"No, I don't think so," I answered.

"You supposedly left the documents at home. Did you use your famous poker face?"

"Yes and no," I said.

"Things went awry, I guess."

"Basically."

"You can't talk. Okay, call you later." Regina hung up.

I hung up too and turned to the sound of Max's voice.

"She's a good cook, Doreen is. She thinks I might die of starvation," Max called out to no one in particular, his green eyes twinkling. "She tries new things."

"Are you playing cards tonight?" I interrupted.

"I didn't see enough of your uncle for one day, so I need to watch him lose at cards tonight." The two brothers were in business together.

"It's good for you."

"Yeah, yeah."

Ty refused to separate himself from the phone and his notepad while Max and I sat drinking Cherry Heering in the kitchen. Finally, Ty was finished with the phone, and he sat down in one of the kitchen chairs; he spread out the pages on the glass tabletop.

"What do you do?" Max asked, examining Ty's face, which was framed by sandy-colored straight hair. He watched as Ty took a slow final gulp of his beer. I shot Max a "be polite" look.

"Investment banking at Goldfarb Magillan."

"The *big shots* on Wall Street," Max said.

"I guess that's one way to put it," Ty answered.

"And your father?"

"Never knew him."

Max glanced my way, muttering, "Typical American family," he said sardonically in Polish. Often, he would throw in some Yiddish expletives for special effect, but not this time.

I saw Ty give my father a funny look. He parted his lips as if about to speak, but stopped.

"Not now," I said to my father.

Max continued. "My stockbroker knows nothing. I can't understand why they pay him."

"Ty's not a stockbroker, he's an investment banker," I corrected.

"They're all the same," Max said, rising to his feet and leaving the kitchen.

I was thankful the conversation was over. "Just ignore him. Max isn't overly impressed with the moneymen of Wall Street. Nothing personal."

Without replying, Ty glanced down and began to use his calculator and beeper, the two vibrating in unison. Later on when Max and I ate dinner, Ty worked at the hallway mahogany desk. I placed a plate of food in front of him. It sat untouched the rest of the evening.

Sam, my uncle, arrived at eight o'clock for the weekly poker game. He had three blocks to walk. Seymour and Willy, friends, followed by a few minutes. The four had met right after the Second World War in Germany as "displaced persons"—all Polish-born teenage survivors of Hitler's "final solution." Forty-four years had passed since their liberation.

"What kind of name is that?" Sam whispered in Polish, referring to Ty.

"Who knows—some Americana name. Be polite. Let's play cards," Max instructed his brother in Polish. The brothers had grown up speaking both languages, Polish and Yiddish, and continued to use them alongside their less than perfect adopted English. I understood all three of their tongues, making it impossible for them to converse in secret.

""First cookies and tea, Max," Sam said, switching to English. "Hope you have some of those good Albanian chocolate cookies left."

"Belgian, Sam. You think Albania exports gourmet cookies?" My father let out a sigh for emphasis.

The balding, short, bowlegged foursome settled in at the dining room table, with sweets in hand, for their game. They exchanged jokes and gossiped as the steam from the tea glasses curled up and around their exposed scalps. During the card games, they made sure Sam won at least every fourth hand; otherwise, he would pout and threaten to go home. When he won, they hollered appreciation for his undisputable acumen. Beaming in response, he would yell, "Doreen, lucky again."

Luck had always played a mystical role in our lives. Since as far back as I could remember, the brothers, Max and Sam, weighed every event by whether it was sprinkled with such. They had been lucky during the transport from Krakow, their hometown in Poland. They had been lucky that Sam was a well-known amateur boxer and scrappy street fighter. They were lucky they were not selected at the entrance to Auschwitz by Dr. Mengele for his sadistic experiments. Over the gates to that camp, in iron casting, hung the words *"Arbeit Macht Frei,"* meaning "Work makes you free." But the young brothers claimed they quickly learned that only luck could make them free. It was the supreme force on earth.

The gold-leafed Louis XV clock in the living room chimed at the stroke of nine. Ty said he was going to give a progress report to "the boys" waiting at the Goldfarb Magillan offices. He bent down to retrieve the phone. He let out a loud scream.

"What happened?" Max and the card players looked over.

Ty's facial muscles were taut, and his eyes bulged, making him look like a fugitive stunned by approaching police car headlights. He clasped his lower back.

"I know. It's his back, just like me. But such a young man, shame," Seymour stated as the four players came over to us.

Ty remained in a twisted shape, like a huge pretzel, with the phone sprawled out on the carpet in front of him.

"I have a bad back. It's nothing a few Advil can't take care of," Ty said, his mouth pinched in pain.

"We need to get him into a position to relax the pressure," I said.

"How about the couch?" Sam blurted but then noticed Max's frown. "Okay, not the couch. Hala's couch—too fancy. How about Max's bed?"

"Don't be ridiculous. What would Max *do* with him in the bed?" Willy asked, his question squeezing through a space between his two front teeth.

"Nobody's doing anything with him in bed. The kid *needs* to be in bed," Seymour said.

"Guys, enough. Just put him in my room before he collapses, and we need to call an ambulance," I ventured as Ty moaned.

"You talk of ambulances and hospitals, *narishkeit*, not good subjects, Doreen," Max reprimanded. *Narishkeit* was one of Max's favorite Yiddish words, meaning nonsense.

Sam, his head barely clearing Ty's elbow, assessed the situation. In his socks, Sam stood at five feet, even. He grabbed Ty around his muscular waist and bent his knees in an effort to gain some leverage.

"Enough with that," Max said. "You cannot pick him up, Sam. You were a boxer, not a weightlifter. Such a stubborn mule."

"Why not? I will put him down lightly on Doreen's bed." Sam wasn't about to capitulate.

"I can make it by myself," Ty said, but he remained stationary. It seemed this was mere wishful thinking on his part.

Sam threw his sinewy arms around Ty and tried to lift him again. The card players converged on the duo as soon as they saw Sam seesawing under Ty's carriage. It took four pairs of hands, knotted and lightly age-spotted, to maneuver the six-foot, three-inch banker into a horizontal position on my bed. After succeeding, Sam covered him with my yellow and navy blue duvet and fluffed some pillows around him.

"I have something in my medicine cabinet for this," Max said as he shuffled to his bathroom. "I don't know what it is, but your mother believed in it."

"I need to get to the office tonight." Ty struggled with his words.

"Forget about the office right now. You rest and soon you feel fresh like a daisel," Sam said, satisfied with his accomplishment.

"Daisy, Sam." Max was back with some brown-coated pills and water.

I leaned over to look at the pills in Max's hand. "Take them. They're muscle relaxants, mild ones. I'll call your office and finish up some of the spreadsheets while you rest for a little while. In an hour or so when you'll feel a bit better, you can head over there."

The card game resumed, and I continued drafting and organizing the documents at my bedroom desk. Another of Sam's "lucky again" bursts made me stop and look up. Out of the corner of my eye I studied Ty, snuggled among the dozen or so pillows, surrender to slumber accompanied by the sounds of clanking tea glasses. I noticed how his skin caved toward the emphatic dimple in his chin, and recalled the occasional flicker crossing his broken left eyebrow. His hair fell on my sheets, and his fingers caressed the soft duvet. He was dozing with his angular jaw facing my pajamas, cashmere sweater, and corduroy pants strewn on my recliner. *Should hang up my clothes more often*, I thought.

Then I noticed that his straight nose was a mere two inches from my jade box, the one Regina had given me years before to keep my ghosts in. I thought that, despite their propensity to monopolize the bedroom, Ty was safe; my spirits would refrain from disturbing the transient inhabiter of my bed. I presumed they had no interest in him. Their interest lay in me and my "carrying on for them," as Tania repeatedly stated.

Then suddenly I caught sight of Tania, her tiny silhouette twirling up toward the ceiling. I waited to see Aaron and Yankel, for the trio usually traveled together. But the boys failed to show up. Glancing back at Tania, I noticed her mouth in pouting form as her index finger pointed at the bed holding Ty. She said, "No, no," before she disappeared through the ceiling.

My father startled me as he stuck his head in the doorway.

"Peter's on the phone," Max said. He must have taken in my puzzled face, because he added, "Remember him? The guy you're supposed to marry this summer."

T HREE WEEKS LATER, LENNY AND I headed to the offices of Goldfarb, Magillan & Company. We had repackaged the Dick Dorf telecom deal after the first was rejected and were set to present the new version to the investment bankers. The possibility of getting an equity stake in addition to serving as legal counsel in the new configuration made Lenny more anxious than usual. He removed his jacket for the subway ride downtown in the hopes of avoiding sweat pellets that would melt his starched new shirt and self-confidence.

Dick Dorf was waiting for us at the thirty-fifth-floor conference room, backdropped by the Statue of Liberty and the New Jersey shoreline. Looking at him, in his tight brown hip-huggers and floral shirt, I figured a New Jersey diner on Route 4 would have been a more appropriate venue for the meeting—over roast beef with gravy and mashed potatoes washed down by milk shakes.

William Rodes, Dick Dorf's cousin Winston, and two younger female associates laden with file folders entered the pristine conference room. The women passed around their business cards. No Ty in sight. Little glass bottles of Perrier and notepads with pens emblazoned with the Goldfarb Magillan emerald green logo were set in neat rows on the polished table. There were phones with blinking buttons in every corner of the room and portraits of former Goldfarb and Magillan premerger partners—all elderly white men—hung on the long wall opposite the expansive floor-to-ceiling windows.

Lenny busied himself unloading from his worn briefcase the documents he had instructed me to prepare and had reviewed word by word with scrutiny. The unusually late hours we had been keeping were getting to me; fatigue was taking its toll. My legs felt rubbery; my eyes were dry and burning. In my more than two years working with Lenny, this was the first time hardcore work had trumped his lusting after Katherine van de Vrande and the late afternoon martinis with his Vietnam buddies.

Dick Dorf began to pitch his business plan to Rodes and entourage, by way of handwritten slides that were projected onto a white screen at the head of the table. His nasal voice rose and fell, taunting my auditory senses, as he detailed his entrepreneurial plan.

"So, you're proposing to buy telecom switches and carry international telephone traffic, transatlantic?" Rodes asked, pushing his chair back from the conference table. "Like MCI?"

"Exactly. The little guys, like me, are entering the field. And there'll be big money to be made." Dick grinned.

"Deregulation is revolutionizing telecom. The entire environment is changing, fast. Dick wants to be one of the early pioneers," Lenny spoke up, his fingers damping his hair.

"I think telecom operations carrying international traffic overseas, emphasis on the word *overseas*, are the wave of the future." Dick smiled. Despite his clever words, his lack of class was palpable.

Failing to get any traction for his initial prepaid calling card venture, Dick Dorf was now coupling his original card idea with a larger telecom play—as an international telecom carrier. He was certain this combination venture would be a success and that Rodes would grab it.

"Some private investors are already on board, but we need more serious financing to play hardball. That is where you come in, Mr. Rodes," Lenny said as he glanced at me.

Rodes studied some of the charts and business models fanned out on the table in front of him. He pushed his chair back again and closed his eyes for a moment. "Nancy, please go get Ty out of his meeting, and bring him down here."

Nancy, one of the young female associates, left the room, and Rodes said as if to himself, "The kid is exceptionally talented. Great creative head."

I opened the Perrier bottle closest to me to douse the hot flashes crawling up my legs toward my neck, despite the blasting air-conditioning. Twisting my earring with my right hand, doodling with my other on a pad, granted me respite from looking directly at "the kid," Ty, when he entered the room. Ty's voice tickled at my earlobes as he approached the conference table and conversed with Rodes. He sat down at the other end.

Rodes indicated that "time was of the essence." He then turned to Lenny. "Will you be available in the next week or two, Lenny?"

"Doreen is better versed in the documents. But, naturally I'll be available for consultation throughout," my boss answered in a voice dripping with sincerity.

"Okay, let's break while Nancy brings Ty up to speed," Rodes said.

I beelined for the coffee and pecan cake on the side counter; it was long past caffeine and sugar infusion time. I needed a boost. Bill Rodes joined me.

"I guess double espresso is for mornings only," I said. Rodes's gaze was firm as he spooned two sugars into his white porcelain teacup. "Ty mentioned your predilection for espresso last time we worked on the Dorf deal," I explained.

"You have a good memory, young lady." The fit banker with graying temples took a measured look at me. I smoothed my skirt. My sling-backs were Katherine van de Vrande's style shoes, but unfortunately they hurt; I moved my cramped toes around.

"Yeah, I have a wonderful memory for people trivia. Scares some folks."

"That must come in handy sometimes."

"Sometimes. Do you have an espresso machine at home?" I asked, changing the subject.

"My wife threw it out because it reminded her of 'number one' too much." He chuckled.

"Your first wife?"

"Yes."

"That makes sense. I probably would've done the same."

"She doesn't take competition lightly."

"Neither do most investment bankers," I said.

Rodes's dark eyes glittered a bit. He glanced around to see the others busy, and then expanded upon his present wife and her ability to handle four children from his previous marriage "to an insane neurotic." They were all grown now and dispersed across the country. His oldest daughter—about my age, he guessed—was a single mother to an eleven-year-old boy, having given birth while in high school.

"He's my favorite, but my daughter won't let him fly here alone from Oakland. She's too nervous. He's her whole world, as you can imagine," Rodes said.

"And I assume she needs to work."

"Yeah, she's in retail. Nice position. Little vacation."

I took a bite of the buttery treat. It was too sweet and pecans never were my nut, but it was better than nothing. "Why don't you go and pick him up in California?" I said with a full mouth.

"What?"

I swallowed the piece and said, "Fly out and get him. Arrange a meeting out there or something and bring him back with you."

Rodes stared at me. My coffee cup rattled a bit—overstepping bounds with a Wall Street shark wasn't recommended. He slapped his cup down and stepped toward me, grabbing my face between his manicured fingers.

"You're a genius," he bellowed. "Why didn't I ever think of that?" He pressed my body up against his dark suit. He smelled of Aramis cologne and cigars.

"It's not very complicated," I suggested in a small voice.

"That's not the point. You actually *listened* to what I had to say and answered. How refreshing."

Everyone turned around. Winston's mouth was locked in an open, frozen position, in the shape of a perfect zero. My cheeks were burning like marshmallows roasting over a beach bonfire. I busied myself with chewing some more cake, as I caught sight of Ty on the other side of the room. His eyes crinkled up around the edges above a toothy smile. He winked at me.

Rodes ordered everyone back to the table for a resumption of the session.

"Ty, are you comfortable with the issues here?" Rodes asked, pulling out a chair at the head of the table. Ty's hair swayed as he nodded in agreement. Then Rodes asked, "When can you free up for this deal?"

"Well, I have the Wagner real estate deal to finish in the next couple of days, and then I can start on this," Ty said.

"That means next week sometime," Rodes said, thinking out loud. "You realize that the end of next week butts up against July Fourth, which means lots of us will be gone. You have a lot of number crunching to do."

"I'll manage," Ty said.

Lenny offered that we work on the papers in the P&S offices, so he could "assist." I wondered how he was going to be of any help from his beach chair at Cape Cod.

T HAT SUNDAY, MY FIANCÉ, PETER Baumgard, was due back from one of his frequent business excursions to Japan. He had a two-day layover in New York before he traversed the Atlantic Ocean once again, this time for the annual pearl trade show in Geneva, which was always held during the first part of July. Early summer was a hectic time for the pearl industry. Peter had invited me on the phone to have Sunday dinner with his family, as he was anxious to see me as soon as he arrived from Kyoto.

The Baumgards resided at 1279 Fifth Avenue, so I hopped on the crosstown bus to the East Side. The M86 bus wound through Central Park, which was filled with joggers and Rollerbladers buzzing alongside on the twisting paths. White-flecked branches heavy with green leaves and spiked pines trimmed the circuitous road. The muggy smell of summer filled the air. The sunlight peeked in and out of the trees as my mind poked at the uneven pieces that made up the puzzle of Peter Baumgard. He was cosmopolitan in manner, handsome in a European way, and engaging, when he cared to be. Yet he was also at times edgy, priggish, and intellectually uncurious.

Chapter 3

I entered Peter's quiet and elegant apartment house and rode the elevator to the nineteenth floor. I pushed his bell, and Teresa, in her black uniform, opened the door. Behind her, I saw the dining area ready for the customary Sunday meal. The dining table was set with formal white dishes and flatware, accompanied by crystal glasses laid out on the plain white tablecloth, which seemed starched into unrelenting cardboard.

The orderliness and predictability of Baumgard family life made me feel secure and unthreatened, like reading the end of a suspense novel before starting the first chapter. No surprises, no anxiety.

Glancing around, I saw Peter's father, a rotund and jovial man, predictably parked in his reclining chair in the corner of the living room and absorbed in *The Economist*. A crystal glass of cognac rested nearby on the side table.

Peter's brother, Eugene, came out of the bedroom he shared with James, the youngest of the three Baumgard brothers, to ask if we were going to have time for our poker game.

"Sorry, Gene, not tonight. Peter and I have plans after dinner," I said, patting his soft, curly hair. "But I hope you're studying that poker manual I got you."

Usually Gene and the younger, feistier James joined me in a few hands of poker after a Baumgard dinner. I loved spending time with Peter's two younger brothers, relished interacting with my adoptive siblings. It was a welcome contrast to the quiet of my life with Max on the West Side.

Peter came out from his quarters to greet me. He resided in the converted maid's area, containing a bedroom, bathroom, and mini-kitchen. His mother, Ingrid, referred to it as her "prince's kingdom." I examined the prince: six feet tall, slim, with dark eyes and black lashes, the kind that made women swoon.

"Doreen, you look too cheery, considering I've been away for a week," he said, kissing me.

"And you look too cheery for someone who should be quite jet-lagged," I teased, realizing that the half moons under his eyes were indeed darker.

Over Peter's shoulder, I watched Ingrid approach us in a measured gait. With her gray hair pulled back in a bun, highlighting her face, which was unadorned by makeup, she was clad in one of her sensible outfits, a dark gray knitted skirt and matching top, in addition to simple pearl earrings. I noticed the immaculate white apron tied around her padded midriff. It was an odd accoutrement, for Ingrid's hands never touched any cooking ingredient or utensil, she simply supervised her housekeeper. Yet it also paradoxically reflected Ingrid's place as matriarch and the notion that all would be nourished and protected in her kingdom.

"Hello, Ingrid. Nice to see you," I said.

"Yes. Doreen, I understand from Peter that your picks were very well received," Ingrid said. "I think you're beginning to understand the techniques involved in dealing with Japanese businessmen."

What's the big deal? The pearl suppliers based in Kyoto love designer labels—the more expensive the better. Hermes scarves and Prada wallets were perfect—obviously.

I shook my head. I had learned to look past her slightly frosty tone, for I understood that Ingrid had my best interests, or at least her son's best interests, at heart. And, for the most part, I appreciated her efforts.

Ingrid had never made a secret of the fact that she was intent upon Peter marrying what she termed a "good girl" after the empty-headed, spendthrift Tiffanys, Ambers, and Crystals he had dated earlier. And she wanted an "Ivy League–type" partner for her son, someone with "real intellect," who would compensate for

Peter's lackluster academic undergraduate record at the University of Miami. It was clear I fit the bill.

It occurred to me just then that Peter's cards had also been on the table when we met two years before. At that time, I was still in law school when my friend Regina had asked me to accompany her to buy a strand of pearls at Baumgard Nikkei. Since my first date with Peter shortly thereafter, I knew exactly who he was.

He was a young man certain that his thermostat of self-confidence had already been set in his youth and would remain as such indefinitely. Gliding through the University of Miami, he had coasted into the corner office at his father's side at Baumgard Nikkei. As the eldest scion of the pearl traders, he had no doubt about his place in the world.

During our first few months, I had enjoyed Peter's certainty in life, his easy cohabitation with his destiny, and his debonair ways in the family business. But as time wore on, in the recessed tracks of my mind, doubts had started bumping into each other like go-carts at Great Adventures amusement park. And I sensed there were already rumblings of disaffection in Peter with his dutiful life, subtle and evanescent. I was apprehensive that ultimately, as the younger Baumgards came up the ladder rungs, climbed into business, and lost their greenness, they would encroach upon Peter's monopoly, eating away at his self-esteem and sense of challenge. The membrane stretched over the drum cylinder, initially producing beautiful sounds, when pulled further would burst into little pieces, spinning to the ground like gooey confetti, worthless for making music.

I glanced up at my fiancé, noticing that his eyes were a bit uneasy and intent on me. Suddenly, I realized that my awkward pause had arrested my dialogue with Ingrid about the presents for the Japanese businessmen.

"I was helped by Regina," I said, clearing my throat. "Ingrid, I accept your compliment on her behalf. She suggested the wallets."

"That's nice, dear." My mother-in-law-to-be closed the subject and untied her crisp apron. "Now, dinner. Please, everyone to the table." She turned to her Honduran housekeeper. "Teresa, we're ready."

The four Baumgard men landed in their regular seats within seconds. The meal, consisting of roast veal, spinach, and tiny white potatoes, was washed down with wine, lukewarm German-style beer, or soda water, designated for the women and minors.

Peter kept his gaze on his father, as Alfred said, "I assume you looked into the Biwa pearls." On the outskirts of Kyoto, Lake Biwa was known for the harvesting of riverine and freshwater lake pearls. "Did Yakimoto drive you out there?"

"As always. By the way, he has a new Jag. Black," Peter said. He swallowed a sip of beer.

"What do you think of the colorful ones?" Alfred asked. His mustache was trimmed with beer foam. I knew he meant colored pearls.

"Supposedly, the Brazilians are big on the orange ones," Peter said.

"That sounds exciting," I said, feeling an urge for Peter to speak of colors: primary colors, earth tones, cool colors, warm ones, metallic colors. Recently, I had been experiencing a desperate thirst for color. The scenes in my life seemed to be playing out in monochromatic tones, and I was feeling restless.

"Colors, no, no," Peter said. "Only black or white. True pearls."

"Absolutely," Ingrid said. "Any other colors are cheap and unsophisticated. Charlatan pearls."

The word *charlatan* made me laugh. I should have known

better than to think the Baumgards would accept the notion of introducing colors into their pearl line. To them, pearls, and perhaps all things, were either black or white. Gray was the only other hue they recognized. Of course, there were South Sea, freshwater, Tahitian, Akoya, stranded, set, and dangling pearls. But, according to them, color-wise, the oyster creations were either in black or white and would remain so.

I watched as Eugene and James sat quietly through the family meal, kicking each other under the table every now and again, as talk of business floated over their heads. Ingrid ate in a deliberate fashion, absorbing the information and nodding.

After a few moments, Ingrid turned to me and asked, "How was the rest of your weekend, Doreen?"

"Friday night, Lulu came over for dinner."

"Is Lulu that doctor friend of yours?" Alfred asked.

"A resident at New York Hospital, oncology," I answered.

"Isn't she the one who wore that miniskirt at your graduation dinner?" Ingrid asked, while frowning at James, who had his elbows on the table.

I smiled at the thought of Dr. Lulu Smith. The tall, slim blonde had been born Leah Rivka Smilowicz, the fourth and plumpest daughter of an ultraorthodox Jewish family. Her name, physique, and attire gradually compressed as she engineered her way through Mount Sinai Medical School, bolstered by the generosity of private grants and the American government.

"She wears her skirts very short," I replied. "Everyone, of course, has their *mishigas*."

Yiddishisms threw Ingrid for a loop, and I knew that. Usually, I tried to avoid launching any into the atmosphere, knowing full well that this was considered a glaring "flaw" on my resume. But, sometimes I couldn't control myself.

Peter gave me a glance.

The Baumgards were Upper East Side Jews, of pure German descent. Third- and fourth-generation Americans. Blue bloods. Elitists. They condescended to those who communicated in the Yiddish language.

"I'm sure your father enjoyed the evening," Ingrid said.

Ingrid often referred to Max as "your father," not by his name, somehow distancing herself in the third person and the formality. I always had an uneasy twinge when she spoke of my family, making me suspect that at times she wished to take an eraser to the blackboard, wiping away the chalk markings of my relatives and leaving the solitary stick figure: a good little girl holding her diplomas.

Ingrid shifted in her chair and took a sip of soda water. "That's nice that you had your friend to dinner," she said, placing a forkful of spinach in her tight mouth.

I knew my Yiddishism had unhinged Ingrid, and she was trying to allay the tension perforating the conversation. Appreciating that, I changed the subject to a neutral one: the movies.

After Teresa served coffee and chocolate cake, Peter and I excused ourselves to go to the movies. Despite his jet lag, Peter insisted we go out together, claiming he could nap during the movie if need be. We had plenty of time, so we strolled down Park Avenue.

"You know, the Oyster Ball is next month," Peter said. "I was thinking you should wear one of our new necklaces." Every year, the black-tie Oyster Ball was held at the Waldorf Astoria, attended by pearl traders and prominent retailers.

"I'm assuming you've decided that already."

"Doreen, come on, you know it's very important for the firm."

"Okay, I was just teasing. What's the design?"

"South Sea pearls and diamonds." Peter pulled me toward him. "You'll look spectacular, honey." He smelled of starched cotton and cologne, refined and expensive. I couldn't pinpoint which of his fragrances it was.

As a five-foot-three-inch gaudy Christmas tree? I thought. "I'll wear it with grace and pride," I said, making light of the task.

Peter looked particularly dashing that moment as a smile crossed his face. One strand of his straight jet-black hair fell over his eyes, taunting his perfectionism, reminding me of his affability on those occasions when he smoothed out his uptightness.

There had been many times when I had indeed tasted his delectable side. Once, we were at the Connecticut shore near Old Lyme, at his friends' beach house. It was late afternoon, and the summer heat was folding into the gentle, murky ocean waves. Peter's friends were out ingredients shopping, so we could all whip up some pasta dishes later that night.

Peter stepped out to the backyard of the white-shuttered house to use the outdoor shower, standing adjacent to a row of neatly groomed knee-high shrubs. The shower looked like a giant whiskey barrel, with dark wooden vertical slats, a swing door, dirt patch flooring, and a hose dripping lukewarm water, hung from a makeshift pole—probably a discarded lamppost.

I heard him greet Aunt Sadi, who resided year-round next door, renting out rooms for the summer season in her double-tiered cottage, yellow-shingled with moss green shutters. Every afternoon, she eased her octogenarian body into one of her rocking chairs, whiling away hours, knitting and napping on her back porch, shaded by a large willow tree, until she welcomed the stars into the summer night. Suddenly, her phone rang, an unusual occurrence at this time of day. She awkwardly extricated herself from the rocking chair and with the aid of her cane, went indoors to tend to the phone.

I was sipping lemonade, standing against the kitchen counter soaping up the leftover breakfast dishes. Peter's voice breezed in through the screened window with his rendition of "Ain't No Mountain High Enough," originally performed by The Supremes. He wove the solo and backup vocals in different pitches.

Peter's eyes were tightly closed as he rinsed out his lathered hair, when I slipped into the whiskey barrel, wanting to join his recital. Before I had a chance to touch him or say something, the shampoo running across his suntanned cheeks, his laugh, my proximity, and the muddy ground underneath must have conspired to cause him to slide, unbalanced, out of the swinging door. He landed flat and taut as a surfboard, front side down, in the neat shrubbery.

My aching sides paralyzed me, cramping from laughter, rendering me unable to help Peter. After struggling for a few moments, he stood up straight, mud all over him, twigs and leaves randomly embedded in his stomach and thighs, and rubbed the shampoo out of his eyes.

"I've always liked chocolate," Aunt Sadi said, back in her chair, rocking rhythmically.

Peter said nothing, not moving, a smile on his face.

With her knitting needles not missing a beat, she added, "And may I also say, frosting suits you well, son."

The next day, Peter purchased three boxes of chocolate-frosted cupcakes and donuts. We joined Aunt Sadi on her porch and closed out the afternoon gobbling the confectionary treats and listening to her stories of growing up in the shadow of the Depression.

We frolicked the rest of the weekend, taking each other in. The sounds of the waves washed over the sun-kissed sand as the Good Humor truck chimed, and the scent of seaweed and grilled hot dogs wafted over us. I almost lost myself in Peter's luscious dark eyes that time in Connecticut. He was loose, witty, and gregarious, making me believe that our pairing could transcend, maybe even mend, strains tearing away at us.

At times like that, I almost believed that Peter's cordiality could extend to my ghosts as well. Throughout our courtship, he had been annoyed with the existence of my spirits. The funny part was that Tania was keen on my making this romantic relationship work, and she used all methods of prodding and pushing me into his arms. It was ironic that Peter's best allies were the ones who unnerved him so much. He believed my haunts were provincial, embarrassing, and indicative of an unprogressive mind. At the beach, I thought I detected a glimmer that Peter might learn to accept my ghosts, or at least see them in a more positive light.

But then, on Sunday night, we drove from Old Lyme back to Manhattan. The minute Peter caught sight of the New York skyline, something twisted inside him. His eyes lost their sparkle and his posture stiffened, his easiness washed out to sea. Pearls, loyalty, Ingrid, obligations, success, propriety, and business crept back toward center stage, clouding some of Peter's flashes of light sweetness.

"And what about setting the date already?" Peter said now, hauling me back to the present, as we stepped into the movie theater.

"Maybe this coming spring."

"You keep promising. It was supposed to be now, *this* summer."

"What's the movie about?"

"Your delays are getting ridiculous."

An image appeared before my eyes. My father staring at me, perplexed as to why I was not rushing to wed this handsome pearl trader. Peter was a financially secure, well-entrenched American of the same faith. Max was ecstatic, so why wasn't I?

"So when are you moving on preparations? How about indicating a month, first. I won't press for a specific date," he said.

"How about saying you love me, Peter," I said, touching his arm.

"Stop changing the subject, Doreen. The guys in the Diamond District are starting to talk," he said, referring to the jewelry manufacturers and traders jammed on and around Forty-seventh Street, known as the Diamond District.

"Don't be absurd. The guys don't spend any time on your affairs, they have their own agendas." I faked a slight laugh.

Peter didn't seem to appreciate my theory, his face contorting in a frown.

Sweat collected on my forehead and in the soft areas at the back of my knees. Strange pounding sounds were getting louder by the second behind my eyes, pressing against my temples from the inside. Slides of Ty Rockwell's dimpled chin were flashing like television images in my mind. In the far distance, I heard Tania scream, "Stop this right now."

"Peter, I'm not feeling too well," I murmured, putting my index finger to my temple. "Headache. It's getting bad."

"You'll be sitting inside. The air-conditioning will make you feel better."

"No, I think you're terribly jet-lagged, and I'm wiped out. You know it's been a tough week for me too—work-wise."

"Skip the movie?"

"I think that's best."

"I'll take you home," Peter said.

"You just got back from Japan; go home and relax. I'll make it just fine on my own." He was shaking his head in disagreement, but I insisted. "Don't worry."

Without allowing time for his answer, I kissed him goodbye, pushing open the glass doors and propelling myself into the damp night air.

As I walked home, tepid waves of nausea began building in my digestive system. Suddenly, I envisioned myself standing in front of Ty's door. A grin pirouetted over Ty's face as he opened the door. He then stepped over the threshold and scooped me up, effortless and nonchalant, carrying me inside. The screen went blank.

As soon as I entered my apartment, the one I shared with my father, I went straight to my room. I saw the light under Max's bedroom door, and I was thankful that he was in bed, undoubtedly reading *The New York Times* or a history book.

I lay on my bed quilt fully clothed and closed my eyes. I heard a stirring and was aware of the presence of my ghosts.

Tania bumped up against my side, her hair brushing against my cheek. "Forget about the banker," she said in my ear.

I didn't answer, nor did I move my eyelids.

"Do you hear me, Dorka?" she asked and poked my waist. Tania always referred to me by my Yiddish name. I was named after Max's mother.

"Go away," I said, letting the two words sputter from my mouth while I opened my eyes.

"Dorka, you owe us continuity. You promised."

"I never promised, you always just assumed," I said with a slight hiss.

"There were so few of us left. Someone must carry on, replace us, remember us."

Weariness oozed through my body; even my fingertips felt tired. I didn't want to hear about the children who were wiped out during the Second World War and my responsibilities toward them.

"I've heard this more than enough times," I said in irritation.

"Obviously not. What are those thoughts about the banker?"

I pushed at Tania's shoulder and sent her spiraling toward the ceiling. I caught a glimpse of Aaron and Yankel near the window, their frightened, childish eyes staring at me.

"Go away," I shouted. I turned on my side and pulled a pillow over my face. I slept in my clothes that night.

Chapter 4

THREE DAYS LATER, I HAD just hung up the phone from my talk with Peter, who was already in Geneva for the pearl trade show, when I received a call from Ty. He informed me that he had finished up his real estate deal and was ready to begin work on the Dorf deal. We arranged to start the following day at my office.

The next morning, Thursday morning, Ty walked into my office in a dark blue suit with a cellular phone pressed to his ear. I realized he had graduated to the use of a cellular phone in addition to his beeper.

"Rodes fucked up my vacation again," Ty said into the phone as he swung the file folder onto my desk.

"No cursing," I said.

Ty looked incredulous. Turning away, he cupped his hand over the receiver and continued, "Listen, John, I'm stuck with this telecom deal. Rodes thinks we should look at this stuff again. So don't count on me for the holiday weekend. Keep me posted on the action." Ty snapped the phone shut.

"Do you have a share?" I asked, assuming that he had a "share" in a house located in one of the fashionable Long Island beach towns. After all, he was an investment banker, and they all seemed to aspire to vacation time in one of the various Hamptons, or Fire Island or Shelter Island or Montauk.

"Fire Island," he stated.

Of course, I thought.

Ty slid his jacket onto the back of the chair facing my cluttered desk, but left his shirt with Tiffany gold cuff links in place. I recognized the brand; I had purchased several pairs for Peter's Japanese business counterparts.

"What was that you said before?" Ty asked before settling into the chair. "Something about swearing."

"No swearing. I hate it. You're on my turf now, so watch the profanity, please."

He did not respond, just gazed at me and then away, opened the file folder, and began reading.

We spent the next few hours and the following morning working on the calculations. I kept myself focused on the work sheets and made my conversation professional, although images of his wink at the earlier conference bopped around in the recesses of my mind.

At about noon, I heard the sound of Katherine van de Vrande's spiked heels near my door. Her auburn hair was swept up in a cool summer do, her blue eyes were the color of a blue jay, hypnotizing, and her alabaster complexion was intensified by her raspberry lips, color-coordinated with her office walls.

"I'm going out," she said. "Want something?" Behind Ty's back she mouthed "del-i-ci-ous," rolling her tongue over her moist upper lip.

"I'm fine. What about you, Ty?" I said. I refused to smile back at Katherine.

"Too early for me—I'll order later." He kept reading, never looking up.

I dug out a Saran-wrapped sandwich, tuna with sliced tomato on rye bread, from the bottom of my bag. "I made you a sandwich too, if you want," I continued, humoring myself aloud. "Yours is on white bread."

Before Ty could respond, the receptionist buzzed. "Regina on line four," she said, chewing gum.

As soon as I picked up, Regina began yapping about the birthday festivities, my birthday coinciding with the nation's, both being on July 4. "Lulu is getting the evening off and maybe the next day as well," she told me. "So we've got to decide what our agenda will be and fast—I'm boarding my Delta flight soon. Can we have our traditional dinner? Does Peter mind?"

"He says we should have it." Before leaving for Geneva, Peter had made me promise to celebrate my birthday with my friends, as always, even though he wouldn't be there.

"Okay, great, so where?" Regina asked.

"What about the Penguins? I'd hate to exclude them," I asked, noticing Ty had stopped working, shifting in his seat.

"Well, I was thinking we bring stuff over to you and have it there with the Penguins. Much more relaxing at home," Regina said.

"Okay, it might as well be at my place." I sighed. There was no point in arguing with Regina. I had known her since we were in the same bunk at sleep-away summer camp many years ago. She was relentless. We divvied up the tasks, which meant I was to do most of the cooking, and we concluded that dinner would start at eight in the evening, giving Lulu enough time to freshen up and travel uptown. Regina hung up in a rush: they were closing the gate at the airport, and she was about to miss her flight from Miami.

"What the hell are penguins?" he asked.

"It's shorthand for my parents—well, my father now—and my uncle and aunt," I explained, sipping some water. "Actually, all the refugees."

"Refugees?"

"The 'displaced persons' of World War Two, survivors of the concentration camps and labor camps. You saw a couple of them at Max's poker game. No doubt you noticed they're all short, squat, with shiny heads—and they walk funny, kind of ambling from side to side, like penguins."

"Uh-huh." Ty stared at me for a few seconds. He moved in his chair and returned his focus to his calculator. I watched his fingers tapping on the instrument; his broken left brow twitched as he again shifted in his seat, without glancing up.

The next day, by the late afternoon, the offices were becoming deserted. I expected tumbleweed to blow down desolate Fifth Avenue, like in the old western movies. The exodus from Manhattan for the long July Fourth weekend went into full swing as the summer sun exploded into a red ball of fire. Lenny had run to catch the 11:45 AM Metro North train to White Plains in order to gather his family for their drive to Cape Cod, where they intended to spend the next week. Katherine's space had gone dark after lunch, when she swung out of her office as she blew kisses. All the other attorneys and staff were gone by the time the orange-frilled sunbeams of dusk splayed across my desk.

Ty worked, oblivious to the rapid changes in the environment. His cell phone and calculator continued to harmonize. The fax machine in the hallway hummed as it spewed out documents on Goldfarb Magillan letterhead.

"Okay, I'm out of here," I pronounced, collecting my handbag and stuffing some papers and sunglasses into it. "See you Tuesday."

"Are you out of your mind?" Ty said. "It's only six o'clock. We're nowhere near done."

"That may very well be true, but I have dinner plans with Max and a poker game later tonight. Holiday weekend. Different planets, you and me. I don't work 'round the clock. Sorry."

"Are you out of your fucking mind? Rodes expects this done, holiday or not."

"No cursing, remember?" I said, rising from my chair. "Seth and the boys count on me for poker. They all manage to get there after long hospital shifts, so why should *I* disappoint *them*?"

Once a week I played poker at Dr. Seth Rabiner's place. Seth had been a year ahead of me at college. For years now, we had been regularly playing poker with three friends of Seth's, all doctors. Usually we played on Wednesday nights, but for the July Fourth holiday weekend we had decided to move the game to Friday.

Ty rolled his eyes, fiddling with some paper clips on my desk. "Rodes, or for that matter, no one at Goldfarb Magillan, cares if you're on vacation, or ill, or anything." His voice then softened. "You heard our conversation at our last meeting. I committed to getting this done. This isn't going to bode well for me."

I was about to say, *But I don't work for Rodes.* But then clouds passed through Ty's eyes, spotting them with dark flecks. He flipped his hair off his forehead and hunched over like a football quarterback losing the Super Bowl.

"Tell you what—tonight and tomorrow morning I've got previous commitments. But tomorrow afternoon ..." I hesitated, studying the piles of papers scattered on my desk, "come over and we'll try to get some more done. Heck, at least this way there'll be less of a workload for me next week."

As I locked up and we left the P&S office building, I reminded him of my home address and phone number.

"The bow tie is here," Max called as he opened the door the next afternoon.

"Max, Max, behave yourself," I shouted, sticking my head out of the kitchen.

"At least I remembered his name, Doreen."

Ty shook my father's hand and gave him a weak smile. Watching him, I realized Ty often moved in a nonchalant fashion, with his left hand in his trouser pocket and his head tilting slightly.

"Come in, Ty," I called, wheeling back to the stove. "I'm making sauce for the salmon in the fridge. Anyway, I thought we should work where the daffodils are." The kitchen wallpaper was bursting with daffodils. I had always done my homework there.

Max excused himself to extend the dining room table, finish the *Times*, and then take a nap—Saturday ritual.

"So how was a night off for you?" I asked.

"It would have been better out on Fire Island, but it was tolerable, nonetheless," he admitted. "And poker?"

"Well, this was the second time I won big recently. This time I trumped Seth's two pairs with three-of-a-kind. Too bad—it pissed him off. And poor Seth was already unhappy after one of his more grueling days. ER. He's a trauma specialist," I said, stirring the tomato-based sauce and tasting it. "Needs more garlic. For a moment, I thought Seth might not show up tonight after losing at poker, but he will."

"How can you be so sure?"

"He likes my friend Lulu, but he doesn't know it yet."

"A meddler, too," Ty said, grinning and seating himself at the kitchen table. The yellow and white wallflowers softened his angular features.

"Not meddling, just nudging luck along. No harm in that."

I put some cookies and two cups of coffee on the glass tabletop. Ty sipped from one mug.

"So where're you from?" I asked, pulling out the kitchen chair to sit.

"Bismarck, North Dakota."

"A little far from the lights of Broadway."

"And a lot less glamorous. I supported myself at the state university as a dishwasher, at one of the only Italian joints, near campus."

"You worked your way through school?"

"My second job was at the popular gas station, pumping gas. Hours were convenient—three to six in the morning."

"How'd you get East?"

"Wharton full scholarship. First in many years for a Bismarck kid. Practically the whole town saw me off."

"The town?"

"Well, you're talking Madison Square Garden and a bit—that's the whole population."

"Tiny."

"Yep."

"Your mom must be thrilled with your accomplishments."

"That's another story." He leaned back on the hind legs of the kitchen chair.

"Why?"

"Well, she worked at the local hospital. Every morning she drove there in her powder blue Chevy, an old piece of junk. But she loved it." His eyes seemed to be glued to the wall behind me. He stared at it for a while. "Two months after I started Wharton, she was killed in a car wreck, early morning. A drunk driver hit her on Route 94."

My eyes started to swell with moisture. Motherlessness was a phenomenon I could relate to, unfortunately—not only for myself but for Regina as well. Both our mothers had passed away prematurely. *And he is a full-fledged orphan. Poor kid.* "So sad."

"I didn't even have the money to get home for the funeral."

"What was her name?"

"Faith Rockwell."

We continued to talk for hours, never even managing a glance at the Dorf papers, when suddenly my friend Regina appeared. By then Ty had agreed to stay for the remainder of the evening, after concluding that the trip to Fire Island, by subway, train, and then ferry, would be erratic and inconvenient, at best, during the holiday evening hours. He decided he would work on the Dorf material tomorrow, possibly on the deck at Fire Island.

Dressed in a leopard top draped over tight pants and bearing a box of store-bought brownies, Regina stretched out her manicured hand in welcome to Ty. As the two shook hands, Regina's eyes scanned the length of Ty Rockwell.

"My, oh my, what has Doreen brought home now?" Regina asked, a grin overtaking her face.

"Ty's from Goldfarb Magillan. We're working on a deal together," I said, wanting to kick her in the leg, but I couldn't under the circumstances.

"Which one?" Regina asked, not even glancing at me; her eyes were stuck on Ty.

"Dorf," I said, knowing I had told her about Dick Dorf on several occasions. "By the way, Regina's an account executive at the cosmetics company Puff Cosmetics. Very successful."

"Sounds impressive," Ty said.

"Should have gotten my law degree," Regina said. "At Puff, all I'm surrounded with are neurotic women and uptight Tinkerbells."

"Stop complaining," I said. "Come on, we need to set up."

Regina helped me set the dining table while Ty became engrossed in *The New York Times* sports section, the only section Max never read. We were using plates pulled together from several sets of casual dishes, because Max and I had refused to use my mother's large set of porcelain blue and gold Rosenthal fine china since the day she left us.

Then Lulu arrived, carrying yellow daffodils. Her hair was still slightly damp, and her clothes consisted of a blue skirt and a sleeveless top.

I introduced Lulu to Ty. Tiny lines crinkled up around her eyes as she said it was nice to meet him and asked, "Are you an attorney as well?"

"No, investment banker."

"So your hours are as bad as mine. Sorry to hear that," she said with compassion. Ty responded with a shrug and a laugh.

The door then opened, allowing my aunt and uncle, Bea and Sam, and my friend Seth to join us. Max came out of his room to greet the guests, kissing his brother and sister-in-law on both cheeks. Regina's current boyfriend, Michael, a massively built ex-football player, arrived last, at the same moment that the antique clock chimed eight o'clock. I expected Peter, still in Geneva, to call after nine o'clock, as he had promised.

Candlelight twinkled and twirled around the faces of my guests as they sipped fruity white wine and devoured grilled salmon with olive and garlic tomato sauce, steamed asparagus spears, and gnocchi swimming in mushrooms. Ty, seated between Seth—still dressed in his crumpled hospital greens—and Regina's boyfriend, was engrossed in lively sports talk with the two of them. *Good seating arrangement*, I thought. Lulu was busy entertaining the rest of the guests with tales of her hospital life.

Regina took her knife to her wineglass, tapping to signal for silence. "Okay, boys and girls, listen up," she said, rising from her seat. "We're all here for one common purpose—and that is to celebrate the birthday of our dear friend." She paused for effect, raising her glass, encouraging everyone to join in the toast. "Lulu and I feel it hasn't been fair to the rest of us that men like you, Doreen, despite your, shall we say, unusual choice of interests. Or maybe, *because* of them." Regina paused and began to circle around the table. Regina always teased me that, despite my seriousness, I had more luck with the opposite sex than she ever did.

"True," Lulu said.

"So we've surrendered and bought you a subscription to the periodical *Foreign Affairs*," Regina continued.

I used to read this publication at the library whenever I got a chance, mainly on the weekends.

"You finally have bought me a perfect gift," I said, smiling. "Hope the lingerie industry can withstand the downturn in summer sales."

Shortly after, Peter called from Geneva saying he was sorry he was missing me and the fun. He had just bought the "most beautiful strand of black pearls the world has ever seen," and said he would deliver them in person as soon as he returned from the trade show. He apologized for the tardiness of the gift, but he was certain I would be as taken as he was with his purchase.

After I hung up the phone, I served coffee and dessert in "free style," as Regina called it, allowing everyone to spread out in the living room. Regina was eating banana cream pie in healthy bites as the two of us stood near the kitchen entrance. I was holding a brownie in one hand and a cup of coffee in the other.

"Big and beautiful," Regina said, looking in the direction of the couch where Michael, Ty, and Lulu were seated, chatting.

"I guess things are heating up between the two of you," I said.

"You dumb ass, I'm talking about the banker you brought home."

Before I had the chance to comment on her choice of language, Max interrupted. "Regina, please, *narishkeit*," he said as he passed from the kitchen with a glass of tea. "Why do you talk like that? Doreen is getting married soon."

I looked down at my brownie. I knew this conversation wasn't going to be pleasant when Max set his teacup down on the dining room breakfront and crossed his arms over his middle.

"I don't think it's nonsense, Max," Regina answered. "He's absolutely delicious looking."

It was a strange coincidence that Regina and Katherine had both described Ty with the identical adjective. I glanced over at Ty. He was laughing at something, his head thrown slightly back, light bouncing off his front teeth and gleaming hair. He *was* big and beautiful.

Max gazed intensely at Regina. "Do you realize what you're

doing? Encouraging your friend here to consider someone like that?" He pointed at me and then at Ty.

"With all due respect, I don't see my friend here rushing to tie the knot with Peter," Regina said, her hand shaking slightly as she brought a forkful of pie to her lips.

"So you think that makes it fine to push Doreen into the arms of a *shaigets?* And one from such a family? *Oy gut,*" Max said. *Shaigets* was an uncomplimentary term for a gentile, particularly when uttered by Max.

"I was just stating a fact. It's Doreen's life. I'm not pushing anything," Regina said.

"Then *zie shtil*," he said. I had never heard Max speak to Regina in such a manner.

"What?" Regina asked, stunned by his forcefulness.

"Be quiet," I translated in a splinter of a voice.

Max and Regina glared at each other for a moment and then whirled away in opposite directions. I tossed a loud sigh into the dense atmosphere.

Chapter 5

EVERYONE, EXCEPT LENNY AND KATHERINE van de Vrande, was back in the office on Tuesday morning. Katherine was nursing her sangria-inspired holiday hangover with bed rest, aspirin, and fluids. Normally, her absence would have sullied the office atmosphere, particularly Lenny's moods, which would have been clouded by irritability. I was glad Lenny was on vacation for the week.

Ty and I conferred numerous times in the following days, coordinating the Dorf materials. On Wednesday and Thursday we met at my office. On Friday we finessed some of the wording and the accompanying charts. The whole Dorf project seemed to be growing exponentially.

Late Friday evening, we continued to talk shop at a café table across from Lincoln Center. Ty had insisted that we "massage" more of the Dick Dorf deal numbers together before he headed to Fire Island the next morning for a beach break, partial compensation for his earlier lost July Fourth weekend.

"I left Bismarck behind, and I haven't been disappointed for one minute since," Ty said.

"Not even by all the kooks and crooks in this town?"

"Not even by those, and there's no shortage," he said.

"Why did you come, really?" I said, concentrating on my profiterole dessert, plucking at the vanilla ice cream, letting the chocolate sauce ooze onto the white plate. I braced myself for the standard French cuff answer: material success, blah, blah.

"Color," Ty said.

"You mean, as in green?" I watched the chocolate swirl into a kind of Rorschach design, waiting for him to talk of money.

"No, I mean colors—wild ones. Diversity, energy, adventure—stuff like that."

Was he kidding? My ears must have betrayed me. He must have been talking about amassing big bucks, power, status, and I had simply misheard. "Say that again."

He did. His words were quite ordinary, yet strung together; hanging in the air between us like mistletoe, they sounded so magical. "How much wine have you had?" I asked, looking at the bottle of Merlot; it was still half full.

His fingers reached across the table to my hand resting on the tablecloth. He gently touched the back of my protruding knuckles.

We continued to talk. Ty's lips moved in animated fashion as his blue shirt lightened his face. His melodious words stroked by my earlobes, my forehead. In truth, I missed some of the content of Ty's utterances, but I sensed his intoxicating spirit; even his drive seemed easy and nonchalant, in tune with his body language.

After dinner, we strolled up Central Park West, gentle breezes ruffling my long skirt. In front of my building, I stepped up on the sidewalk curb to narrow the divide in our height and pecked Ty on the cheek. Repositioning his head slightly, he kissed me on the lips.

I floated upstairs.

The next morning, the ringing of the phone sliced through my deep sleep.

Ty shouted at the other end, "Doreen, are you there? I'm at Penn Station, was about to catch the train out to Fire Island, but reconsidered. I think we should try to finish up the business plan together. Do you have some spare time?"

Rubbing my eyes, I sat up in an attempt to get my brain functioning. The digital alarm clock on my nightstand read 10:30; I was perplexed that the previous night had been peaceful and ghost-free. I scanned the room for any evidence of Tania or her young male companions. "Weren't you supposed to be out of here already?"

"I got stuck on work late last night, tying up an oil exploration project, and didn't go. How about trying to finish Dorf with me today? I have more analysis to incorporate. We can make some intriguing predictions based on my new figures."

The way Ty said "intriguing" made my heart flutter like butterfly wings. "Well, I was going to hang out with Lulu tonight. She's not on call." I avoided mentioning Peter's return from Geneva tomorrow night.

"Can you give me some time, just a bit?"

"This is a perfect example of why someone like me refuses to join the legions of French cuffs, starched white shirts, whatever." I glanced at my clock again. "You *never* stop."

Ty didn't answer right away, but I could hear him breathing in a steady tempo. He finally said, "Listen, how about we work at my place. I've got a slow computer, but a computer nonetheless. I'll make you a tuna sandwich."

"That's an offer a girl can't resist. I guess." I sat up in bed thinking for a moment. "Alright, I'll come down later on. Tell me your address and what subway gets me there."

I knew that he knew that I knew we had no real need to meet right then at his place to work on the Dick Dorf deal.

Under the blazing noontime sun, I ambled from the West Fourth Street subway station, my old law school stop, three blocks to Ty's place. The ragged park benches in Washington Square Park lay bare of people, the cement chess tables baked in the sticky canary rays of sun. The whole area steamed with heat and naked emptiness.

Ty had a third-floor walk-up studio furnished in quintessential bachelor style: uninspiring couch, oversized television, messy coffee table, and tiny kitchen devoid of appliances. In contrast, colorful sheets, lots of pillows, and a matching quilt in cobalt blue and lime green spiced up his bed, alcoved on the side. Neat and cheery.

"Welcome to my palace." He bowed low upon opening the front door. "Lunch is now being served."

I dropped my bag on the floor and approached the little corner table. It was set with plates of quartered tuna sandwiches, a pitcher of lemonade, and coleslaw salad in a blue bowl. A bunch of yellow daffodils was stuffed into an empty plastic Coke bottle, as a decorative centerpiece. "That's so sweet. How did you know I love coleslaw?" I said.

As Ty came toward me, I noticed how the sunlight spilled into the room and onto his smooth sandy hair. His head was slightly askew, his button-down shirt was untucked, and his left hand was buried in his khaki shorts. I pulled his head toward me with one hand, kissing his lips. He kissed me back, longer. Katherine van de Vrande and Regina had indeed been right.

All of a sudden, I had no clue what to do. Maybe I should bolt for the door. Run.

"Would you care to see my brand-new sheet set?" he asked in a quiet voice.

That somehow made me giggle. But I couldn't get any verbal response to leave my lips.

"How about trying them out? Give me your opinion on the quality. I went up to Bloomingdale's last week for these," he said, as he led me by the hand to the bedroom. "I've never been there before, and I've lived here for more than five years. It took me an hour to figure out the sheet sizes."

He dipped down and spread himself onto the bed surface, lying flat on his back.

After a minute, I slid down next to his muscular body, concentrating on his relaxed breathing. "Feels like *excellent* quality," I whispered, running my fingers over the pattern. "And the fit's most definitely perfect."

The swooshing noises of my ghosts began. I sat upright and swung my feet over the side of the bed. The spirits thumped at the furniture and exploded against the mirror, which was supported by bronze brackets on the opposite wall. Their shrieks and moans ricocheted off the ceiling, hitting me like darts.

Putting my hands over my ears, I said, "Can't do this."

Ty turned over on his side to face me. "Are you okay, Doreen? You look pale."

"This isn't your problem." I pushed my hair back; my neck was getting sticky. "When I get in a sleeplike position, things start to happen."

Ty extended his hand to touch my arm. "Nothing happened yet."

I waited a few seconds for the frenzied yelling to subside.

"You see, by day my life was and is normal." I paused and turned to look at Ty, starting again. "My days were always full of friends and school and fun. But when darkness fell, there were different forces. You could never understand nor should you want to."

"Try me."

"Why should you bother with someone else's demons?"

"That's how you get to know someone."

Aaron, the youngest ghost, grazed my forehead. He then hovered over me like a helicopter. The two other ghosts were treading air around the light fixture hanging directly above the bed.

I kicked off my sandals and brought my legs up on the quilt, crossing them before saying, "As a kid, when I couldn't fall asleep, I'd crawl to my bedroom door, lie on the carpet, and listen to the Penguin tales of survival."

"Tales?"

"Stories of young people living through the worst hell on earth. But yet, oddly enough, most of the stories were funny. Eccentric characters and hilarious antics despite the fact that it all occurred in concentration camps and the like." I paused, waiting. Peter would always change the subject about now, telling me it was destructive to dwell on the past, particularly a "horrible" past. Failing to get any reaction from Ty, I continued. "At night, Tania, Yankel, and Aaron would float over me, laughing, yelling, crying."

"Ghosts?"

"Yes."

"Be specific."

"They're kids dressed in tattered clothes. Tania is the most verbal, often speaking to me," I said, hesitating for a moment.

"Strange names," Ty said. "Are they made up?"

"No."

"Elaborate, please," Ty said softly.

"Tania was my father's cousin. Taken by the Nazis."

"Then?"

"Never heard from again."

"The others?"

"Aaron was my father's young nephew, his only nephew." I knew Ty was going to ask what happened to him. Before he could, I answered. "Killed, Auschwitz."

"The other one? Forgot his name," Ty whispered.

"Yankel, Aaron's bunkmate at Auschwitz. Died right after his liberation while in another camp called Dachau. Typhoid. He was twelve."

"You learned about them by listening to the Penguins?"

"Yes. I listened for hours. Then I would drift off to sleep with my ghosts tucked in next to me. Most of the time, Tania would wrap her skinny arms around my waist."

"Sleep's a good escape."

"Not really. Once asleep, I often dreamt of the piles of hair at Birkenau."

"What's that?"

"The death camp of Auschwitz, the gas chambers, the ovens. The dreams were in gray tones, except for the long chestnut hair at the top of the pile outside the chamber doors."

"Yours?"

"Right."

Ty played with my hair, twisting it gently. A feather of compassion seemed to rustle behind his eyes. After a few moments, he said, "Everyone has demons."

"Even Presbyterians?"

He smiled broadly. "Who said I'm Presbyterian?" He raised himself on one arm. "Mini, I think your past has made you unique. I've been watching you. You suck people in with your personality."

"Mini?"

"Reflects both your mini status, as a penguin, and your petiteness." Ty grinned broadly. "Good pet name."

The room became relatively tranquil. Aaron and Yankel sat on the edge of the dresser, impish legs dangling; they started to doze off. Tania was pressed up against my back. I was expecting her to say something, like "Dorka, run now." Before she had a chance to, I shooed her away.

"Maybe we should go out for a walk," Ty suggested after a few minutes. "Get some fresh air."

I failed to answer for some time, staring at the colorful quilt pattern. "Nah." I then kissed his eyelids in slow motion, drinking in his masculinity.

"You sure?" Ty asked.

"I have other plans," I whispered as I touched his chin with my fingers.

"Really?" His lips turned up gently at the corners.

"Don't worry," I said, unbuttoning the first button of his shirt. "I'm going to make sure we have quiet for a while."

My life was about to turn upside down.

Chapter 6

WEEKS PASSED. I WORKED WITH Ty on and off during that time. Often Peter was out of the country on business. I spent many of those evenings with Ty, at dinner, talking late into the night and beyond. He was fascinating, intelligent, humorous, and different from Peter. He was also undeniably wrong for me in many ways.

Whenever I was with Peter, I noticed that everything reminded me of Ty, making me long to call him, see him, touch him. That posed a serious problem, being that I was engaged to Peter, and I remained determined to somehow make that marriage happen.

After the summer breezes gave way to fallen leaves and tweed suits, I realized Thanksgiving was fast approaching and my caseload was becoming overwhelming.

One cool autumn day, I was on my way to get a certain client to agree to a divorce settlement. The judge in the case had given us a deadline, which was looming.

Lenny, in a state of fury, had dispatched me solo to obtain Madame Sanne's approval for our latest pleading in her divorce case, because otherwise, if present himself, he would have been "compelled to strangle the old bitch." He wanted to avoid litigation, and she was pulling in the other direction.

I was repulsed by the thought of his hands wrapped around the old lady's neck. True, Madame Sanne was irritating, with her pointy face and her voice of grating intonations. But, on the other hand, she had named Lenny executor of her estate in her last will and testament. Executors make fat fees for probating estates, especially one of a seventy-year-old eccentric containing over fifteen million dollars in blue-chip stocks, with no human descendants.

For exercise, I walked the thirty blocks from my office to her home. The sky was a dazzling blue, the color of a robin's egg. When I reached her building, I plopped down on the couch in the center of the art deco lobby with its two-storied ceiling. Despite the crisp weather, beads of perspiration had accumulated on my upper lip, like raindrops bubbling up on parched soil. A few gulps of water from my plastic bottle alleviated some of what seemed to be my overheating under my winter coat. Afterward, I checked my face in the lobby mirror; Max's green eyes looked back at me. I took the elevator up to Madame Sanne's penthouse.

The elevator doors opened directly into her ten-room apartment. A sweep of taupe marble floors and matching walls stretched behind Madame Sanne, like the Great Wall of China. She was draped in a flowing pale peach dressing gown with a feathery collar. Her puffy bouffant-style hairdo looked as if it were about to topple her diminutive body.

"I don't want to sign," she announced to me. "I told Lenny that earlier today. Why should I compromise with the vile Dalck? He lived off of me long enough," she huffed, walking into the living room with tiny steps as if she were afraid to crack the floor tiles.

"We should talk this out, Madame Sanne. Let's sit down." I followed her to the living room, settling into the salmon-colored couch in front of a marble fireplace with bronze cupid firedogs. "Such beautiful antiques," I said. "You have exquisite taste."

I thought of the rare times I had accompanied my mother, Hala, on antique shopping expeditions. She had gracefully tolerated my lack of enthusiasm.

"Do you love antiques?" she asked.

"I've shopped for French antiques. But I don't know if *love* is the right term."

"I see." Madam Sanne paused, scanning my facial features for a few seconds. "Some coffee, yes?"

So yes, we had coffee and little petit fours from Café Ambrose. She talked of Paris and uncouth American manners. Her heavy French accent somehow made me envision globs of butter slathered on baguettes.

"I enjoyed your company today, but I cannot sign a divorce settlement paying that gigolo money. Call your Lenny now and make that clear," she told me. Her bouffant bounced from side to side as she repeated the word *gigolo* several times.

"As far as I can tell, Madame Sanne, you're an intelligent person with savvy business skills," I said. "For the sake of argument, let's do some calculations together." I grabbed a notepad and a pen from my bag. "You married Dalck, seventeen years your junior, and stayed together for how many years?"

"You know from the pleadings." She looked the other way.

"Twelve years. And what would you say is the reason you stayed with Dalck for most of that time?"

"Nothing."

"No, really. Take a moment to think back."

"Well, I guess ..." She hesitated, rearranging her collar with her spidery hands. "I guess you could say, *pleasures*." She stretched out the word.

"Very well. And how many of the twelve years were filled with pleasures?" I asked, keeping a straight expression on my face.

"Maybe ten."

"So if we divide the $500,000 proposed settlement amount by the ten years, we get an even fifty K per annum. Why don't you look at it as severance pay for each year of, as you say, *pleasures*," I ventured, looking at her quivering chin.

"Go ahead," she said, not meeting my gaze.

"Considering your impressive assets, which you were brilliant enough to amass, it seems like a pittance to me. And please don't forget your mounting legal bills. I mean, Lenny does not work for free."

About an hour later, I strolled back into the P&S offices with the signed Sanne papers tucked under my arm.

Two weeks later, the judge's clerk phoned to confirm the meeting in Justice Walter Teller's chambers. Patty Mahoney, the clerk, reminded me, for what seemed like the thirtieth time, that her boss was intolerant of lateness or "any other indication of disrespect."

As I was preparing to head out, the phone rang. It was Ty; he wanted to know if we were going to have dinner that night as we had planned. Peter was in Rio.

I hesitated. I was unsure about dinner, but even more so, I was unsure about our relationship. Actually, I was unsure about almost everything at that point. It was getting too complicated to continue seeing both him and Peter. My schedule—not to mention my conscience—was sinking under the weight of a double, two-timing romantic existence, kept secret from all others. I was experiencing many headaches and periods of anxiety-induced exhaustion.

"Actually, Ty, I kind of feel that …" I started and stopped. "I think we need a break."

"You mean you do."

"Okay, I do." I realized I was deluding myself that this duplicitous arrangement was going to work. But I couldn't get up the courage to end it—maybe because I really didn't want to.

"Are we going to talk about this?"

"What's to talk about? You are what you are." I glanced at my watch. "I don't know. It's all so confusing. But right now I must leave. Can't be late."

"Okay, what's next?"

"We'll talk later." Escaping the subject was my goal right then.

"You know I'm working on a wireless telecom deal, and it's pretty much around the clock—no real breaks unless I squeeze one in."

"Understood. I'll let you know. It can wait until you wrap up the deal. Anyway, I need time to sort things out. Sorry." I hung up without even saying good-bye.

I left the office in a hurry, grabbing that day's *Times* and ample unfinished files for the waiting period. My face was dotted with cold perspiration droplets. The subway ride provided me with an opportunity to do some breathing exercises, clearing my mind of my personal quagmire.

The New York State Supreme Court, a white marbled building taking up an entire city block in Lower Manhattan, stands in splendor on Centre Street, dominating the other courthouses and governmental buildings in its proximity. Its massive Greek pillars and stone statues at its front preside over expansive marble steps, a triangular park, and several subway stations. Climbing up the steps, I thought of all the practitioners of justice, and the clients, criminals, clerks, reporters, and spectators who had climbed these stairs before. For a moment I was proud to be counted among them.

That emotion was quickly dashed when I entered the building. The contrast between inside and outside temporarily blinded me. After adjusting to the poor lighting, I noticed the security areas with tired security guards, metal detectors, stained walls, scuffed dark linoleum floors, and the strong smell of burned coffee and mildew, all shouting—shabbiness.

I rode up in the elevator to the fifth floor, crammed between a group of clerks and their files. The hard wooden bench in the hall facing the Honorable Justice Teller's chambers, Room 540, was cold and uncomfortable, but I sat down and stayed seated nonetheless. The air smelled stale, and bleak light filtered through the soot-smeared courthouse windows. Sporadic footsteps and slamming doors resonated in the background, while I waited for opposing counsel as well as our clients to show, busying myself with the *Times*.

They arrived within a few minutes of each other. Opposing counsel, an attorney with a small Staten Island firm, was in his rumpled brown striped suit with tie undone. His client, the slight Dalck Major, Sanne's soon-to-be ex-spouse, slithered up right after him, hair greased back, donned in a greenish jacket over a black shirt and tight jeans. My client, Madame Sanne, did not disappoint in her shocking purple suit and diamond brooch. Above her face, caked with foundation, a mound of hair was pinned up with rhinestone hair clips. Just then, she reminded me of a hooker who had not had a paying john in a very long time.

I pulled aside opposing counsel, Craig O'Leary, in order to gauge his willingness to finish this matter, once and for all. We seemed in agreement on the settlement numbers and payment schedule, leading me to believe the hearing would be relatively painless. I eased back on the bench near Madame Sanne, who was studying her hand, particularly the ruby ring hanging loosely on her finger. A few feet away, back plastered against the mustard gray wall, Dalck sulked with head bent downward, apparently taking in the floor tiles, while his attorney, O'Leary, was struggling with a pile of papers unloaded from his briefcase.

A few minutes later, at 10:40 AM, Patty summoned us into the judge's chambers. Justice Walter Teller, in shirtsleeves, seated in a leather chair in front of the oversized desk strewn with blue-backed motions and opened casebooks, did not look up as we filed in. Degrees and honorary plaques hung askew behind him near bookcases groaning under the weight of the jurisprudence texts. His black robe drooped on a wooden old-fashioned coat hanger near the narrow window, the sole source of faint natural light. The room, about the size of a large walk-in closet, smelled like pastrami, recently consumed—as was evidenced by the mustard stain on the judge's pudgy right cheek. *Pastrami in the morning.* The thought made my stomach wretch.

"Ladies and gentlemen, have we finally reached a settlement?" Justice Teller asked, peeking over his half-eye reading glasses.

"Judge, we believe we've come to a number mutually agreed upon by both our clients," Craig ventured, turning to me for support.

"Your Honor, we've settled on a half-million-dollar figure to be paid out in two equal installments by my client," I added.

The judge lowered his head to scan the settlement documents

Patty had placed in front of him. His comb-over reminded me of the nasty weeds that grew over the limestone slabs in the back of my apartment building.

"Mr. Major, do you fully consent to this settlement amount?" The judge focused over his glasses.

"It's a very miserly amount, Your Honor, but considering I'm about to remarry now, I won't argue," Dalck said, massaging his chest with the palm of his right hand.

"You revolting scum," Madame Sanne hissed, jumping up from her chair. "How dare you remarry without notifying me about this?"

Craig and I exchanged glances. He mopped his brow with the back of his shirtsleeve. My breathing began to change pace, quickening. All of a sudden I pictured my boss's puffy, agitated face dripping with perspiration; it loomed in front of me as if in a nightmare.

Justice Teller leaned back in the chair, pushing his glasses up on his nose. "Mr. O'Leary, the court would have liked to know about this development before …"

"I had absolutely no idea about my client's upcoming marriage," Craig interrupted, glaring at Dalck, who was suddenly deep in contemplation of his black suede loafers. "I would like to request a few moments to learn the details, in conference with Mr. Major, and share them with the court thereafter."

The judge granted a ten-minute break. Craig shoved his client out of the chambers. They were to confer at the far end of the hallway. The fuming Madame Sanne clasped her skinny, crinkled arms together as I led her back out to the benches outside the judge's chambers.

As soon as I stepped into the hallway, I was stunned to find Ty pacing up and down. He was dressed in a charcoal gray suit and blue shirt with tie loosened. Approaching him I asked, "What happened?"

"Nothing. Just needed to talk. You can't just notify me it's impossible for us to go on and hang up."

"Not now," I said, pondering my poor judgment in having aired my ambivalent feelings on the phone that morning, until another, fresher thought slammed into my consciousness. "Wait a minute. How did you even know I was here?" I made a habit of never telling anyone outside the office, particularly Ty or Peter, my work schedule. And I knew I had not mentioned my precise destination to Ty in our earlier conversation.

"Your office," Ty said. "Well, actually, Katherine wouldn't tell me, but Lenny told me that you were down here."

I envisioned my boss's supercilious grin: no doubt he was glad that he was somehow bonding man-to-man with Ty of Goldfarb Magillan. And, maybe he was even doubly thrilled about the possibility that his associate's life might explode in her face.

"Who is this *delicacy*?" Madame Sanne questioned, making sure the words sounded very French as she neared Ty, pressing her face up close, trying to get a bird's-eye view of the unfamiliar male specimen.

I introduced her to Ty in a perfunctory manner, names only. She made Ty kiss the back of her extended right hand, as a blush crawled up her neck to her hollowed cheeks. Wanting to ask her for some privacy, I began to speak, but then decided against it. It was clear she had no intention of budging.

Ty brushed his hair off his forehead. He moved up without touching me, his nose aligned with the top of my forehead, his back to Madame Sanne. "Doreen, you need to get serious," he said, his soft breath stirring the hairs at the top of my head.

My laugh echoed down the hall, bouncing off the lackluster

walls. Madame Sanne arched the small of her back, and I felt her eyes penetrating my profile as I said, "This is definitely a first. No one has ever accused me of lack of seriousness before." If anything, since I was a child, people had commented on my seriousness as way beyond my years.

"No joke." Ty didn't smile. He glanced back at Madame Sanne, about to say something to her, but apparently he thought better of it. He leaned over, bending down, and said in a whisper, "Marry me."

Madame Sanne gasped and opened her Chanel purse to take out a tissue.

"I need you to marry me, more than I've needed anything in my whole life. There is no other way that I can really have you."

"Who said I want you to *have* me?" My voice rose a bit, as my hands grew moist and blotchy. Craig and Dalck, still in conference several feet away, stopped talking and turned to look at us.

"You know you love me, Mini. You make love like you love me—that can't be faked."

My cheeks must have gone cabernet red, the heat ignited like a lit gas burner behind my forehead. *What an inappropriate subject for the consumption of these clowns*, I thought. "Fine, Ty," I said, feigning calmness by regulating my breathing. *Stay calm and postpone topic to another time and venue.* I noticed Craig and Dalck starting to inch over our way.

Patty came out of the judge's private chambers, saying, "The judge is ready."

Saved by the court, I thought. *Finally got something positive for myself out of the justice system.*

"Just a minute." Ty turned to her. "This is more important." He whirled back in the other direction and said to me, "I want an answer now."

"Too many ghosts. Let's discuss this privately later on today," I said, lowering my voice, trying to be inaudible to the group.

"So you'll settle for some boring life with Mr. Cultured Pearl and his frigid clan?" Ty raised his voice. "You're going to sentence yourself to a colorless existence, for what? To satisfy your father?"

"*My ghosts*. Forget about Max. And this is certainly not the time nor the place." I hoped this would truncate the exchange.

"Just capitulate and marry Peter—that's the solution," Ty was going on.

"You think things are so simple. I'll just marry you and everyone will be happy, including me?" I could have used an exit plan right there and then. Wiping my palms on my skirt, I clasped them together in back of me. "What about my past? And my obligations?"

"No one can change the past. And it was really horrific, incomprehensible to the human mind. But it's over. Are you willing to doom yourself and your descendants until the end of time?"

"I didn't doom myself; it was done for me."

"Your ghosts can come along for the ride; I've no problem with that. But let me come along as well," he said, his voice cracking.

Ty looked haggard. I ached to touch his beautiful face and stroke it, fold his muscular chest into my small frame, somehow melt him inside me. But I knew I couldn't, not then. "Find a nice, blonde, uncomplicated girl. You can have an easier life. You deserve one, Ty," I said, realizing that even Justice Teller was out of his chambers now and listening. His narrow eyes absorbed the scene. The little spectator circle tightened around us, eyes moving back and forth between us as if they were all watching a riveting cross-examination, *Perry Mason* style.

"I know what I want," Ty said, pointing at me. "You—to make me think and make me laugh." His brow was beading up, and he removed his tie, throwing it on the bench.

"Ms. Lowe, would you care to explain to me what is going on?" Judge Teller said.

"It's a bit complicated, Your Honor, but I think we're almost done." Turning to Ty, I said, "Okay, tell you what. I'm willing to consider the offer. We can discuss it again in a few days."

"Oh no, no you don't. Once I let go here, that'll be it. You'll run, finding all kinds of reasons why this won't and can't work." Ty looked around at the audience.

Finally, one of the spectators spoke up, his voice teasing the air around us. "Listen, we don't have all day. I've got another conference scheduled at noon," Craig O'Leary said, looking at his watch. "Get married right here and now. Can you perform the ceremony, Judge? Then we can finish and get on with things."

"Sure, my powers include matrimony, not just divorce," Justice Teller said, patting his comb-over with his fingers. "But we're in the midst of a hearing in another proceeding ..."

"I love weddings." Madame Sanne perked up, stepping toward Ty. "You know, that would make it a fait accompli."

I cut in. "Very funny, guys. Hate to ruin your entertainment for the day, but this doesn't seem to fall into my book as a suitable wedding."

"*Suitable?*" Ty said, his raised voice uncharacteristic but authoritative. "You've got to be kidding. You hate pomp, you couldn't care less about fancy things, and now you suddenly have problems with the wedding itself?" Ty sat down on the bench with a thud. He cradled his chin between his hands, his eyes misting up.

I hope he doesn't bawl in front of these people.

"I tell you what, Mini. Let's get married here and now and stop the sneaking around. Then, if you want, we can throw a big party, whenever and wherever you say."

"What about the Penguins? Will this be fair to them?"

Madame Sanne and the rest of the group looked puzzled by the addition of an unfamiliar animal into this "circus." Patty said, "Penguins?"

"Ms. Lowe, you have caused this entire proceeding to get out of hand," Teller said, his voice peppered with irritation.

Ignoring all of them, Ty said, "I understand the Penguins may be upset."

"*May be*? Have you been with me or someone else for the last few months?"

"Life's unfair—some are lucky, some not. You always say that. Maybe the Penguins won't be happy, but what about you, Mini? You love me, god damn it." Perspiration was forming between Ty's nose and upper lip. "For once don't be so sensible."

In my mind, slivers of childhood flashed by on eight-millimeter film, like the old home movies I've watched countless times. My mother, strawberry blonde Hala, dressed in a flowered skirt, smiling directly into the camera as her daughter danced in front of her, with a big lollipop in hand and red stains on her crisp white dress. Emblematic of my earlier life, I could never do any wrong. Just my breathing was reason enough for my mother's light smile.

But that was long ago, and she was gone. Now, I craved blazing colors to fill my adult palate.

I looked at Ty, the gregarious, gentle gentile who had dubbed me Mini. His cowboy swagger and speech, at times laced with profanity, belied his compassion and soulfulness. He smelled of raw humanity; his desires were infectious: life sprinkled with adventure and mirth. He refused to travel solo on his journey, yearning for a partner. If I rejected his proposition now, my fate would undoubtedly be sealed: a bleak existence in the North Pole. My toes started to numb from frost, yet my cheeks were on fire.

"Alright, I think I'm ready," I said in a low voice. "Maybe." I wasn't sure about what I was doing.

Ty pulled back my hair and kissed my forehead. Madame Sanne blew her nose in a tissue, mumbling. Patty whispered to her boss to get his robe back on and convinced him to officiate, as she ushered the little party back into the justice's chambers. Justice Teller postponed the Sanne hearing until the following month.

With Madame Sanne as my maid of honor and Craig O'Leary as best man, Ty and I took our vows in a ceremony presided over by Justice Teller. Madame Sanne made a weepy toast, most of which was incomprehensible quasi-French. We drank Chivas Regal, retrieved from the judge's upper right desk drawer, in Dixie cups supplied by Patty from the communal water cooler.

Then I maneuvered Ty into the judge's private bathroom, closing the door behind us. We could barely fit into the tiny space alongside the toilet, rusted sink, and mirror. Putting down the toilet seat cover, I slid off my heels and stepped up. I drew Ty toward me, folding my arms around him, my nose pressing against his forehead. I kissed his eyebrows and then each of his eyelids, before getting to his lips.

"Okay, Ty, you said I make love in a certain fashion. Well, then …" I said, my fingers moving swiftly to open the top two buttons of his shirt.

Bringing his hands up, he grabbed my fingers. "Stop, Mini, enough," he said, although an enormous grin remained painted upon his face.

"We'll lock the door; they won't mind. It'll be memorable

in the judge's bathroom," I said, freeing one hand and opening another one of his buttons.

"That's for sure. But no, no, not now," he said, kissing me again. "Not a good idea here."

"Why not?" I said.

Ty moved his head against mine and whispered, "Because you're much too loud."

Laughter tumbled out of my mouth, forcing tears to well up in my eyes. My legs became rubbery, barely holding me up.

Ty squeezed his arms around me, chuckling. "Understood? Besides, I've already held up the boys long enough. I should be home sometime tonight, because the IPO documents are going to the printer, with one of the other guys. He'll be there all night proofreading, but I'll be off until early morning," Ty said, buttoning his shirt. "Got to get back to the office. You going to be alright?"

"I guess. I'll call Lenny and take the rest of the day off," I said, kissing his dimple. I truly did have plenty to do. "Thanks. It's been a lovely morning, a fabulous fait accompli."

There was one downside to the fait accompli: it was going to come as a seismic shock to everyone else in my life.

B IDDING TY AND THE REST of the wedding party good-bye, I headed for the nearest subway platform, a hint of liquor on my lips, having decided to break the news of my marriage to the outside world—solo. My oldest friend, Regina, was going to be the first to hear the news, in person.

I climbed aboard the subway headed for Puff Cosmetics headquarters, at the top of the "Lipstick Building" on Third Avenue. The rhythmic clanking noises of the train were a welcome respite after my unorthodox wedding, crowding out all other voices in my cerebrum. It was a few days after Thanksgiving, yet the city air still stirred with talk of turkeys and family gatherings. Even the Hindu straphangers, sandwiched near me on the train, bantered about cranberry sauce and traffic jams linked to national Pilgrim Day. I had spent the holiday at Sam and Bea's home, as always, enjoying loads of food and entertaining conversation with them, with Max, and with my cousin Sally, Sam and Bea's only child, and her family. Peter had been with his clan crosstown; Ty had been steeped in a project, working most of the day.

And now, I was hitched to Ty for life.

Chapter 7

On Third Avenue, I stood looking up at the thirty-two-story, oval-shaped building covered in coral-colored stones, with its numerous bands of windows. The building was divided into three sections, each ascending section narrower and set in further than the one beneath, looking like a colossal lipstick to the gods, hence its moniker.

As I stepped off the elevator on the top floor, the Puff receptionist, Lizzie, a petite bleached blonde with blue eyes like sliced blueberries, noticed me through the glass doors and waved. She was gabbing on the phone, elevated behind a bubblegum pink reception desk designed to resemble a giant powder compact. The baby pink walls of the reception area and the halls shooting off from there, as spokes of a bicycle wheel, were decorated with oversized Warhol-like photos of Puff products: lipsticks, eyeliners, and the company's signature sparkling eye shadow in stick form.

Two bored New Rochelle housewives had founded Puff a decade earlier as a lark, parodying the dominant cosmetic firms. To their surprise, the high quality and whimsical packaging caught on like a ferocious brushfire, jettisoning them onto both the national stage and the New York Stock Exchange. Regina was their second hire; she rode out the Puff bonanza alongside the founders, enjoying every minute of it. The firm now boasted twenty-three domestic sales offices and was poised to launch its first overseas operations, in Paris.

As soon as I swung into Regina's office, she signaled me to sit in a chair, parallel to her desk, as she brought a phone conversation with a buyer to a close. Open cosmetic boxes, order sheets, and a hairbrush lay on her antique pink desk with silver top. A sunshine poster hung behind her. She twirled a lipstick tube between her red-wine-coated nails.

"What brings you here? And during regular working hours?

Quite amazing," Regina said as she hung up the receiver and straightened up. "Don't tell me you dumped Peter?"

"Why do you say that?"

"Well, you've been rather distracted the past few months. I'm good at sensing your moods," Regina said. Lizzie buzzed her with another buyer from Houston; Regina instructed her to take a message and hold all other calls. "Well, what gives, Doreen?" She leaned toward me and fixed her gaze on my face.

"I got married."

Regina's eyes widened, and she sat forward in her chair. "So I was wrong, it was *not* Peter who was bugging you."

"I didn't marry Peter."

The color drained out of Regina's cheeks. She twirled her chair around and catapulted out of it. Between her desk and her window, high above Third Avenue, she paced, shaking her red-highlighted hair. Taxi horns and bus noises, in faded form, filtered through the large hermetically sealed window.

"Give it to me slowly," Regina said.

"I didn't marry Peter."

"I got that part."

"I married Ty Rockwell."

"The gorgeous banker?" Regina asked as she removed her jacket and draped it on the back of her chair. "But you told me you had dinner with him twice and that's it."

"Well, much more than that," I said. "Couldn't bring myself to talk about it."

I noticed that her turtleneck was tapered, accentuating her ample bust. Regina abruptly left the office, returning after a few seconds, carrying two mugs of sparkling water, and sat back down. "Drink this, then tell me what got into you," she said, sliding one bubblegum pink mug across the desk. She kept her fingers wrapped around the mug handle, knuckles whitening. We sipped simultaneously, allowing time for reflection.

"I couldn't marry Peter, as planned, this summer," I said. "And I couldn't marry Ty."

"But you did."

"Right."

"Help me out. Be-cause?" Regina set her mug down near the order forms. She folded her hands in front of her on the desk. Somehow, she reminded me of my fifth-grade teacher, Mrs. Mermelstein, who used to fold her manicured hands in similar fashion on her desk right before she lost control of herself.

"Because he's my one chance for combustible transformation."

"Skip the fancy talk. But you just said you couldn't marry him."

"I couldn't in the traditional sense of planning a wedding and going through all the usual motions. Too many opportunities for change of heart, you know … outside pressures." I played with one of the lipstick samples. "So I married him, spontaneously, during the Sanne divorce hearing in court. He showed up there and, well, things just evolved. It's a long story, sounds weird. I guess now it's a done deal."

"Holy mother of shit. I don't believe this." Regina unfolded her hands and put all her fingers through her hair, stretching back in her chair, glancing toward the ceiling. "Jesus, how many boyfriends have you had? I mean serious ones."

I knew where this was going, but answered nonetheless. "Four."

"I can't believe my fucking ears." Regina ignored my raised eyebrow; she was obviously not interested in curbing her profanity. "I've had twenty-three boyfriends so far. Losers, cheapskates, nogoods. And you have had four, two of them fighting to marry you." Regina shook her head. "You are one fucking lucky girl."

"Don't you see any problems with this?"

"What with marrying a charming hunk of a man?"

"And the rest?"

"Doreen, dear, I may not have any luck with men, but I'm not stupid." She leaned toward me, our eyes level. "You'll find a way to reconcile this with the rest of your life. Maybe, somehow, you'll finally figure out a way to use the jade box."

Two weeks before my sixteenth birthday, Regina had presented me with a jade box. She had been sprawled out on my bed comforter, her wavy hair—reaching down to her waist—pulled back in a glittery band, her T-shirt damp from the humidity and heat outdoors. It was mid-June. She had come from New Jersey into Manhattan for the weekend, making the trek by bus to the Port Authority Bus Station and by subway from there.

Inside the wrapped package she had withdrawn from her knapsack was a box of inlaid green jade, rectangular in shape, about the size of a loaf of bread. Shiny gold brackets were fastened at the four corners with tiny golden nails. "Turn it over," Regina had said. Fitted into its underbelly in a compartment, was a key. As I fingered the tiny key, a summer ray of sunlight glinted off of it.

"I saw it in the window of a store on Fifty-seventh Street a few weeks ago, in one of those phony liquidation sales, 'Everything Must Go.' I grabbed it. I knew it was perfect for you," Regina explained.

"The most beautiful jewelry box I've ever seen."

"Not jewelry—it's for your ghosts. The minute I laid eyes on it, I thought, *Holy crap, this is for Doreen*. You could put each ghost, one by one, inside the box, when you feel ready."

"For what?"

"For safekeeping. Once they're all in there, and you feel confident that you can part with them, you take out the key and lock the box. Forever." She beamed at the notion that she had devised the ultimate, foolproof plan for my "bothersome spirits."

For years, the jade box sat next to my bed on my night table. I fingered it before going to sleep most nights, tracing the lines of the jade pieces and brackets, sometimes cupping it in my hands as I lay near the door listening to Penguin tales. But it remained empty.

Regina looped around her Puff desk now, snapping me back to reality. She wrapped me in her arms, hugging me. She wiped teardrops from under her eyes. "Forget the ghosts for now. You really deserve a great guy, Doreen. I'm glad you got rid of the one with the stick up his ass." As she released me, she asked, "How're you going to get through telling everyone else?"

"I'm not sure. I'm going to find Lulu next and then work up my courage to tell Max. Afterward, maybe I can think about the overall ramifications of this. Or maybe not."

"Your father's not going to take this well."

"That's an understatement."

New York Hospital was a cluster of high-rise buildings abutting the East River. The light-colored buildings were connected by third-floor glass-enclosed walkways spread like octopus tentacles over First Avenue, which was pulsing with traffic—a giant East Side anthill of health-care activity. Lulu was in the midst of her three-year oncology residency at "the wards," housed on the fourth and fifth floors of the hospital's main building. Cancer was big business.

As soon as I swung through the revolving doors, the odors

of disease, chlorine, and recycled stale air assaulted my nose. The elevator taking me up was cramped with an elderly patient in a wheelchair, his mobile IV stand, his orderly, and an extended Latino family clasping a bunch of blue balloons, which were vying to escape toward the elevator's high aluminum ceiling.

On the fourth floor, at the nurses' station outside of the operating theater, I inquired as to Lulu's whereabouts. The young nurse, her hair in cornrows, instructed me to wait in a chair near the elevator banks; Dr. Smith was delayed in surgery. Being too agitated to sit, I decided to explore Department 400, the cancer ward. The light pumpkin-painted corridors did little to quell the palpable suffering. Respirator breathing noises reverberated down the hall, mixing with the rhythmic beeping sounds of the heart monitors. Patient and nurse murmurs drifted from behind floral curtains, which were sloppily drawn around the occupied beds.

I suspected Lulu had chosen this field because she found schizoid solace in her patients' struggles, especially those with poor odds. She likened it to her battle to escape the overbearing strictures of ultra orthodoxy. In her insular world of Williamsburg, Brooklyn, severe limitations were placed on women's rights; women were expected to have early marriages and endless children. Her father, a modestly remunerated diamond cutter, had never envisioned his Leah Rivka Smilowicz practicing medicine out in the vast secular world as Dr. Lulu Smith.

"Doreen, checking out the depressing environment?" Lulu asked.

I turned to see her walking toward me. Her blonde hair was pulled back in a thick, long braid, revealing cheeks etched with fatigue and dark half moons under her brown eyes. Her delicate features reminded me of an exquisitely crafted Fabergé egg. Long, shapely legs extended from her white hospital coat down to her scuffed clogs.

"I've a few minutes for a cup of coffee," Dr. Smith said. "Why don't we head to the cafeteria?"

On our way down the stairs, I asked, "How's Ely?"

Ely, a five-year-old leukemia patient, abandoned by his family—who had been unable to cope with the financial and emotional ordeal of his looming death—had been lying in Room 407 for thirteen consecutive weeks, alone.

"I think I'll stay tonight. It looks like it may be his last," Lulu said. "Would hate to have him die by himself. Someone ought to hold his hand."

"This is why you never get any rest, not to mention a decent social life," I said, trying to put a lighter spin on the topic.

"You're probably right, but I can't help it," Lulu said.

We bought a tuna sandwich, to share, and two cups of tomato soup. It had been hours since I last ate. The steamy soup warmed my face from inside, healing the tips of my fraying nerves. As Lulu spooned some soup into her mouth, I informed her of my morning activity.

"This morning I married Ty while at a divorce hearing," I said. I explained the rest of the details in a succinct manner.

"I think you've outdone me," she said, without breaking her soup tempo. Then she took a bite of the tuna sandwich and chewed. I waited for her elaboration; none followed.

"That's all you have to say?" I asked.

Tiny wrinkles creased around the rim of her eyes. "Your escape, maybe rebellion, is more brilliant, subtler than mine was."

"Did you notice I married Tyler Rockwell of North Dakota? Subtle, huh?"

Lulu put her sandwich down and smoothed out her napkin.

"My childhood world was stunned by my actions, but I have no regrets. Remember when we met, I was a dumpy religious girl—big glasses, long skirts, afraid to look anyone straight in the eyes. So little exposure to the outside world. But something inside me was pushing me to get out of Williamsburg."

Five years earlier, an acquaintance had asked me to help "this religious college kid get a cheap apartment." This kid, four years my junior, turned out to be a soft-spoken and intelligent adult, drawing me in with her refinement and compassion. Taking her under my wing, I introduced her to my New York City life, including Regina, who managed to mastermind Lulu's aesthetic and social transformation, particularly during the time I was steeped in law school studies.

"What am I getting out of?" I asked.

"You tell me."

"Max claims my luck is Peter."

"And you say?"

"I'm afraid to end up like Ely."

"You mean dying alone?"

"Being unlucky in death. Something deep down makes me think with Peter I would get to the end and regret it all. Die lonely, sad, even alone."

"You need luck in death like in life." She looked around the cafeteria. She pushed her hair back and shook her head, like she was releasing her ponderings into the atmosphere. "You once said that I was brave to trust my instincts, so trust yours." She brushed my arm with her hand, her gold charm bracelet sparkling in the fluorescent cafeteria light. "So, now all we can do is wait."

"For what?"

"To see if your instincts were indeed right."

Her beeper purred. Dr. Smith was requested back on the

cancer floor. As she made her way out of the cafeteria, at least one thing was clear: we would have to wait to make any judgment.

Once out on the street, I stopped at a pay phone to call Ty. By now it was dark. I apologized, letting him know I was going to be held up for a few more hours. He was kind enough to say he was planning to watch a football game.

The snow and salt crunched under my boots. As I came out of the subway, the wind smacked at my head, tangling my hair in messy clumps. I proceeded down Seventh Avenue toward Twenty-ninth Street.

Although my father and uncle dealt in imported glass for specialized commercial use, their office/warehouse had been situated in the heart of the fur district, south of Penn Station, since as far back as I could recall. Despite their financial success, the brothers had never moved their offices to a "better" neighborhood, so as not to antagonize their luck.

The smell of burning animal fur wafted out of the doorways of the few furrier establishments still left in the neighborhood, meshing with the smoke of kebab and other questionable meats cooking on the street vendors' grills. Entering the dilapidated doorway, I took the elevator up alone. No need to disturb the superintendent dozing in the folding chair. On the third floor, the locks creaked and the metal door swung open after I knocked several times.

"Doreen, you're here so late? And it's not even Wednesday," said Max, as he let me in. Since I had begun working for Lenny, I still came on most Wednesdays to help out with light office work, including correspondence, catalog editing, and some filing. It was a good way to stay connected with these two Penguins.

"Sam, Doreen's here. Get down from there and say hello. Give a kiss," my father instructed his older brother.

Sam, with hammer in hand, up on his tiptoes on the desk, was attempting to fix the air conditioner, which was protruding from the top of the dirty window. His choice of instrument was ludicrous. "So late. Maybe I should take you out to dinner," Sam said, blowing me a kiss with his free hand.

"Another brilliant idea came into your uncle's head," said Max. "This time, he decided to fix the air conditioner. I hope he doesn't believe we need it in forty-five-degree weather." He chuckled. "His repairs again. He thinks a hammer and some banging will make it run. In the end, he'll fall off the desk and break his head. *Akshun*."

"I'm not stubborn, but lucky. I know how to fall. When I fall, I fall very light," answered Sam, swinging at the unit's flimsy metal underbelly.

Under his breath Max muttered choice obscenities about his sibling. Sometimes the five years between them did not invoke the traditional respect of seniority. Sam abandoned his handiwork and climbed down to greet me. Despite the sixty-two winters under his belt, I could see his amateur boxing abilities in his nimble movements. My pint-sized uncle had been renowned in his youth for intense rage and fast fists.

"How about a candy? Strawberry?" Sam asked, as he put five into my hand and more into my black bag.

"Sam, I don't need so many."

"So give some to Peter," he replied.

"I don't think he'll want any candies, at least not from me."

"So tell him they're from me," Sam said, smiling, smug at having resolved the issue.

"He won't want any candies"—I paused—"because I married someone else today."

"Married?" the brothers said, in unison, looking at each other for a second and then away. Max folded and refolded the *Times* on his desk, while Sam rocked himself in a standing position. The clock with the Allstate Insurance logo ticked in what seemed like desperate attempts to fill the awkward silence. Glancing at it, I realized it was close to eight o'clock.

"I married Ty in a civil ceremony, this morning." I decided to skip the details; they were far more than the two needed to digest now. With no way to soften the blow, I just laid out the bare-boned facts.

"The bow tie? The *shaigets* bow tie? Is that possible?" Max said, again using the Yiddish for non-Jewish male, negative connotation. "Have you lost your mind?"

My uncle pulled up a chair with two widening holes in the upholstered seat. Sam sat down without taking his eyes off Max, who was slouched over the desk, rubbing the lids over his bloodshot green eyes, their vibrancy having leaked out in the last few minutes. His body seemed smaller and more shriveled like the prunes he regularly popped into his mouth.

Max sighed and said in a low voice, "What happened to you, Doreen? Did you forget who you are?"

"I want to find out who I am."

"By throwing everything away?"

"No, by taking everything with me, just on a different path."

Max turned to his brother. "She could have been married into such an elegant family. A fine family, with a great business." He stood up, pulling his loose pants up around his middle.

"Look what she picks." He sighed. "Good your mother isn't here to see this."

A chill flitted at the back of my neck. "I think Hala would have blessed it."

"Never," Max said, his voice quivering. "This is not how we raised you."

"Hala believed in taking chances. So did you, Max." I imagined her face, wide-boned and freckled, her brown eyes steady and compassionate. I imagined her talking about trusting my own instincts, like Lulu, and living to the fullest.

"I'd go with a sure thing—my own kind, and established, and rich," he said.

"You married Hala, an orphan just like you, but with a chronic heart condition, with no guarantee of her longevity, nor producing children, for that matter. She had open-heart surgery when I was four. No sure thing."

"Those were different times. Don't compare," Max said, turning away from me. "You're ruining your life, Doreen."

"Possibly," I said, afraid to look at my uncle, Sam, sensing he was on the verge of ripping wide open. There seemed like nowhere to turn, an ominous dead end.

My parents and I had an implicit understanding that we functioned as equals, like the black and white keys (and the foot pedals) on the piano, somehow making it seem only natural that I should call them by their first names, instead of the more traditional labels of Mom and Dad. They showered me with every opportunity and luxury, while I served as their protective talisman, shielding the survivors of the unbearable against more forces of evil and pain. As cocaptain of the ship, I was charged with navigating the treacherous waters of their new culture and society, while pervading their universe with tastes, giggles, and sounds of little girl experiences. In later years, the traffic of girlfriends, boyfriends, and poker buddies and their laughter filled up the voids of sadness and anxiety, especially on the days Hala lay ill.

Rising to leave, I gathered my bag and began to move toward the door, my legs wooden, fearing that any prolongation of the conversation was going to suck us into a vortex of accusation and hostility, from which we would be unable to extricate ourselves, whole, as the tight, albeit truncated, family we had become. I scribbled down Ty's phone number at the margin of Max's *Times*, before leaving. "My new number. I'll see you next Wednesday."

Lacking the energy to navigate the subway stairs, I boarded a downtown bus instead, crawling in the direction of Ty. It was a cold night, a sliver of moon in the dark sky. The few people riding with me looked tired from the long day. I walked the four blocks from the bus stop, rain falling in sporadic spurts, knocking at my hair as my heels kicked at the puddles swollen with melted snow. I slid the key Ty had given me several weeks before into the lock, turning it, and entered the premises, dim light coming from the alcoved bedroom.

Ty was sitting in bed, his face bent down engrossed in a book. The reading light caressed his profile, throwing an elongated shadow over the rest of the former bachelor space. I flung my coat, tweed suit, and stockings onto the couch, leaving on my turtleneck. I suddenly realized I had no other belongings in the apartment.

"The most exhausting day of my life," I said, winding around the alcove bend and slipping under the quilt. "My head's all fogged."

Ty closed his book and slid it on the nightstand, stretching out his arm so I could get comfortable with my head on his T-shirt, barely concealing his broad, muscular chest. The scent of his cologne induced my breathing to slow. Tears trickled from my eyes in a steady stream, dampening his T-shirt; he stroked my hair. My body felt limp, as if chunks of energy had been hacked out and swept into the city gutters.

"Sorry," I mumbled. "This isn't going to be a typical wedding night."

"Perfect, because it wasn't a typical wedding either. At least we're consistent." Ty smiled. For a second, a laugh begged to burst through the surface of my face, but my mind boycotted the attempt. My weariness must have been evident, because Ty said, "Don't fret, Mini. Get some sleep now. Are they here?"

I nodded my head as Tania pressed up against my back, digging her boniness into my thighs, her right arm slung over my waist. She whispered in my ear, "You've betrayed us."

Too tired to shoo her away, I shifted position to lessen the pressure from her knee, then twisted her arm so that the white underarm was no longer visible. I could not bear to see the small tattooed "A-2112." It was Hala's number, the one that had been branded in blue dye on her forearm when she entered Auschwitz. Aaron floated by and settled at the end of Ty's legs, curling into a tight fetal position, making suckling noises, his thumb deep in his mouth. Yankel sat on the floor in the corner of the room, crying.

My lids began to close, blocking out the sights and sounds of my new life, when they abruptly sprang back open. *Oh my God, I forgot to tell Peter.*

Chapter 8

T HE NEXT DAY AT MAX'S apartment, while Max was at his office, I was collecting clothes, my hair dryer, the jade box from Regina, and the latest issue of *Foreign Affairs,* and putting them into a duffel bag, when I suddenly remembered Peter's gifts.

Opening my bottom dresser drawer, I withdrew all the Baumgard jewelry and placed them into an old Stride Rite shoebox, stuffing the box into the duffel bag. The diamond and pearl necklace, the pearl double strand, the Tahitian black pearl drop necklace, the Rice Krispie-like pearl triple-stranded necklace with matching earrings, and the popular "Jackie O-style" pearl bracelet jangled in the cardboard box throughout my cab ride. *Thank goodness I emphatically discouraged Peter from buying a formal engagement ring. One less item to return.*

Earlier that morning, I had placed a call to my boss, Lenny, telling him I would be in late. Afterward, I phoned Peter, asking him to meet me at the coffee shop situated at the bottom of his office building. The line had been riddled with hesitation, as his day was jammed with meetings with new Brazilian buyers, including a catered lunch for the group in the Baumgard Nikkei conference room. In reluctance, he proposed we snatch a few minutes right after lunch, when the Latin Americans were scheduled to take a walking tour of the skating rink at Rockefeller Center. I had jumped at the offer.

At the Baumgard Nikkei offices, Marina, the elderly receptionist, greeted me with a cheery smile. She limped, one leg being shorter than the other, around the reception stand and pecked me on the cheek. We had become friendly during my time with the younger of her two Baumgard bosses. She liked to talk about her seven grandchildren, and I was amenable to listening. Marina indicated Peter had asked that I wait in his office; he promised to be out as soon as possible. I dragged the duffel bag with me into his office.

Swiveling in his executive chair, I surveyed the dark gray room, gravitas and Ingrid written all over it. Along the walls, pearls in every form—strands, brooches, wrist bracelets, earrings, tiaras, ankle bracelets, headbands, cuff links—hung on ebony backgrounds encased in black cabinets, like constellations flickering in a mythical galaxy.

Bright afternoon rays of sun sliced across Peter's desk, which harbored tidy stacks of order slips, a travel schedule for the coming two months prepared by Marina on her electric typewriter, and a sales brochure for IBM computers. On the walls were pictures of Japanese snow-topped mountainous scenery; under these Peter kept one personal picture of the Baumgard clan, including me, all of us decked out in black-tie attire. The photo had been taken during last year's annual Oyster Ball at the Waldorf Astoria. Baby pearls intertwined with miniature oyster shells garnished the picture frame.

I remembered the first time I had met Peter in this office. Regina had called one morning requesting my company in purchasing some pearls, in an effort to "conservatize" her look.

We had met in the lobby of an office building at the corner of Forty-sixth Street and Sixth Avenue, home to the pearl wholesalers called Baumgard Nikkei Traders. Regina had found out from a colleague that she could get quality pearls at a discount from the firm. Getting there first, I had been waiting for a few minutes in the lobby, watching people strutting in and out of the building. I was getting warm, so I unbuttoned my coat and straightened out my turtleneck. I noticed my leather boots were scuffed, but only the tips were noticeable under my corduroy pants.

About to take the *Times* out of my bag, I caught sight of Regina pushing the revolving doors on her way in. She came toward me in a white down-quilted coat and high heels. She opened her coat, revealing an emerald green suit with leopard trim. Her bag was of a matching animal print with gold buckles.

We immediately took the elevator up to the twenty-first floor. The receptionist—then a younger Marina—had led us into this very same office. We entered to find a slim man with his back to us, his hand extended into one of the black cabinets. I had been transfixed by the pearl displays stretched across the walls of the room. As the man turned around, I remember being surprised by his youthful age and good looks; somehow I'd been expecting a different, much older gentleman.

Obviously feeling the same way, Regina exclaimed, "What have we here?" She smiled and extended her hand. I knew Regina had switched into flirt mode.

He stepped forward to shake her hand and then mine. His eyes focused back on Regina. "I'm Peter Baumgard, but if you prefer, I can bring my father in to help you out."

"Quite the contrary. I enjoy dealing with your kind much better. By the way, how old are you?" Regina asked.

"I assure you I'm way beyond the minimum drinking age,"

he said, a faint smile on his lips. It was clear he was not about to divulge any more information.

"Good enough." Regina had removed her coat and draped it over her arm.

"Please be seated and we can get started." Peter indicated we use the chairs planted in front of an elegant glass desk, with the pearl showcases lining the wall facing us.

"What would you like to see?" he asked, folding his fingers together. I noticed his cuff links protruding from his blazer were sprinkled with diamonds. I figured they were real.

Regina told him she was interested in a strand of pearls, but had no idea what kind, quality, or hue. In short, she was here to browse. Peter decided to start by showing her the less-expensive strands of cultured pearls. He stepped to the furthest showcase and unlocked the cabinet, taking out a few samples. He walked back toward us, explaining some attributes of the necklaces as he put them on black velvet pads, which he slid to the middle of the desk in front of Regina.

I figured Peter and Regina would be hunkered down for a protracted session; neither of them was conversing with me anyway. So I reached for the *Times*, deciding I might as well catch up on some news. I mumbled some apology to them for any unintended rudeness, and then I opened the newspaper.

After a while, I glanced up to find Regina "modeling" pearls in front of a mirror on the sidewall. I watched Peter handle some pearl strands, authoritatively but lovingly. He seemed to move with grace through his pearl kingdom, content and comfortable.

Suddenly I heard Regina's voice. "The point is I'd like to appear conservative—you know, professional," she said.

My eyes followed Peter's as he slowly looked over my friend from heels to red lips to big hair. "And you think a strand of pearls is going to do the trick?" His tone was tinged with humor, charming, not chiding.

I couldn't help but burst into laughter. After a few seconds Peter joined in. He had maintained a serious facial expression until then. His laugh was refreshingly genuine.

"Laugh it up, Miss *Foreign Affairs*," Regina said, smiling at me in the mirror, a double strand of pearls swaying from her neck.

"Why do you call her that?" Peter asked.

"It's bad enough she's about to finish NYU Law School, but she also likes to read periodicals like *Foreign Affairs* in her spare time, for fun," Regina said, sighing for effect as she fingered another strand of pearls with matching earrings. "Crazy, huh? Look at her. Seriousness is written all over her."

And look he had. An hour later, Regina left the Baumgard Nikkei offices with one long strand of perfect cultured pearls, and I left with a date for the next Saturday night.

Now, Peter entered the office, his eyes remaining distracted with his morning business dealings. "Hi. Let me finish something and then we'll talk." Opening his cherrywood file cabinet, Peter flipped through two files and scribbled notes into one before putting them both back in place. Shutting the file cabinet with a thud, he turned to me. "Okay, what's the important issue?"

Peter looked striking in his navy Brooks Brothers suit, custom-made shirt, and tie with dancing elephant print.

"You know the wedding I'm supposed to be planning?" I heard myself say.

"You picked a date, finally. That's great, honey." He already had one foot out the door.

"No. I don't know how to tell you this, but it isn't going to happen."

"You need more time," he stated, probably presuming I was delaying the event, once again.

"No, it's not about time." I paused, swallowing hard. "I married Ty yesterday."

"Who?"

"Ty Rockwell, the banker at Goldfarb Magillan."

"What the hell are you talking about?" Peter looked directly at me, his eyes frozen; they seemed to have lost their blinking abilities.

There was a knock on the door, and his father, Alfred, stuck his head in. I watched his mustache sweep up and down as he told Peter that he was accompanying the Brazilian contingent to Rockefeller Center. After perfunctory greetings to me, he left us alone again. Peter sighed.

"Remember, I worked on the Dick Dorf deal—the lowlife with the telecom ideas. I met Ty then." I kept my voice steady.

"And then you married him?"

"No, not right away. I saw him for a while."

"You *saw* him while we were engaged?" He stepped up to the desk and bowed his head, getting so close a whiff of ginger sailed at my stiff face. "I think there are names for that—*tramp, cheat, whore*. Or maybe *traitor* would be a better word. Take your pick." Peter pounded his fist against the desktop, the vibrations sending papers in random directions, some cascading to the floor.

Betrayal. I had avoided confronting that particular issue head-on, since the day I first laid eyes on Ty. Betrayal was a loaded term, one that I had great difficulty in swallowing, let alone digesting. But by objective standards, that's what I had done to Peter. His cards had always been on the table, since the day we met over two years ago. The dynamics of his life had grown apparent to me by our third date, at the latest, and yet I hung on, deceiving him and myself—like wearing costume jewelry to the Oyster Ball. I had continued despite a constant uneasy twinge in my breastbone.

The kaleidoscopic patterns twirling prismatic colors of commitment to Peter for so long had come to a screeching halt in my mind, transforming into a clear, static picture, uncircumventable. Perfidy. Infidelity. My body's natural cooling system kicked in as if I were standing in the middle of Death Valley. Droplets dribbled under my sweater and itched at my skin, but I was afraid to remove my blazer for fear that any sudden physical movement would somehow further ignite Peter's rage.

"I betrayed you. It's unacceptable. But it wasn't intentional, Peter."

"Great, I can take that to bed with me in the future."

"Someday you'll have someone wonderful."

"I hate that shit. Stop it." He paced around the room with both hands stuffed into his pants pockets. "Don't be patronizing."

"No need to curse."

Peter hesitated, his brow twisted. "For years you accompanied me to pearl events, socialized with my family, brought me to Max's, asked my advice, traveled with me, slept with me." His eyes were blazing. "And now you're leaving me for some Wall Street white trash after knowing him for all of two minutes?"

He lifted the picture of all of us at the Oyster Ball and chucked it at the opposite wall. The glass splintered across the carpet, a few of the decorative pearls rolling off. One hit the heel of my shoe; I gazed at it: white, sweet, innocent, vulnerable.

"You don't even know him," I said quietly while dwelling on the two words "white trash," as if it mattered what Peter thought of Ty.

"You honestly believe this banker can live with your peculiarities?"

"Well, at least he doesn't feel compelled to tell me to shut up about them."

"He can never understand you, Doreen—your ghosts, fears." He was calmer now, his eyes becoming clearer, his braided brow unraveling a bit.

"Maybe not, but I need a life of vast possibility. Vivid colors. Things I don't think you understand, Peter. Despite your good intentions, these are terms outside of your lexicon."

He turned his back to me and stuffed his hands into his pockets again. "My mother was right all along. You could never be pliant."

The unbendability accusation baffled me. Weren't he and Ingrid the unyielding ones? Weren't they the ones who saw the universe in two shades, with no room for flexibility, creativity, Technicolor?

And in an epiphany, what was suddenly unmistakable to me was the disaster that would have reverberated throughout my planet, if it had continued to revolve in the Baumgard solar system—consequences Peter could not or did not want to foresee.

Peter was wide open, with no corners, like flat cornfields. He would follow the life trajectory that Ingrid had already predesigned, predestined, preprogrammed. But Ty was a labyrinth, right angles coming at me at every turn, his destiny yet unmapped. Instinctively I knew I could plot some of the movements, take hold of the steering wheel for part of the course, and that he would welcome, even savor, my involvement without paying heed to suffocating decorum and duty.

"Maybe Ingrid was right," I said softly, bending down.

I unzipped the duffel bag, pushing the jade box to the side and grabbing hold of the shoe box, yanking it up on the desk.

Without looking up at Peter, I removed the Stride Rite lid. Reaching in, I began to take out the jewelry pieces one at a time. The diamond and pearl necklace clinked on the desktop, throwing some brilliant sunrays at my face. Suddenly Peter's hand swept in front of me, knocking the shoe box over. The jewels scattered over the desk, scrambling the stack of order slips.

"Doreen, you're going to regret this and come running back to me," he said.

I glanced up as Peter turned away to open the door. "I'm really going to miss your brothers. Please tell Gene and James for me." A tickle scratched at my throat. I coughed.

"Show yourself out; you know the way." He slammed the door.

PART II

.

Chapter 9

FIVE YEARS LATER, TY ROCKWELL decided to gamble it all.

Just as the eleven o'clock news was about to broadcast one night, Ty flew into our apartment. "I think this may be it, Mini—no more Goldfarb Magillan," he said.

Looping around the alcove, he checked on sleeping Jack, who was breathing in his blissful peacefulness. Kissing his forehead, Ty tucked the quilt under our three-year-old prodigy's chin. Jack had come into the world fifteen months after we were wed by Justice Teller. He weighed in at ten pounds, with beautiful skin, a light blonde fuzz atop his head, and a set of healthy lungs. We chose his name because it was succinct, masculine, and of indeterminate ethnicity.

Another fait accompli, Madame Sanne would have said. *The single greatest moment of my life*, I thought.

"So what happened?" I asked.

"Jerrold and I had dinner at Gabriel's," Ty said. For the past several weeks, Jerrold Wagner, the New York real estate tycoon, had shown compelling interest in the prospect of partnering with Ty. It was the summer of 1994 now, real estate was in a major slump, and Jerrold needed to diversify fast.

Beforehand, Ty had served as investment banker on several ventures, with Wagner as developer. He had shared pieces of his telecom dream with Wagner, ideas which had crystallized while he had worked on the Dick Dorf deal. According to Ty, thanks to Dorf, not only had he gotten hooked on telecom, but he had gotten intractably hooked on me as well.

"And?" I said.

"And here is the diagram I drew for him." Ty showed me the napkin, with his diagram on it looking like a spider web, fiber transatlantic and national lines crisscrossing the face of the globe with switches at their numerous junctures.

I clicked off the television as Ty came back around, as it was clear to me that television world affairs would have to wait. He sat next to me on the couch, whose striped colors had long faded into monotony.

"I think I convinced Jerrold that this is the time to pursue telecom with my plan and he agreed," Ty said. "The big providers are in for a shock. You know, the telecom field is about to burst wide open."

"He's willing to invest in your idea. That's wonderful."

"A guy named Avery Beekman will invest along with him. They've been investing side by side for years. Actually, Beekman is like a junior investor."

"Okay, that's fine."

"But, this means we may not be living high and mighty for a long time."

"We're not exactly living the opulent life right now, Ty."

We had recently moved into a small two-bedroom apartment in the same building where Ty had rented his first studio,

increasing our monthly rental payments. My old firm, Pellier &
Spielman, had moved to Westchester at the end of my pregnancy,
so we had amicably parted ways. I had not returned to the
workforce since then, savoring motherhood for the past three
years. With one salary, albeit a good one, we remained careful in
our expenditures.

Looking around the apartment, I noticed Jack's yellow-
wheeled tricycle parked near the high chair, and the aging
television perched on bricks. My feet were bogged down in
colorful blocks and Matchbox cars. I got up and walked over to
the kitchen to wipe down the countertop and wash out Jack's
dishes and cups.

"Jerrold offered the equivalent of a year's salary and an office
in his space," Ty said.

"Great."

"Salary—no bonus included."

"Isn't your bonus 50 percent of your salary now?"

"Yep."

I suddenly understood the implications of Ty's remark about
our future lifestyle. Thoughts shot up to my frontal lobe, thoughts
I hadn't entertained for a long time. If I had wanted a secure
financial future, I would have been Mrs. Peter Baumgard right
now, instructing my very own "Teresa" about housekeeping and
dinner guests. My apartment would be stretched across the front
length of a Park Avenue building, between Sixtieth and Eighty-
sixth Streets, not below and not above. Ingrid, my mother-in-
law, would be on the line giving out instructions for the next
pearl event and my duties. Peter, handsome in dark suit with tie
tightly fastened, would come home from the office, brush my
head with a kiss as he stiffened, catching sight of the toys strewn
throughout the living room.

I rinsed out the last of the cups and dried my hands on the kitchen towel. "So then I won't get my nails done every week."

"When was the last time you got them done, Doreen?" After several seconds, Ty's face relaxed, the corners of his mouth forming a grin.

"So then, what's the problem?" I asked.

Actually, I wished nails were my problem. My ghosts took that spot.

I turned to put the dried cups into the cabinet. I couldn't help but digress into pondering my ghost predicament. My spirits remained shaken by my marrying Ty. Many nights they kept me awake, pressing into me or simply hovering close to my face and disturbing my sleep. My verbal altercations with Tania about "my betrayal of the ghosts and our people" was the substance of many of my nightmares.

There had been a short reprieve when Jack first arrived. At his birth, Tania had kissed his cheeks, and Aaron had been ecstatic about the entrance of a new Lowe descendent into the world. At night, I would find them sleeping soundly, tucked in at his crib corners. I suspected Tania made sure Jack was always covered with his baby blanket.

But the euphoria had only lasted for a short time. Our détente deteriorated in a slow and steady fashion until my recent visit with my doctor. Thereafter, things took a severe dive toward full-scale disaster.

A few weeks ago, I had sat facing my gynecologist, expressing doubts that there would be any more Lowe-Rockwells. She had agreed with me that chances were slim. I had suffered serious complications during Jack's delivery, which had very likely resulted in stubborn secondary infertility. So far, our efforts to produce a sibling for Jack had failed.

There were indications that my ghosts were not taking this news well at all. They were growing more petulant. Tania's whining was eroding my tenuous equilibrium. "Dorka, this is another terrible thing you have done. First, Ty and then this."

Thankfully, my aunt and uncle, Sam and Bea, unaware as Max was of the gynecological news, remained happy. They had their daughter, Sally, and three granddaughters. The addition of a male into the Lowe clan was a blessing and "rounded out our family," according to them.

Max was a different matter. I had been aware of my father's ambivalence since the moment he had walked into the Mount Sinai maternity ward. When he saw Jack as a one-day-old infant, his tears had welled up. From his mumblings I had gathered he was devastated that Hala was missing this experience. And, even more so, he was upset at the mixed genetics of his new grandson.

Too bad Tania and Max couldn't talk directly to each other, I thought. *They have a lot in common: disdain for me.*

After the Labor Day weekend and without fanfare, Ty moved into an eight-by-four-foot office down the hall from Jerrold Wagner, at the pinnacle of the Chrysler Building. His desk swallowed most of the space. No secretary sat outside his office, but the panoramic view of Manhattan to his south kept the North Dakotan "inspired and buoyant," as he claimed.

For months, Ty seemed to spend inordinate amounts of time in pensive mode, with few meetings and no significant business travel to speak of. Frequently I asked him what he was doing, confused by his work schedule, which consisted of holes reminiscent of Swiss cheese.

But as winter approached, the enigmatic nature of his days fell to the back of my mind, replaced by my new priority— Regina's January wedding. It was a fortuitous opportunity for me to plan a lavish wedding without being the one in white walking down the aisle. Regina's father was in a nursing home besieged by Alzheimer's disease, and her mother had lost her fight to breast cancer when her only child was a freshman in college. That left the "highly functional wounded," as Regina called us, responsible for all the wedding preparations.

A master of manipulation, Regina arranged convenient business meetings at New York's finest ballrooms, with florists, photography studios, and dress shops, often with me posing as assistant. She not only arranged her wedding, but her Puff sales soared during this period.

On a bleak December afternoon, we finished the third fitting of Regina's wedding gown at Bergdorf Goodman; she managed to look both slutty and sophisticated in the Vera Wang piece. Swinging out the revolving door, we headed down Fifth Avenue. Regina grabbed my arm in a firm clasp.

The snowflakes caressed our faces as we zigzagged across the intersection of Fifty-seventh Street and Fifth Avenue under a giant illuminated snowflake, hung above the traffic, made of endless strands of white lights, like giant versions of Peter's pearls. The holiday decorations, Santas, and colored bulbs twisted around trees and lampposts like candy canes intensified the festiveness of the scene, with the shoppers whirling by us, balancing gift-wrapped boxes and store bags. Many seemed quite taken with Regina's smile, her face glowing with enticing kinship.

Regina was wrapped in a mink coat, zebra-striped gloves, and suede mocha boots with high heels. I couldn't help but smile remembering the chubby girl in summer camp, where we had first met when we both turned twelve. She would spend hours wrapping her kinky hair around aluminum cans, usually the used pickle kind, to achieve "drop dead sexiness." The "do" did not last more than an hour in the stickiness of the Berkshire Mountains, but that never dampened Regina's enthusiasm.

My energy began to wane, as did the winter sunlight fading on the sidewalks oozing streams of slush. In need of resuscitation, we turned into Fabio's for some coffee and cheesecake. "White Christmas" was playing as we settled at one of the tables.

"Love the Christmas songs, though this isn't our holiday," Regina said, sipping her latte.

"You should love them; after all, you were the star of the Christmas pageant performance."

Regina threw back her head, her signature throaty laugh tingling my ears as we reminisced. At seventeen, topped by an afro, Regina had belted out "White Christmas" to more than two thousand New Jersey suburbanites in the school auditorium. I had come to watch Regina perform. She had worn oversized white Styrofoam wings tied to the back of her mother's long silver nightgown.

I peered into my cup as if some answers could lie in the grounds spiraling at the bottom. "Irving Berlin's obsession with Christmas really used to freak me out," I said. "I could never understand why this Jewish kid tried so hard to fit in. And you know what the irony is?"

"What?"

"Maybe that's what I'm doing."

"I wouldn't mind," Regina said.

"Sometimes I lie there in the middle of the night, staring

at the ceiling, wondering how the only child of Max and Hala ended up sleeping beside this *shaigets*."

"It's better than having to make do with someone else's hand-me-downs." A tremor of self-pity rustled behind Regina's eyes.

Normally I would have changed the subject from Ty, to consider (for the hundredth time) Regina's predicament in marrying a man eighteen years her senior, with an ex-wife and two kids in the wings, but I was deep in narcissistic melancholy.

"Ty claims he's a nonpracticing Christian, doesn't care about Christmas and all. But then I ask myself what happens to Jack? Will he understand what all the Penguin suffering and pain was about?" I rambled, pulling my woolen coat tighter around my body, a shiver running up my spine. "How will he understand the destruction and redemption?"

"Jack has a great and normal life," Regina said.

"So that's it—just normal?" I mimicked her tone for *normal*.

"Your mother would've thought that's more than enough for her adorable grandson." Regina edged forward in her seat. "You're a lucky girl, Doreen. And Hala would've been damn proud." She slurped the last of her latte and set the cup on the table.

"You don't know that for sure," I mumbled.

Regina studied my face as if she might somehow decipher an answer in my features. "What I do know for sure is that someday when we're close to the end, we should go see the real penguins."

"What brought that up?"

"You know—Penguins and penguins. The other day, I overheard this woman talking about her trip to Antarctica and the penguins. She said she could leave the earth contented after that."

"So I'll be able to leave contented thereafter?"

"Maybe." Regina shook her head, pressing a strand of hair behind her ear. "Promise me we'll go."

It was impossible to refuse Regina. Her smile was infectious, her requests so sappy and sentimental. I figured it was easy to acquiesce now; there were so many years to go.

"Okay," I said.

I guess she felt she had accomplished what she wanted in our conversation, because she abruptly rose from her seat, swinging her mink over her shoulders. She glanced at her watch with bemusement. "Ready? We've got an appointment to keep. Anthony is waiting for us. You're getting your hair styled, dear." Anthony of Hair Magnifique on Madison Avenue was Regina's longtime hair stylist.

"You made an appointment without my knowing?"

"Oh yeah. Stop thinking so much. Get up—we're out of here." She scooped up her zebra-striped gloves.

I looked out the picture windows at the flakes coming down at a quickening rate. I was not about to argue with Regina; there was never any point. I grabbed my hat and bag and followed her out.

In late January, on a blustery moon-inspired Saturday night, Regina Astor became Mrs. Marc Sandler. She looked like a royal princess as she stood beside Marc, a successful mortgage broker. At the ceremony, Lulu and I walked down the aisle in floor-length raspberry gowns, the shade of Katherine van de Vrande's office walls.

I studied Marc—tall, slim, and balding, with fashionable spectacles on his ski-slope nose—as he took his vows. Generous with money, but not of spirit, he managed to compensate for the wide age divide between him and his spendthrift bride. No matter how hard he tried to be engaging and funny, he struck me as uncomfortable in his own skin.

At the reception, hundreds of orchids and roses in varied shades of red stood in huge flower arrangements on the tables as the 318 guests sipped from champagne flutes, under chandeliers dripping canary crystals. The air filled with the trumpet and saxophone sounds of the twelve-piece orchestra while guests devoured red and black caviar. The smell of duck cooked with oranges permeated the stratosphere of the Saint Regis Ballroom.

Max and Sam in tuxedos, and Aunt Bea in a black gown, were there. *Penguins actually looking like penguins.* The thought made me want to giggle for a moment. But then sadness pushed up, like the tips of icebergs protruding through the ocean blue. Hala was absent. I imagined her, the personification of refinement and elegance, enlivening Regina's wedding, happy to have married off "beloved Regina," as she called her.

As I watched Ty greet guests at the ballroom door, I thought of Hala's impeccable hostess etiquette. For an instant I regretted leaving Jack at home with a babysitter. I could imagine him, in a tiny tuxedo, skipping through the crowd smiling at everyone.

Marc's teenage children from his first marriage glared at Regina. I wondered how it must feel to lose a parent to another person rather than to an act of God. I felt pity for the youngsters, who refused to give Regina a fair chance. She, of all people, would have been receptive to any offer of kinship, being way short on relatives herself.

As I ruminated about the complex predicament of familial relations, my eyes drifted over to Aunt Agnes, her mother's aunt, Regina's closest living relative. The childless widow had flown up from sunny Sarasota to participate in the nuptials, promising to control her usually wicked remarks. But the vow unraveled as soon as she ventured past the subject of weather.

Seth Rabiner, my old friend from Johns Hopkins and my poker buddy, slid over to me at the rim of the parquet dance floor, plump with couples swaying to the crooning sound of Frank Sinatra. He was decked out in black tuxedo and red bow tie; I was taken aback by his transformed imprint. In clean-shaven form, his features were pleasant.

"Almost didn't recognize you without your ER greens on, Dr. Rabiner," I said. It was rare to see Seth out of his crumpled hospital greens; he even wore them during our poker games.

"How does it feel to be giving Regina away?" he asked.

"Fabulous—great to be at her wedding."

I wanted to suggest that he dance with Lulu and was about to say something when I noticed that his dark eyes, hooded by blotchy eyelids, were streaked with pinkish lines. The fetid smell of bourbon whipped past my face. As my one shoulder strap slipped down, Seth put it back in place, leaving his hand on my shoulder.

"It's wonderful to put an end to Regina's troubled history with the opposite sex. Need I remind you what a mess that was?" I added.

"What about *your* fucking mess?" he said, dropping his hand from my shoulder. He studied the parquet near his shoes.

Although startled, I knew this discussion required quick termination, preferably with minimum casualties. Mustering my thoughts, I said, "Any self-respecting doctor would recommend coffee at this point, because, otherwise, someone might say something regrettable." Smoothing the creased front of his shirt with my hand, I decided that commenting about cursing was inappropriate when dealing with a sauced friend.

"No one here has the guts to tell you, your life's a complete fraud," he continued. "What happened—you saw a dimpled chin and threw your giant conscience out the window?" Seth's cheeks were getting greener by the moment.

I scanned the room, pinpointing Max near the ballroom's French doors, talking with Aunt Agnes. I almost felt sorry for Max that he was missing Seth's enlightening observations, which he no doubt shared. Seth had managed to stab my Achilles heel well even though he was stone drunk.

"After five years, you suddenly remember to give me your opinion," I said.

"Five days, five years, a hundred, the issues haven't changed. Ty is a great guy, the type most guys love to hang around with—but as your husband?! For Chrissake, Doreen, you used to see everything through the lens of history, Penguin history. And then puff." He snapped his fingers in the air. "All gone."

"How do you know that's changed?"

"Get real. Don't try to feed me bullshit." His last word fired out with a drop of spit at my cheek.

"You've some nerve, Seth, criticizing my choices with such ease, considering you've yet to prove capable of any romantic connection with …"

Ty sashayed up next to us, interrupting. "You two look very serious. What's the topic?"

My whole life spilled onto the slippery deck of a ship, heaved from side to side by storm waves. Crumbling into pieces, my soul slid overboard, in fragments, gobbled up by the tungsten gray waters. Needing to climb back up to the surface, I used Ty's smile to hoist myself. After a few seconds I heard my own voice. "Actually, we were discussing the AIDS epidemic and how it is affecting Seth's hospital procedures …"

Ty waved his hand. "Okay, got it. The world's problems can't be solved here, not at this party. So, if you'd kindly pardon us, Seth, I'll invite the young and charming Mrs. Rockwell to dance."

He whisked me onto the dance floor, wedging us between two Puff executives and their partners. I pushed my head into Ty's collarbone. Throbs of pain pounded my chest as shards of broken soul scratched the inside of my cranium. My stomach churned with angst-laced acidity, threatening to spew out duck all over Ty's new tuxedo. I kept my head steady so that Ty would not catch my eye and make inquiries, leaving my mind time to regroup.

Seth had been rude, and drunk, but he had certainly not said anything I hadn't pondered since Ty entered my life. *Isn't this what those around me really think, even without the assistance of several drinks?* I breathed in Ty's masculinity, his cologne, wanting his nonchalant confidence to pass through my fingertips into my bloodstream, like heroin shooting through the veins. On most days his energy was intoxicating and liberating, compensating, to a great extent, for the undercurrent of anger and disappointment, particularly on Max's part.

Yet there was no way of escaping it. I had committed an act of supreme fraud, on my parents, my family, and my history. And on myself. Was I fooling myself that it was otherwise?

"You know, your new hairstyle's going to come in handy now," Ty said in my ear.

"Why? Am I going to work in a salon?" I touched my new shorter cut, tucked under at the chin. I felt thankful for the humorous topic.

"The new sophisticated look is perfect for your legal position at our first telecom acquisition."

"You bought a firm without me knowing?"

"It was a long shot and, besides, you were preoccupied."

I felt a pang of guilt for having expended so much energy on Regina's wedding. "Details, please," I said.

"Twenty-five million revenues a year, no profits," he said.

"And?"

"You've got to straighten out the legal mess there. Part time should be enough. You need to go over ASAP." Ty twirled me around counterclockwise three times and then dipped me. "Hope you won't have difficulties with the president."

"I think I can get along with pretty much anyone."

"Good to be positive," Ty said.

"Why?"

"Because Dick Dorf is president."

"What?"

"He'll be your new boss."

Chapter 10

TWO WEEKS PASSED BEFORE I mustered the courage to even think of traveling down to Dick Dorf's Village Telecommunications Solutions, known as VTS. But first, I hired a babysitter for the workweek, with the exception of Wednesdays, the day I traditionally brought Jack with me to Max's office. Through an acquaintance, short, round, Ecuador-born Fernanda Gonzalez came to us, with limited English but bountiful warmth and energy. Jack took to her immediately.

With child care taken care of, I ran out of reasons not to show up at VTS. So one Tuesday morning in early March, I found myself staring at the directory in the lobby of 60 Hudson Street, searching past MCI, ITC, GTE, PTW, and other alphabet trinities before finding VTS. Later I would realize that three-letter acronyms were de rigueur in the burgeoning telecom universe. But my head was focused elsewhere then—on tactics for surviving Day One, and all the other days thereafter, with my new boss.

The square building on Hudson Street in TriBeCa was the epicenter of the telecom universe on the East Coast. All telephone and data traffic destined to cross the Atlantic and end up in a home or office in Europe, or beyond, had to pass through huge gateway switches housed in this redbrick behemoth, taking up a whole city block. In the innards of the basement, running along baseboards through racking equipment, up columns and under elevated flooring, highways of fiber-optic and copper lines buzzed with millions of minutes of telecommunications traffic.

VTS operated out of the back quarter of the thirteenth floor. Aluminum double doors opened onto a reception desk with a large space visible behind. Lucinda, the receptionist, seated at the desk, told me Mr. Dorf was expecting me. The brunette sported an unmistakable Brooklyn accent, and a beeper was clipped to her Lycra top to the right of her Dolly Parton-like cleavage. I wondered what messages she needed to receive via beeper technology rather than through the traditional phone, which she answered all day long.

Following Lucinda's swishing hips, I strutted past the well-lit "switch room," where large mainframe machines nested on elevated turquoise flooring. To me it looked like a space-age Laundromat. Lucinda stopped at a bright turquoise door; the sign next to it indicated Richard N. Dorf was indeed president of VTS. Before I even stepped inside, my composure was shattered by the sound of a familiar nasal voice.

"Darling, I never thought we would get to work together again," Dorf blurted out. "Isn't it great?"

"Fabulous." I smiled in feigned excitement as I entered the office, stark and ultramodern.

Dorf circled his desk. In contrast to the sleek metal piece, Dorf looked like a throwback to another time. *His fashion sense would easily unnerve most of the human population, at least in Manhattan,* I thought. His brown striped polyester shirt was unbuttoned to its middle, revealing two thick gold chains intertwined with his chest hairs. Topping off the couture, a Yankees cap was planted over graying temples, tufts shooting out from under the worn, dirty rim.

"Let's settle in the conference room, so we can catch up," he suggested. "Lucinda, be a doll and get us some ginger ale."

He led me to a bland room, carved out from a corner of the switch pit, separated by glass walls. The conference table looked like someone's discarded dining room table, which it turned out it was. Lucinda's cousin had swapped the furniture, including the chairs, black vinyl upholstered, for four months of free long-distance service. Lucinda came in, placed two mugs on the table, and left.

"So, you snagged Ty, a Goldfarb Magillan star," he said, slurping from his mug. "Didn't think you had it in you, Doreen."

"I guess I'm just a lucky girl." I resisted sounding too facetious.

"It's not every day a Wall Street star gets swept up by a ..." Dorf stopped, taking a sip of his drink.

"Can't find the right words, huh?" I asked, about to help him out with some terminology, but I decided against it. No reason to indulge him in this discussion. Dorf was straightening his gold necklaces.

"So here we are. Wagner is chairman and your man is president of the holding company of *moi*," Dorf continued with a smile. "Who would've believed?"

I certainly wouldn't have. I drank from my cup. Jerrold R. Wagner, real estate tycoon, fluent in four languages, a man of continental manners, in business with Dick Dorf, slime exemplar. Life certainly was full of surprises. "I guess your telecom hunch was a good one—at least Ty thinks so."

"And you not?"

"Time will tell."

He smirked at my answer as he swallowed more ginger ale.

"Ty thinks I can help you with your legal load," I said, nudging the conversation into a more productive lane.

A head of dark, thick hair poked into the room. "Dick, I'm going now. Thought I'd stop by first."

"Good, good," Dorf responded. "Come in, Claude. Meet our new legal eagle, Doreen Rockwell." Dorf turned toward me. "Claude Thomas is our controller; we couldn't live without him."

"Lowe's my name, professionally speaking," I said, nodding.

"Nice to meet you," the stout Claude said. "Anxious to work together. But right now, you must excuse me. Need to get up to Washington Heights." Looking to Dick, he elaborated. "Told Harry if the money isn't ready when I get there, I'm throwing his computers and printers into the U-Haul. Hope we can use some of his Compaq computers here."

"Make sure you count before you leave Harry's," Dorf said.

"Don't bet too much on my walking away with cash, so plan on replacing our computers instead." Claude tipped his head to me and ducked out of sight.

"Good guy. Knows how to collect on the accounts receivable," Dorf said.

"Isn't that a tad illegal, removing property from your customer's premises?" I asked, trying not to appear appalled.

"They owe us money—it's been more than eight months. I don't need to supply free international phone service for Harry's call center. The Dominicans are a tough crop."

"And Claude does *all* your collections?"

"Yeah, it's fabulous. You're going to love him." He headed for the door, saying, "Let me show you around."

Dick Dorf walked me through the rest of the VTS offices, introducing me to his management team: Louey Spitelli, Frank Macroni, Gino Ventaletti, and Bernadette Civale. Ethnic diversity seemed lacking here with the exception of Claude Thomas, a Lebanese, sprinkled into the sauce.

Frank Macroni, vice president and Claude's direct boss, was designated my point person to guide me through the maze of legal documents and field my questions, in addition to serving as my conduit for work from the rest of the company.

I followed Frank to his office at the end of a corridor of identical, lackluster rooms. The desk held pictures of his family and overflowed with papers and binders. Even his desktop computer had piles on the keyboard and more papers barely balanced atop the screen monitor.

"First, let's have some Turkish coffee," he said, bending over to light a portable gas burner. Near his chair, a plastic table held the burner, along with a tray of small, ornate, handleless coffee cups. He put a few tablespoons of Turkish roast and three spoons of sugar into the aluminum coffee urn and set it on the fire.

I noticed his large, round eyes behind thick glasses focused on the activity, and his head of hair and beard, brown with red highlights, which were neatly trimmed. He took a call on his direct line, stroking his beard with two fingers during the conversation, mainly emanating from the caller's side. He hung up and poured two cups of the brew, the aroma sending tingles through my nostrils. He handed me one cup across the sloppy paper divide.

"Well, then, where should we start?" Frank asked.

"Tell me how the legal work was done until now."

"We used outside counsel for much of the the work, a firm called Bacci & Bacci."

"How about your sales agreements?"

"We have lots of those, which I'll show you soon." Frank was peering into his coffee cup.

"Excellent coffee," I said, figuring another tack was necessary to jump-start this conversation. His answers so far had been rather undernourished.

"Thanks." Frank seemed pleased, his eyes brightening for a moment.

"What's the immediate issue for me?"

"Let me give you the legal files so you can go through them. Make an index of them so they can be referenced when need be. Then we'll take it from there."

Fair enough, I thought.

Frank began to go through the disaster called his desk, collecting three piles of documents, which if stacked together would have towered over Michael Jordan. He called two assistants to move them out to one of the empty cubicles in the open area housing the sales team and wished me luck.

"What about a computer?"

"You'll have to borrow one, find one not being used. Sorry, don't have any extras."

I suddenly hoped Claude would be picking up some Compaqs in Washington Heights. "And a telephone?"

"Eventually."

Isn't this a telecom company? I wondered.

My surprise must have shown on my face, because Frank said, "Local service is provided by the local phone company. We're solely a long-distance, international phone company. We can't seem to get enough regular phone lines."

I sat down in the cubicle and took a glance at the papers in front of me. They spanned the corporate legal spectrum: offices leases, sales agreements, carrier agreements, vendor contracts, confidentiality agreements, bankruptcy creditor filings, switch purchase paperwork, fiber leasing documents, and employee contracts. Many were unsigned, some were missing pages, lots had spelling mistakes even in the first few paragraphs, none was filed in a labeled folder, and all were frayed at the edges.

Rubbing my eyes, I settled back in the chair. Little throbs of anxiety were drumming at my temples. *Okay, first things first.* I got up and went in search of some paper and pens. Eyeing a seemingly abandoned computer station, I made a mental note to ask to use it later on. Circling back to my cubicle with some supplies and a cup filled with tea, I lodged myself between the upholstered cubicle walls and began to weed through the paper heap. About two hours later, faint spasms climbed up my legs. I figured I might as well stretch with a walk and stop to update Frank on my progress.

The executive offices were all devoid of their regular inhabitants, and the switch room was quiet save for the constant humming of the mainframe metal structures and air conditioners (the space needed to be kept at very cool temperatures). Lucinda's chair was pushed back and still indented from her behind, as if she had just fled in panicked haste. The switchboard phone system on her desk was ringing, with lights flashing frantically across its front. The digital clock on the desk read 1:30. I picked up her receiver, pressed one of the outside lines, and dialed Ty's number.

"How're you, Mini?" he said when he picked up. "I tried calling you, but the receptionist said she had no idea where you were."

"I'm in some cubicle in the sales area."

"Hold on a minute," Ty said.

I heard the ringing of his cell phone in the background. I

shuffled papers on Lucinda's desk as I listened to Ty's voice speaking into the other phone. He was apparently trying to get off the other call, and his voice was strained. I realized this was not the first time I had overheard Ty's uncomfortable, rushed murmurs into his cellular device. After a few more seconds of conversation, he hung up the cell phone and returned to me.

"Who was that?" I asked. I was usually averse to prying, but this time I couldn't overcome my curiosity.

"No one," he said. A second or two passed. "Well, actually, it was a guy who wants to get some business from us. He's from Morgan Stanley."

"Really, who?"

"No one you know," Ty said and quickly added, "So, what's your impression of the Dorf operation so far?"

Ty's response seemed a bit odd, but I figured now was not the time to get into it. So I answered, "Well, I could ride a skateboard, *naked*, down the halls here. I believe lunchtime is a holy affair, work forbidden during the siesta."

"Guess our job of streamlining is urgent. And, you know, on top of that, their numbers are weak," Ty said.

"I'm plowing through the documents that the VP, a guy named Frank, handed me."

"And?"

"Tons of cleanup. You didn't exaggerate at Regina's wedding."

"That's why I volunteered you." Ty laughed. "By the way, I'm interviewing a guy for the CFO position here. I like him; we'll see what Jerrold says. Maybe Beekman will interview him as well. His name is Brad Barkow." Last week, Ty had mentioned it was time to bring on a chief financial officer at the parent company, JRW Communications.

"That will make six employees under you," I said. "I hope you spawn more kids other than Dick Dorf's firm—otherwise, you may go down in history as the saddest start-up story ever."

We hung up. I sauntered back to my work space, passing through the telemarketing section. *Even telemarketers leave for long lunches and all at the same time*, I marveled. By about half past three, most of the VTS staff members had meandered back to their stations. There was a series of conversations zapping at me from different directions, mainly concerning recently ingested lunch. The rest of the afternoon, with darkening winter shadows filtering in through the slatted blinds, and plenty of yawns, the salespeople handled phone calls and tapped at their terminals. At one point, the dozen or so salespeople crowded around their manager for a "pep talk" on boosting sales strategies. By five o'clock, the stampede to the elevators was in high gear.

"Anybody here know what work is?" I said out loud, my voice echoing down the abandoned hallway and snaking into the empty switch room. I took my bag and headed out.

Chapter 11

T HE NEXT MORNING, ON WEDNESDAY, I bundled Jack into his jacket and zipped down, as usual, to my father's office, with toys and snacks in tow. Jack loved the motley faces on the subway. The building's superintendent rushed to greet "my little man" with a high five. As soon as the elevator cranked open, Jack pattered to the rusty metal door reading "Saxx Glass Importers," banging away with his hand, shouting. Max opened the door slowly, and the two squealed with delight.

Wednesdays were my customary days at the family business. Now more than ever they filled a deeper vacuum. Since my marriage to Ty, Max had refused to come to my house and I had limited my visits to his apartment. The full absence of Hala and the self-imposed distance of my father were often too vivid and painful to bear. In resolution, we clumsily settled for sharing Jack on the no-man's-land of Max's office, under the guise of my helping out.

Sam, neatly dressed with some lonely hairs plastered across his scalp, grabbed our coats and hung them in the closet. He went behind the aluminum shelving and came back with fistfuls of candies. In a preemptive strike, he said, "Don't tell me they're not good for his teeth, Doreen. His baby teeth will fall out anyway."

Jack climbed up on the worn leather desk chair and began to unwrap the toffee candies, his face beaming. Sam shoved a whole assortment of flavors into my bag, saying, "This pocketbook is too heavy. Look, Max, this must weigh at least twenty pounds and then she has the other stuff for Jack."

Max and Sam passed the bag back and forth in somber fashion. I studied my father—his hunched shoulders, his enormous black sneakers. His shorter, older brother was still erect in posture, bringing them closer than ever before in height.

"Small women should not carry bags of this size," Sam said in Polish looking at Max.

"But where should I keep all my things? You know I'm always prepared for emergencies. Nobody's getting younger," I answered.

As long as I could remember, they had total disregard for their advancing ages. The two men chuckled at my comment. Jack giggled along, happy to participate.

Max flipped through the file he had on his desk labeled "Doreen," containing material gathered throughout the week, prompting Sam to remove Lego blocks and toy trucks from the blue bag. Sam and his great-nephew were going to play on the carpeting, as Max dictated correspondence for me to type on the typewriter.

The phone rang, and Max answered. Judging by the quickness of the shadow that swept over my father's creased face, I knew it was Ty.

"For you," Max said, thrusting the phone into my hand.

"Sorry to call you there, but I wanted your input before we make the final offer to bring Barkow on board," Ty said. He explained that Jerrold Wagner was agreeable to the new CFO hire, but Jerrold's opinions were grounded in quicksand reasoning. He used benchmarks involving an interviewee's affinity for art, the type of paintings he favored, and the restaurants he frequented.

Jerrold's coinvestor and the more serious of the two, Avery Beekman, was in the hospital, having undergone a gall bladder operation; he was thus unavailable to interview Barkow.

In contrast to Jerrold, Ty now tried to focus on Brad's qualifications, which indeed were impressive. Young, bright, and hungry, Brad, more than any of the other candidates, believed Ty's company would succeed in a short time frame.

"Hire him," I said.

I hung up to find Max busy straightening out glass samples shelved in the corner, and Sam playing "hide-and-seek" with Jack.

After I called out for Max to continue, he shuffled over and sat in the chair with holes in the seat, and said, "I don't think much can come of this telephone idea. People simply buy AT&T, the giant."

"Not true anymore. Maybe if you'd study the situation with an open mind, you'd have more faith," I said. "You read the *Times*, so you must've been following the developments." There had been sea changes in the telecom arena.

"He'll need tons of luck." Max always referred to Ty as "he" or "him." "And he needs financing."

"Max, how many times must we go over this? Ty has backing from Jerrold Wagner, the scion of one of New York's richest real estate families. And the luck part—he's working on it."

No reaction. My father pursed his lips and sat quietly for a while, leaving me to pound the typewriter keys and wonder if time or luck would somehow resolve some of these issues.

While redrafting a letter to an overseas supplier, I said, "You know, Jack's getting older. In the fall, a preschool program."

"Already?" Max said, a mist fanning out behind his eyes, the green speckled with more yellow dots now. The crevices chiseled on his forehead seemed to deepen as we spoke. I realized he thought that meant Jack's regular Wednesdays at the office would cease.

"Well, your grandson's very inquisitive," I replied. "Hanging around with Fernanda isn't going to be enough."

"But when will I get to see him?" he asked.

"He'll be in school three days a week. But, I'm still going to bring him on Wednesdays."

Jack ran over to us; he wanted to look at his book of trains. Sam opened up the reclining chair, softened from years of use. Jack climbed into the seat, curling up with his hands wrapped around his book. After a few minutes he dozed off, his sandy hair falling on the vinyl folds. Jack was a miniature of his father, only with Max's eyes.

All of a sudden I remembered watching Ty resting in my childhood bed, long ago when his back had gone out at Max's apartment. I never admitted to anyone, not even to Ty, that I had been smitten from that first moment.

"If you gave Ty a chance, you might even like him," I said.

"This isn't why we survived."

Sam tripped over a box on the floor, the bang jolting me. "You see, Max, I trip very lightly," Sam said, glancing at Jack to make sure he hadn't disturbed his nap. The little Rockwell was sleeping by then, faint snores drifting out of his mouth, lips separated for passage of air.

"Again with the falling lightly nonsense," Max said, straightening out his envelopes and lining up the paper clips in perfect rows across the desk.

Sam stood with his back against the window, his gaze focused on Jack's chest, which was moving up and down with each breath. "Maybe you should stop with your *narishkeit*, Max. Consider yourself lucky."

"This lucky?" Max moved toward the window, straining to see through the smeared panes. "Do I need to remind you, Sam, of what *they* did to us?"

"Ty's from North Dakota," I said. "It's a different story. This is America, *goldene medina*, land of golden opportunity, you always say," I declared, knowing full well that despite my comments, war memories were going to cascade out anyway.

"If they only would've left us alone—even to run in the forests, so many more of us would have survived," Sam reflected. "But no, they hunted us down like dogs and turned us in to the Nazis. Volunteered—happily, proudly. No coincidence Hitler put the death camps on Polish soil—he was a clever, evil man."

"For a pound of sugar they took Tania, only twelve years old with such nice pigtails," my father said, his nostrils flaring out and his cheeks turning blotchy in texture. "Beautiful honey hair." His cousin Tania later perished during a march to a nearby labor camp.

Sam walked over to his brother, putting his arm, laced with veins and thick tendons, around him, and whispered, "Shhhh, Max. We're in another place now. No more Poland. And we got another Aaron."

"*You* speak total *narishkeit*." Max raised his voice, flinging Sam's arm off, his eyes steely with fury. "Don't you *ever* mention *him* like that again."

Fifty years had passed since they lost Aaron; it had been the single worst moment of their horrendous war years. Luck had betrayed them then. The brothers never spoke of him with anyone, including me, only to each other in the darkness of late night, over tea. I had slowly pieced together the fragments of Aaron's fate.

He had been the only child of their older sister, Sally (after whom Sam's daughter was named). With her light brown hair, fierce green eyes, and hourglass shape, Sally cut a striking figure in their neighborhood. More impressively, she had kept the family financially afloat in the aftermath of their father's bankruptcy. Sally had moved her husband, Ben, a tailor, and baby son into her parents' home in order to pool their meager resources.

Regarded as a talented portrait photographer, Sally toiled at her employer's studio for fourteen hours each day, six days a week. The family stayed fed and clothed through the efforts of my namesake, Dorka, my grandmother, her back-wrenching housework stretching Sally's modest salary. The two women even squeezed out enough *zlotas* to send Sam, seven years Sally's junior, to the private gymnasia school, a privilege not bestowed on many adolescents in 1939 Krakow while Hitler was shouting words of war in Berlin.

During the first few transports of Jews from their city, Ben and Sally were taken to meet their death by gassing in Birkenau, the extermination camp adjacent to Auschwitz. On the main Krakow train platform, with thousands being loaded into foul-smelling cattle cars, the brothers had sworn to Sally they'd use every fiber of their beings to watch over Aaron. "I've complete faith in the two of you," were her final words.

And so they had. For four years, through the labor and concentration camps, the teenage uncles fulfilled their promise.

Sinewy Sam, propelled by fury, pulverized boxing opponents in makeshift rinks for the pleasure of the SS officers. His prizes of extra tepid soup, made of water and potato skins, and lighter work shifts softened Aaron's sobs. On Christmas Eve 1943, in a stunning performance and against all odds, Sam whipped his Russian POW opponent to a pulp. Aaron received five days off from trench digging, while word of Sam's victory spread awe and elation throughout the Auschwitz barracks.

Then in the winter of 1944, the coldest one since der Führer marched into Poland, the American bombings became more and more frequent. The explosions were sweet music to them, lulling them to peaceful, dream-filled sleep. With each passing day, they began to inhale the glorious, intoxicating scent of possible liberation.

But while Sam and Max were digging trenches in frozen earth, their nephew was found to have a raw potato hidden in his rags. He had discovered the potato behind the kitchen shed. Yankel, the boy who shared his bunk bed, a narrow wooden plank with no blankets or pillows, saw him last, before heading out to his laundry-shed duties. Aaron had been rustling his rags around in a frenzy, his eyes burning bright, illuminating his pallid, sunken cheeks. He looked at Yankel and said, "Later when you get back, I have a surprise to share."

Thirty-six days short of freedom, Aaron was hung between the double fences, barbed and electric. Snow was falling, while the crematorium spewed burning human flesh. His frail, tiny body twisted in the icy wind. The potato protruded from his loose, lifeless mouth.

Aaron had turned nine the day before.

REGINA AND LULU WERE WAITING at our favorite restaurant, Pomodoro, in my old neighborhood on the Upper West Side. Passing the outdoor tables and umbrellas stacked together and secured with metal chains, I noticed the restaurant windows were all steamed up. In clement weather we loved to sit, shaded, under the umbrellas sipping wine and eating Caesar salads, watching the Columbus Avenue traffic whiz by, bus and taxi fumes blowing at us.

Inside, the mulberry-colored walls were decorated with Italian ceramic plates and a large, picturesque mural of Tuscany. Regina and Lulu had grabbed a table in the front corner of the crowded little place and were drinking red wine in goblets. I squeezed between the tables and pulled out one of the wooden chairs between my two friends.

"Doreen, we've got to toast Regina's weekend trip to Barcelona," Lulu said. Her hair was up in a bun. "Her one-month anniversary."

In a flash I pictured Marc Sandler's grinning face. "You'll love it there," I said. "Any specific plans?"

"Second wives equal shopping plus sex," Regina answered.

Chapter 12

"Fascinating," I said, for lack of a better response.

"Anyway, Marc and I need to live it up now," Regina said. "Soon I'm going to start working on a baby."

"Didn't you say you were going to wait some time before that?" I asked.

"I think I did."

"Well, this is only your first month of marriage."

"Yes, but I need something more concrete besides the designer clothes in my closet," Regina said.

"Sounds romantic," Lulu said in an irritated tone.

"Regina's just entertaining us," I ventured.

"None of this relationship thing is serious to you," Lulu said. "Are you just using Marc?"

"Girls, now, let's calm down," I said, turning my head to Lulu. I realized what was irking her. "Mike is still bothering you, I'm guessing."

Lulu had dated Mike Epstein, a radiologist at Mount Sinai, for several months. They had broken up right before Regina's wedding. He had trouble with her earnestness. I suspected he had more trouble with himself.

"Well, at your next workplace, there'll be lots of doctors to choose from," Regina said, obviously ignoring Lulu's last accusation.

Lulu had accepted a staff position back at New York Hospital, where she had years earlier completed her internship. In between, she had practiced at Mount Sinai Hospital.

"This seems like a great time to suggest, once again …" I started.

"Don't even go there," Lulu said, a sigh leaving her lips.

"Excuse me, I think it opportune to mention Seth now," I said. From time to time, I had attempted to impress my idea upon Lulu—that she try dating my college friend, Seth Rabiner. I believed they suited each other. But I also knew that Seth would never initiate the relationship; my only hope lay in Lulu.

"On the rare occasions when we have met, sparks were not flying," Lulu said. The two met infrequently, at my birthday dinners and more recently at Regina's wedding.

"You can *make* them fly," Regina said.

"Force myself?" Lulu looked at Regina with a stricken face.

"Well, maybe not. After all, now that I think about it, he is quite melancholy," Regina said. "And unkempt."

"Stop, Regina," I interjected, turning to Lulu. "You and Seth have so much in common. But you need to make some kind of first move."

Lulu stared at her cutlery and then took a sip of wine. The waiter came over and we ordered. After he left, Lulu glanced back at the checkered tablecloth.

"Look, Lulu, all I'm saying is that you and Seth are both compassionate doctors, really committed not only to the profession but to your patients," I said in a gentle voice.

"By those standards, I can date half of any hospital," Lulu said.

"But there's more to it." I tried to choose my words carefully. "You're both shy people, but underneath there is intellectual depth, much passion for life. Your backgrounds also seem similar. Seth's parents thought he was nuts to go into medicine."

"Yeah, his father is a mailman," Regina said. "I forgot about that."

"He made it through med school on his own, emotionally and financially." I remembered Seth's face as he sat on my dorm rug, when he told me for the first time that his father believed a civil servant job would be the ultimate accomplishment for him. To this day, his folks were opposed to his career decision.

"I thought medicine was every Jewish parent's dream," Lulu said.

"Really?" Regina replied, her eyebrows raised.

"Who am I to say?" Lulu asked rhetorically. After all, her parents still remained enraged by her choices, including her professional ones.

"Don't let Doreen's suggestion about Seth keep you from checking out the doctors in your new position," Regina said.

"I haven't officially started yet," Lulu said. She was scheduled to begin the following week. "Besides, who'd be interested in such a serious person?"

"Just because Mike wasn't for it, doesn't mean there isn't someone who can appreciate you," Regina said.

"Hey, if Ty can handle living with my ghosts, why can't someone find your earnestness attractive?" I said. "And don't forget, Ty gets the pleasure of living with two kinds of ghosts, the real flesh-and-blood kind *and* the translucent." *And none of them approves of him*, I thought.

I reflected on the miserable state of my relationship with my spirits. They were bothersome and whiny, furious at my decisions, and more difficult to tolerate. Definitely not a topic I wished to delve into just then with my friends.

I decided I was going to change the topic to my new job just as our appetizers arrived. While the waiter set them down I thought about my day at VTS. It had only been my second day, but judging by my headache it seemed more like my second year.

Earlier that day, I had realized that my poker face was going to come in handy during my stint at this firm. It had served me well at poker games. It served me well at Max's office on Wednesdays, masking my uneasiness with a quick smile and cordial talk. Now, my gut told me that I would be employing the same poker expression at Dick Dorf's place.

Case in point, the last meeting of the day.

Just before four o'clock that afternoon, Bernadette Civale had asked me to join her and Claude Thomas. When she and I walked into the conference room, Claude was already waiting, drumming his fingers on the bartered table. He flung a clump of papers across the wooden surface to me.

"This is a carrier arrangement we just closed with ITT out of Florida. Great numbers," he said.

"Should I review it?"

"Now." Claude's almond-shaped eyes moved back and forth in his broad face, like car windshield wipers. "Please."

While arranging the pages in order, I noticed the blank spaces atop the signature lines. "This is unsigned."

"Yeah, that's okay," Claude said, waving the issue away.

"You said you closed the deal, so I assume you'll be signing this shortly."

"Doubt it. ITT doesn't want to sign." ITT was a small telecom company operating out of Jacksonville.

"May I ask why?"

Bernadette volunteered, "They have an exclusive with MCI, and this wouldn't be good."

"You mean it would violate their agreement with MCI?" I interpreted her eloquent statement.

Neither answered for a few moments. Then Claude said, "We just want your opinion on the terms."

Although I wanted to pursue the issue of ITT's non-signatory intentions, I decided to hold off. Instead, sitting back in the chair, I read through the document, which set forth the terms by which we would carry thousands of international minutes of the

Floridian firm overseas. While I concentrated, Bernadette made a call to her mother to find out about her latest chiropractic visit.

"The terms seem straightforward to me," I announced, after she had hung up. "So what's the problem? There was obviously more than just the violation of MCI's contracts, which in and of itself was bad enough.

I sat for a few seconds without either one meeting my gaze.

Finally Claude cleared his throat. "We don't have the network to carry the traffic."

You don't have the network? Then what in God's name are you selling? I was feeling an ache in my chest, and I hoped it was building heartburn, not the prelude to a heart attack. *What am I doing in this place?* "That poses a problem," I said in a restrained voice, no expression visible on my face.

I began to suspect they had mistaken me for Mary Poppins, with transatlantic cable and other tricks in my carpetbag. Bernadette maintained a blank look on her face, as if she had just joined the meeting. Claude's eyes shifted—unfocused, like the antique clocks whose figures had swiveling porcelain eyes. I attempted to suppress the rising fear that this place was a freak show.

"I know ITT doesn't need us, but *we* need the revenues—to make our numbers," he said.

"How about profits?" I ventured to question.

"Nope."

Nope. No profits! Right then, the cardinal rule of telecom crystallized in my mind: revenues ruled, not profits.

And then I established my own rule: a sphinxlike facial expression was to be my modus operandi.

I had popped two Tylenol caplets into my mouth before leaving the office, but they had not kicked in yet. I rubbed my temples.

Then I looked at my salad. I plucked a piece of arugula and plunged into the topic. "Okay, so are you guys going to ask about my first days with Dick Dorf?"

"How was?" Regina said.

Lulu straightened up, checking her buzzing beeper. She indicated it was fine to continue the conversation.

"Well, Dick Dorf was as to be expected. But he has this controller whose methods leave something to be desired," I said.

Regina giggled. "Surprise."

"Not funny," I added. "You can't imagine the mess. How these guys have stayed in business this long is beyond me."

"It's good—builds character," Regina said. "Besides, challenges are your forte."

"When were you *not* surrounded by strange circumstances?" Lulu asked. Her smile was laced with traces of commiseration, maybe compassion.

"I hope I won't be there longer than a few months. Ty thinks it won't take more than three months, part time," I said. "Six months, tops." He had convinced me this was going to be a short, easy stint.

Fat chance.

I knew I was deluding myself.

Chapter 13

B Y THE EARLY SPRING OF 1996, Wagner and Beekman had grown tired of financing JRW Communications from their own pockets and were ready to go to the capital markets.

And so, the "beauty pageant" had commenced. Namely, a steady stream of investment bankers flaunting their sex appeal had marched to the JRW Communications offices at the top of the Chrysler Building. Decked out in Rolex watches, Armani suits, and gold cuff links, carrying their computers and presentations, the bankers had pitched their attractive abilities with no inhibitions, hoping to raise millions from the public equity markets for JRW. Ty's old employer, Goldfarb Magillan, had won the contest, beating out the numerous other investment houses.

The beauty queens were now meeting with several of us from JRW Communications for the purpose of rehearsing the upcoming European "road show." Ty and his cohorts had crisscrossed the United States, presenting their company to potential investors. They were now scheduled to cross the Atlantic and sell their wares in Europe. About twenty French cuffs were seated along the length of the conference table on the top floor of Goldfarb Magillan's Park Avenue offices. Scents of aftershave and cologne collided with the culinary fumes of grilled lamb chops and tenderloin.

I was hoping the rehearsal would be fast, because I had a pressing meeting set with Claude Thomas. But earlier this morning, Ty had insisted on my hearing the presentations, and I was complying with his request.

Dick Dorf's VTS had been renamed JRW America as part of the growing family of JRW Communications. Truth be told, JRW America's operation was languishing. There were too many big fish—like Sprint, MCI, and Frontier—in the crowded American sea. Recently, Ty had opened a London office, because countries bordering the other side of the Atlantic were poised to expose their monopoly-dominated telecom markets to competition. He believed Europe was the new frontier.

I now watched Ty, clothed in a herringbone suit and yellow shirt, speaking about the opportunities that he foresaw his company reaping on the European continent. I couldn't help but reflect on his healthy physique. The broadness of his shoulders was perfect for carrying my heavy phantom baggage.

I thought of Max's rejection of his son-in-law. Ironically, despite their disparate backgrounds, the two had much in common: obsession with family and fearlessness in business in order to provide for them. *Family, family, family*—those were the words that poured out of Max's mouth several times a day throughout my childhood. Amazingly, once Ty *was* family, Max could not push past his faith and differentness.

I gazed out of the windows behind Ty. The clouds were fluffy, streaks of pink and violet light spinning through them, reminiscent of the cotton candy I used to gobble at the seashore. Thoughts of Hala pushed up to my consciousness. I wished my mother were still around, to smooth out the rough edges in life. She was good at that, a woman of irrepressible warmth and soft words, camouflaging the river of anxious fear that ran through her core.

Once when she was sewing a skirt and I was dawdling over my third-grade homework at the kitchen table, she rested her needle on the glass, speaking past me as if to the daffodils on the wallpaper, saying, "Maybe we should put an end to it, once and for all." At the time I had thought she meant sewing or housework. Years later, it became clear she had been talking about ending the suffering. She had survived the concentration camps bereft of all relatives, and refused to utter a word about it. Even when the other Penguins gathered and exchanged stories, she remained silent or left the room. Late one night, I overheard her implore my father to consider ways to save the future innocents from more horror. She had said the word "conversion," a word I had never heard before or after from her. In fierce whispers, Max told her she was "talking *narishkeit*, talking crazy. This is not why we survived."

Now, I shook my head, chasing away the memories. I stared back down at my plate to distract my mind. Then cutting my lamb chop, I considered the cuisine. I couldn't help but feel awed by the meals the starched shirts regularly consumed. No wonder they all looked so pumped up, eventually plumped up, by the sirloin from Morton's, veal strips from Daniel, roasted quail and parpadelle from Il Mulino. Ready to take a bite, I placed my knife down and skewered the piece of meat with my fork as my neighbor leaned close to me, his musk cologne assaulting my senses.

"I'm Lance Cranson, M&A," he said, the white glare from his teeth almost blinding me. I knew he meant the mergers and acquisitions department of Goldfarb Magillan.

"Doreen Lowe, JRW America. Nice to meet you."

"Finance?"

"No, legal."

He surveyed me for a few seconds. "Are you by any chance the wife of the CEO of the firm?" He pointed at Ty. I noticed his Montblanc cuff link.

"Guilty as charged." I smiled and looked back at my beckoning chops.

"I've heard you work together. A bit unusual in the high-tech world."

Unusual is a good word for it, I thought. "I guess so, but I actually work at the subsidiary downtown under Dick Dorf—not directly under Ty." I thought I noticed a glow of arrogance scrawled upon Lance's youthful face. But then again, I always intuited that when in the company of Wall Street bankers.

"Any kids?" he asked.

"Yes."

"How many?"

"One."

"Really, that's it?"

It was as if he had taken a sledgehammer to my heart. I swallowed a piece of tomato without chewing, feeling as if a stone were plummeting down my esophagus. I planted my utensils beside my plate and kept my eyes focused on the speakers throughout the rest of the conference. When the session was over, I signaled Ty from afar that the hour was late, pointing at my watch for emphasis and mouthing that I would call him later. I quickly left the room.

On the street, my feet went in the opposite direction from JRW America's downtown offices. I strolled up Park Avenue, with the towers on both sides housing thousands of paper pushers in the form of attorneys, accountants, secretaries, and executives. Queries streamed through my neural loops. *How many are satisfied with their profession? How many are having chicken for dinner? How many know that one and a half million children, like Tania, Yankel, and Aaron, were gassed, burned, tortured, just because they were unlucky enough to be born into the wrong faith?*

My mind wandered, taking in the rows of daffodils in the middle of the avenue, trying to escape more troublesome reflections. At an intersection, I crossed to the pedestrian island, bending down, jutting my nose into the Little Gem daffodils, attempting to breath in rejuvenation. Spring was here, crowding the air with the promise of regeneration, teasing with possibilities of fecundity, and depressing me to no end.

The sun was beginning to set, shadows falling across the skyscrapers, the breezes turning cooler. The streets filled with people in light coats, heads turned down, briefcases tucked in at their sides, intent on escaping the travails of the office, exchanging these, at least for the few hours of the evening, with the conundrums of home life.

I glanced at my watch and saw that it was five o'clock. Jack's babysitter, Fernanda, finished her day in one hour. I realized I had been absent from my office for hours, the meeting held by Claude Thomas long over. Pulling my raincoat tightly around me, I began the trek home. By the time I unlocked my front door, Fernanda had her jacket on and her bag slung over her shoulder; she rushed out waving good-bye.

Walking over to the couch, I placed a kiss on Jack's head; smelling of baby shampoo and innocence, he was engrossed in a video. I debated dinner for Ty, knowing that Jack had already eaten—I had prepared, early that morning, chicken with peas for Fernanda to heat up. The baby lamb chops of the meeting earlier that day drifted through my mind, morphing into baby carrots, then baby corn, baby carriage, baby crib, transforming into crying babies, the images whirling at the rim of my cortex.

Retreating from the living room, in search of reprieve from an escalating headache, I slid into the bathroom. My stockings, in varied textures, drying on a hanger in the shower stall, seemed like aliens, just landed. The walls began to warp. I reached out to open the mirrored medicine cabinet, when a pang of pain in my side caused me to double over. Easing myself onto the floor, I spread out on the bathroom rug.

As I lay there, Hala's smiling face moved across the tiles at the base of the tub. Her mouth was open to speak when Tania bumped into her, her feet trampling my mother's face. Yankel then flitted by, signaling Aaron to follow. The three formed a tight circle, grasping each other's arms, and danced, their gray sack coverings stretched out behind them as they turned, faster and faster.

"What are you doing, Mini?" Ty asked, towering over me. It seemed as if he had just sucked all the air out of the room; my breathing became labored.

"Resting—not feeling too well."

"You're lying on the bathroom floor, in your suit and everything. Come on, get up." He stretched out his hand.

"Not yet. Maybe in a few minutes."

"I'll help you get up."

"No, no, just a few minutes, then I'll be back out. I'll want to get Jack ready for bed."

Ty studied me for a few seconds and left the bathroom.

I sighed, figuring I should follow. But my eyes closed instead. I was hopeful Hala would return, but nothing happened. I sighed again and heaved myself up to a standing position. Turning on the faucet, about to sprinkle water droplets at my forehead, I leaned closer to the mirror. My skin looked paler than normal, my green eyes darker and tired; black, hard pupils stared back at me. Smoothing down my skirt, I hauled my tired bones to the living room.

"Mommy, guess what happened in school?" Jack said, pivoting to look at me.

"Your crayons turned into ice cream cones."

"No, silly," he said, a smile widening across his face.

"Your chair turned into a magic carpet and flew away."

"No, silly." Jack giggled while he poked me in my thigh with his hand. His complexion and green eyes brightened with each giggle.

"Okay, I give up. What then?"

"Henrietta had babies."

"Henrietta, the fat rabbit?" Jack's preschool teacher, a woman who mesmerized her young students with her singsong voice, had brought the rabbit to school a few weeks ago.

"Yep, four babies. And we got turns to hold them."

"That's so wonderful," I said, tussling his hair as I turned toward the kitchen. *Babies, babies. Can't people stop talking about them? Even Jack has been recruited to unnerve me.*

"Mini, feeling better?" Ty asked, sipping a Corona from a glass. As a concession to Max, Ty used a glass when having a beer. This reconciliatory act was lost on Max, but to me, most times, it was a beautiful offering. Right now, though, I couldn't be bothered with appreciating it.

"I guess." I swung open the refrigerator door and stood there transfixed.

"Don't bother about me. I'm going back to the office to finish the presentations," Ty said.

"Can't you have dinner first?" I heard myself say. Why was I asking? I didn't have the energy to prepare anything, let alone sit down with him and eat. My stomach was tied in knots.

"Brad is waiting with the Goldfarb Magillan crew. We need to finish up. Remember, part two of our road show starts tomorrow," Ty said. Brad Barkow, the CFO they had hired, sat in the office adjacent to Ty's.

"What's a road show?" Jack asked, racing his cars around on the floor.

Ty explained that he was going on a trip to London, Stockholm, and then Berlin, and back to New York in five days to raise money from investment fund managers. This was the second leg of the road show, the international piece. Ty had already presented his company in several domestic cities. "And you know what, I get to call you anytime I want using the phone on the airplane. Isn't that great, big boy?"

Jack seemed satisfied with that.

"I'm taking a carry-on with me now, Mini. We've got a long night of preparation ahead, and I need to be at Teterboro Airport by eight tomorrow morning," Ty said, moving to our bedroom; he indicated that I should follow him.

Sitting on the edge of our bed, I watched him pack. He counted out undergarments, white shirts, two blue ones, several ties, and toiletries, all the while glancing to gauge my reaction to his bantering. Ty sounded distant, his voice muffled, as if he were speaking through cotton. I must have been convincing in my performance of listening, because he easily bid me farewell at the front door, saying he'd call later.

I turned back to the living room, where Jack was preoccupied with block building. Sitting down on the couch, I kicked off my shoes and watched him, his tongue sticking out a bit, finagling some pieces into one of the tower steeples. The back of his head, the two hair spirals, reminded me of him as a baby, cheerful and chubby. I scrunched up the couch pillow under my head. My ghost Aaron walked by, turned to his right, and lost his balance, scraping against the television set.

"How about somethin' to eat, little buddy?" Jack said, mimicking my usual question.

"Mommy doesn't feel so great right now. Don't worry about me, just play."

He turned to ponder my face, peered down at his work in progress and then back at me. "Me serve," he said, rising to his feet. "What do you want?"

"Let me have Chateaubriand and asparagus tips," I said.

"Okay." He marched into the kitchen area. After rummaging through the pantry and banging some cabinets, he came back with some crackers and set them on the coffee table.

"Looks excellent," I said, taking a bite of one of the crackers. "Yummy."

"What now?"

"How about some porcini mushroom risotto with truffles," I said, remembering dishes from restaurant meals with bankers, analysts, CEOs, board members, prospective employees, and Jerrold Wagner.

Jack returned with a jar of pickles. His feet pattered, and his hands maneuvered supplies until the table overflowed with Fig Newtons, a glass of milk, grape jelly, hot dog buns, three types of crackers, and a bottle of ketchup.

"Jack, I'm going to rest my eyes, and then we'll get ready for bed. Okay?"

Exhaustion had taken hold of me, my energy tangled in an undertow yanking me toward its core of darkness. I noticed Tania sitting on the edge of the couch coiling caramel hair strands around her fingers, while Aaron circled the room. I watched them for a while until I must have fallen asleep.

"Mrs. Doreen, what happened?" The sound of Fernanda's voice startled me. She was shaking me hard as I struggled to open my eyes. "Mrs. Doreen, ju sick?" Her worried brown eyes were close to my face, the smell of coffee on her breath.

An answer eluded me. I had no idea what she was talking about. Pulling myself up on my elbow, I realized I was still on the couch in my suit and Jack was fast asleep on the living room rug, curled up in a ball, fully clothed in yesterday's wear. All of the provisions from last night lay strewn on the coffee table, and Jack's project was still standing, partly built.

"What're you doing here?" I heard my raspy voice pose a question.

"Ju not good, Mrs. Doreen." She placed her hand on my forehead. "You told me to come to help out in the mornings, you have to be in the office very early the next few days. Big show for Mr. Ty, remember?" She pulled her hand back from my forehead.

Even though I wasn't warm, she thought I might have the flu and helped me get into bed. I knew it wasn't the flu, but it might as well have been. Waves of hot and cold flashes washed over me, sweat dripping from my forehead followed by periods when my teeth clanked together from frost. My hair was plastered to my head in straggly clumps, reeking of perspiration, and my pajamas were wrinkled and damp.

Phones were ringing in the background, the answering machine clicking from time to time. Ty's voice drifted past me, fragments of his messages piercing my semiconsciousness: "going well," "good responses." Also, the familiar sounds of Regina's voice, as if she were shouting from a mountaintop far in the distance, prickled at my ears.

The next evening, Fernanda stayed late and put Jack to bed. "Mrs. Doreen, I go now; it's nine o'clock. Make sure you drink this." She placed a mug of some steamy substance on the night table. She told me Ty had called to remind me he was due back the next morning.

I lay engulfed in darkness with no concept of how much time had elapsed, staring up at the ceiling. Yankel was tugging at the books on the shelves, while Tania perched on the ledge of the windowsill, kicking her legs against the wall like the beatings of drums.

Aaron flew by, whispering. At first he sounded like the buzzing of mosquitoes, but after he had tapped at my head several times, I recognized his words: "betrayal, betrayal." I was stunned to hear his childish voice; he didn't speak too often.

Tania joined in with, "We waited all these years; how could you?"

"Go away," I said. "Enough."

"Marrying Ty, not Peter. You betrayed us, turning your back on your world," she said. "For what?"

"How about love?"

"Don't use that word, Dorka. You had responsibilities beyond selfish needs like love." Tania shook her head. "Millions are screaming to have their deaths, their senseless murders, vindicated."

I heard weeping. I knew Yankel was crying, but I refused to look over at him. "We've gone over this. It's done."

"And now, another catastrophe: no more descendants. No more souls to substitute for those snuffed out by unbelievable evil." Tania sounded angrier.

Aches crawled up my legs, crisscrossed my chest, as I heaved with guilty frustration. Words tried to escape my mouth. *It wasn't intentional. Things went wrong.* I thought of my conversation with my gynecologist.

"This is important to me, not just to you," I finally said.

"Who will replace us?" she asked.

"In vain, all in vain," Aaron said, his voice almost a whisper.

Wiping a tear from her eye, Tania said, "You forced the reality of Ty upon us and now this. How much can we bear?"

"Stop it. What do you want from me?" I shouted, propping myself up on the pillows.

I was feeling just as disappointed and devastated as they did. I scanned the night table with the mug and jade box. My fingers reached out and closed around the smooth green rectangle. I lifted it up. Tania became hysterical in her screaming. Yankel stared with fright. I changed my mind, putting the jade box back where it had rested for two decades, as moisture trickled down my cheeks. After a few seconds, my hand found the brass reading lamp. With one swift movement, I launched it at the opposite wall, smashing the mirror. An avalanche of glass tumbled to the floor.

Silence. None of us moved.

After a few moments, shuffling noises came toward me. Jack entered the room, his pajamas twisted around his legs, his hand rubbing at his eyes. He had obviously been awakened by the crashing glass. I motioned for him to come over to me, explaining that the mirror had fallen down, but it wasn't anything to be worried about. He crawled onto Ty's side of the bed as I covered him.

As he fell back to sleep, my heavy head descended slowly onto the cooled pillows. To the ticking of the alarm clock and some car horns outside, I shut my eyes. The last sound I registered was the noise that Aaron made sucking his thumb, as he lay on the shelf of the bookcase.

"Get up," I heard a voice say.

"Go away," I said, repositioning my head on the pillow.

"Fernanda called me when I landed—she was worried that you're very ill," the voice spoke again.

I realized it was Ty. I opened one eye; the alarm clock read seven o'clock. I rolled over and found Jack still fast asleep next to me.

"I'm putting up coffee. Come to the kitchen," Ty said as he turned and walked away.

I closed my eyes again while listening to Ty putting coffee in our percolator, and then rummaging in the refrigerator. I heard him fiddling with the toaster.

I slid out of bed carefully, not wanting to wake Jack. Putting on my bathrobe, I tiptoed to the kitchen. As I sat down in a chair, Ty poured coffee into mugs and placed some buttered toast on the table.

"Fernanda called from her home, on my cell, as soon as I landed this morning—we were approaching the gate. She said last night you seemed even sicker. She was afraid by the time she gets here at eight this morning you may ..." He paused. "After seeing the state of our bedroom, I think she's right."

I pictured him earlier, standing over me, analyzing my downtrodden mental state, considering meds, electric shock, and sanatoriums in the Catskills.

"Really?" I asked.

"Mini, I'm worried about you."

I bit into some toast, the flavor tickling my throat, thinking how much I didn't want to discuss my fragile state. "How was the road show?"

"We still have the luncheon in New York left to do this afternoon, but it looks like a success so far." He sipped his coffee. "We'll be oversubscribed. Rodes figures we'll raise much more than we originally asked for."

"Great, " I said, realizing I didn't sound too convincing. "And Brad?"

"He was terrifically effective."

"Making his own luck, huh?"

"How about we address *yours* now," Ty said, leveling his gaze at me. "What's bugging you?"

"Don't know."

"I think you do. Try."

I chewed my toast. "Maybe, disappointment," I finally mumbled.

Ty stood up and went to the refrigerator, returning with currant preserves and a knife and sat back down. "I figured this would come eventually," he said in a murmur. "You're sorry about your life." It wasn't posed as a question, but a statement. He tilted forward in his chair, fingering his toast, not looking up.

A tiny sound passed my lips. I had been so wrapped up in

my own misery, it never occurred to me how those closest to me would interpret my downward spiral. "It's not you, Ty."

"Then what?"

"No more kids."

"What are you saying?"

"I can't have any more—malfunctioning system," I said, gulping coffee in order to stifle the sobs. I took a bite of toast with preserves, concentrating on the flavor, tart and sour.

"That's it?"

"More than enough, don't you think?"

"I can think of worse things."

"Like what?" I asked.

"Like having none."

"Alright, I'll give you that. But that doesn't change the fact that my predicament stirs up my friends." We both knew I was referring to my spirits.

"Granted." Ty flipped his hair back. "But, is our situation hopeless?"

"Not completely, but probably."

I watched Ty's face, grooves of tiredness lining his cheeks. His eyes were bloodshot and his shirt wrinkled. "This afternoon we have the last of the road show, the New York luncheon. Then we close the round."

"I know that," I said, getting uneasy. I didn't want to discuss telecom now.

"My point being that after that we'll have time to think. And besides, hell, we're young. Doctors don't know everything. They've been wrong before." Ty gave me a warm smile.

I couldn't help but respond by curling my lips up a bit. "Forever the optimist."

"Why don't you get dressed up, come to the luncheon? Your

favorites, the French cuffs, will be there in droves. And, even better, maybe you'll get to hear Jerrold make a fool of himself."

"For a change."

We both laughed.

Ty stood up, extending his hand. "Let's get in the shower, Mini. Lord knows we both could use a really good scrubbing. Fernanda will be here any minute—it's almost eight."

Chapter 14

S EVERAL MONTHS PASSED. I BELIEVED I had perfected my poker face, both at work and with Max.

But, at poker games that remained another matter.

I hadn't been at Seth's poker game since our falling out at Regina's wedding. I had never divulged the details of my spat with Seth to Ty or anyone else, but the rift between us was apparent.

Now it was Wednesday, a week before Thanksgiving. Seth was on the line. "Come play, Doreen, please," he implored.

I refused his offer politely and then hung up.

"This is his way of apologizing," Ty said. "Go play, Mini. It's been a long time."

"No time," I said. "Too much to do."

"I appreciate your sense of responsibility, but you need a break. The stuff, whatever it is, can wait." Ty looked around the cluttered apartment. "I've been on the road so much recently. You should get out." He had just returned from his fourth transatlantic trip in as many months. He had raised a massive amount of capital since the New York road show luncheon the previous spring.

"I'm fine, really," I said, starting to collect Jack's

cars into the red plastic bin. "Anyway, after work, it's tough to get out again at night."

Ty removed the bin from my hand. "I think I can handle this. There's a hockey game on tonight and Jack's asleep already. Besides, Brad will be calling later from Australia."

"Australia?" I had forgotten that JRW Communications was looking to set up shop in Sydney, and Brad Barkow had been dispatched to evaluate the opportunities Down Under. By now, November 1996, Ty's company had four European countries in operation.

"Brad thinks we should acquire a going concern in Australia—fastest route to revenues," Ty said, pouring a Corona into a glass. "Go play poker; do me a favor." He went over to the couch and settled into the cushions.

"You're feeling better, right?" Ty studied my face, attempting to determine if my mood was indeed as buoyant as my exterior indicated. It had been months since my "procreation meltdown."

"Yes," I said, walking toward our bedroom, intent on convincing both of us. "Alright, I'll go to Seth's."

Shedding my suit, I pulled on pants topped by a pink turtleneck sweater, the color of Puff Cosmetics packaging. As I flung my jacket over my shoulders, Ty glanced up from the television.

"Mini, take my cell phone," he said.

"I don't need it. You know I hate those gadgets."

"But this way I can check in, see who's winning," he said. "And besides, after Brad calls we may need to speak."

"Call on Seth's line."

"Rather not. Remember he always gets antsy, claims he needs his phone free for hospital calls."

"What about your other cell calls? You seem to get quite a few of those strange ones—mostly in the evenings." I was thinking of the rushed conversations that Ty avoided explaining. He always claimed they were unimportant business calls.

"It's after nine o'clock. No one calls." Clearly he was not about to explain those now either.

I reluctantly went over to remove the cell phone from Ty's hand and kiss him good-bye.

"Hope you remember how to use it," Ty said.

"Thought it was idiot-proof."

Seth lived at 110th Street and Riverside Drive. His one-bedroom apartment was not too far from his emergency room at Presbyterian Hospital, and the rent was cheap. More importantly, he was smack in the middle of the Columbia University "action," a perfect place for someone who had, so far, failed to get his life on an adult course, preferring transience and noncommitment instead.

Seth opened the door with gusto. He was in traditional unkempt form: crumpled hospital greens and stubble indicating he hadn't touched a razor for some time. His hair was combed back, accentuating his fatigued features. Only his eyes seemed animated.

He pulled me toward him. "Sorry, Doreen," he whispered in my ear, still cold and stinging from the outdoors. A mixture of sweat and Old Spice wafted past my nostrils.

"It's okay, Seth," I said. "You made some valid points."

"I was out of line at the wedding." He released me from his

hug and whirled me around. "Look, guys, our poker princess is back."

I curtsied as cheers came from the poker regulars seated at the table in the living room. The three of them had been Seth's roommates during medical school. I had returned to New York for law school, while Seth had gone up to Cambridge for medical school. After we had all settled into permanent professional positions in New York, Seth reestablished the weekly poker game, with one princess thrown in for diversity.

"Welcome back, Doreen. It hasn't been the same without you," Jay said. He was dark-eyed and bearded, the most intelligent of the bunch.

"Cut the crap, Jay. She's the funniest amongst us. Jesus, we had to settle for Seth's stories while you were gone," Howie said, rolling his eyes.

"Yeah, they almost brought us to tears. Painful," Ricky added.

"Just plain fucking bo-ring," Howie added.

"Watch the cursing, the poker princess is back," Jay said, taking his regular seat at the table.

Seth headed to the kitchen for nuts and beer. I watched his gangly shape as he moved, and was reminded of our college days when we had sat until the wee hours discussing the purpose of life. His tall, awkward legs had been splayed out on the floor as we talked, eating popcorn and listening to the sounds of Bruce Springsteen. I realized then that Seth's melancholic, disheveled façade was undergirded by thoughtfulness and intelligence.

I threw my coat and bag on the couch and took my regular seat.

The makeshift table was set up as it had been for years, constructed from a round piece of wood that Seth had found discarded on the sidewalk. Placed on a folding table, the wood was draped with a thick velvet cloth Seth had ordered cut to specifications at a local housewares store. Flashy purple and blue chips were stacked in front of each player. Seth was proud of his poker ambience.

"Deal the cards already," Ricky said.

Howie, an unlit cigar in his mouth, distributed the cards.

We picked up our respective hands. Mine were bad cards— all low, no pairs. "I fold," I said, putting my hand down on the velvet.

I watched the others play. Howie moved his cigar around in his mouth as he contemplated his next move. Ricky told a series of jokes, humoring himself more than anyone else. Seth's smile lit up his face as he trumped all with a flush.

The scene carried me back to childhood poker. Max had taught me the game when I was about seven, in order to keep us engaged during Hala's struggles, her operations, various cardio-procedures, and numerous simply bad days. Max and I had had plenty of downtime. Sometimes my aunt and uncle, Sam and Bea, would join us for a round or two.

For years, I thought poker was purely for Penguins. Only when I was a teenager did it become clear that it was a popular card game for non-Penguins as well. In college, my card-playing reputation traversed the campus gossip channels, gaining me entry to the otherwise all boys club.

"I want to hear about the big stuff—Wall Street," Howie said to me. He gathered the chips toward him, having just won the round with a hand of hearts.

"Like what?" I asked.

"Ty has raised one hundred million already, right?" he said.

"Three hundred," I said.

"Holy shit," Ricky said.

Seth put his finger to his lips and pointed at me.

"Wow, soon you won't want to play poker with commoners like us," Ricky said.

"When's it going public?" Howie asked, dealing the next hand.

"Actually, they're having another beauty contest soon," I said, recalling the tense energy during the last contest, when the French cuffs traipsed up to Ty's office with their ammunition. I peeked at my cards; they were good ones, three-of-a-kind.

"What's a beauty contest?" Jay asked.

"Seduction by way of analyst connections, private jets, best pricing at the close of the round, stuff like that," Howie said. "Those investment guys'll promise you anything."

I believed he was right; so did Ty. I doubled my bet. Jay and Seth got out. Howie studied me for a few moments and folded.

Howie threw his hand, three-of-a-kind, onto the table after I showed him mine. His was a higher-valued three-of-a-kind hand. "Lucky bastard that you are," he said. "I can't believe I fell for that look on your face. Christ."

After five more hands, two of which I won, we broke for a few minutes. Seth went into the kitchen and came out carrying a tray with more beer and cookies. Hands reached for the refreshments.

"Someone's cell is ringing," Jay said, his mouth full.

"It's your pocketbook," Ricky said to me.

"Your cell phone?" Seth looked at me. "I thought you hate those."

"Ty's. He made me take it along." I headed toward the couch. Fumbling through my bag, I found the phone and flipped it open.

"Hello," a woman's voice said.

"Hello."

"I'd like to speak with Ty, please," she said, her voice hoarse like a smoker's.

"He's not here right now, but I'll be glad to give him a message."

"Who's this?" she said, sounding a bit irritated.

"Who is this?" I responded in kind.

Ricky and Howie were arguing about the Giants record this season. I waved my hand for them to lower their voices. The line was crackling with static.

"Are you a friend of Ty's or a business associate?" she asked.

"Sort of both." Not knowing what to answer.

"Well, then, please tell him his mother called."

I felt my legs weaken. "What?" I said, my voice cracking as my free hand came up to my forehead. Ricky and Jay turned to me.

"*His mother?*" I said, loud.

"His mother."

"But, you're dead."

"I hope not."

"Is this a prank?" My fingers becoming sticky around the phone, I transferred the piece to my other ear, and sank into the couch cushions. The room was spinning.

"No, it most certainly is not. I need to talk to my son."

I looked around, the walls swaying back and forth, as I said, "What's your name?"

"Faith Rockwell, and yours?"

"Doreen Rockwell"—I paused—"his wife."

There was silence for a few seconds. Faith's breathing was hard and rhythmic in the receiver. "I never knew he was married."

"He'll call you back," I heard my voice say. I hung up in fright.

"Holy crap, was that Ty's mother?" Howie said, coming to sit next to me.

"Don't overreact," Jay said. "There could be a great explanation for this."

Seth said, "Why don't you just call Ty?"

I sat there immobilized, listening to my breathing. My legs had gone leaden, cemented into the couch. I stared at the posters hanging askew over a dusty stereo. Jay's mouth was moving, but he was inaudible. Images were revolving: Hala and Max and Ty and Jack somersaulting over Seth's carpet, hitting the walls. I had a sudden urge to inhale some fresh air. I jumped up, swooping up my personal belongings, anxiety propelling me to the door.

"You're not in any shape to go anywhere," Seth said, following me with his long legs.

"Going home. Alone."

"Not a good idea," Jay said.

I opened the door to leave.

"Are you taking the subway?" Seth said.

"No, cab."

"Okay, at least that's better."

Chapter 15

I HAD NO IDEA HOW I made it back home from Seth's, but at our front door my brain began to explode with questions, like corn kernels over fire bursting into popcorn. I threw the door open to find Ty engrossed in a hockey game, legs crossed in front of him. He had changed into a T-shirt and sweatpants, his hair still damp from the shower.

"Are you out of your mind?" I said, approaching him at rapid speed.

Startled, Ty glanced up at me. My expression must have reflected my agitated state, because the color drained out of his cheeks. He sat up and grabbed the remote to shut off the television. "What happened?"

"Your mother," I said.

Ty tilted his face downwards. He did not raise his head or speak.

I collapsed into the armchair, near the couch. *My whole married life has been one big, fat lie.* "How could you?" There was no verbal reaction from Ty; he was cradling his face in his hands, the same hands that had touched me so many times. "Start from the beginning. Who are you?"

"Tyler Rockwell."

"At least your name is true." I stared at the floor. "You assumed I was never going to find out about your mother." My palms went clammy, and hot flashes were climbing my neck. White specks whirled in front of my irises. "The whole story, Ty," I said. I felt his body stretch as he cleared his throat. *This might spell the end of my sweet life as Doreen Rockwell.*

"As you know, my father was a traveling salesman passing through Bismarck. He was around for about a year and then split town," Ty said. "My mother worked at the local hospital."

"As a nurse."

"No, as a nurse's aide—menial work, low pay."

"But you told me she was a nurse." I paused. "So you were ashamed?" I asked, incredulous. *Can I have fallen for a man so shallow as to be embarrassed by his background to the point of feigning orphanhood?* The thought sent a shiver down my spine. "For that, you deprived Jack of a grandmother?"

"No, it's much more complicated." Ty stood up and shoved his hands in his pockets. He began to pace. "My mother worked long hours and was constantly stressed, although in her own way she tried for me, the best she could, but there were forces …" He hesitated and went over to the window. He stared down at the street for a few seconds. "Most of the time I was with a sitter."

"So?"

"My grandfather."

I sat there frozen, in my gut knowing this was only a prelude to something ominous. Queasiness was beginning to spread through my nervous system like an ugly, dark oil spill in the clear blue ocean.

"My grandfather was a Polish immigrant, a housepainter."

"What year did he come?"

"1927."

At least before the Second World War, before the destruction of the Penguin world, I thought, relieved for a moment.

I stared ahead of me. "His name?" I just needed to hear the syllables to seal the authenticity of the tale.

"Pavel Zbezinky."

"You're not Presbyterian."

"Half."

"And half Catholic."

"Yes."

"So you actually know Polish?" I asked.

"Just a few words. The rest I blocked out as a child."

"But you never admitted that." I felt woozy. "Is anything besides your name true?"

"She drove a powder blue car."

I couldn't speak, sensing there was more coming and that it wasn't going to be good.

Ty cleared his throat and continued. "We lived together. He was a tyrant; my mother was like a ghost. He spent his whole life bitter, ranting about the unfairness of everything, his lack of advancement, his crappy life."

"I could have lived with that." *So, what's the big deal?*

Ty paused. "He blamed all his woes on the Jews."

And there it was. A knife to my back.

Bolting out of the chair, racing to the kitchen, I felt like throwing up. I peered at the stainless steel sink and the dirty coffee cups. I was perspiring and my mouth tasted like dirty socks. Opening the faucet, I threw water onto my face and neck.

Vivid images of my father flashed before me. Max talking about the ties binding us to the past, the lost members of our family. *Family, family.* I was now positive I had married into a family of Penguin haters. Without searching too far within Ty's extended family, I was certain there would be Nazi collaborators, willing accomplices, even Penguin murderers: those who had pointed out Tania, those who rounded up Sally and my grandparents, those who operated the gas chambers, those who did nothing to save the children, as blameless and innocent as Jack. *Oh, poor Jack. My joy, my jewel, now tainted Jack—a fusion of the Penguins and their haters.*

My ghosts were nowhere around. The one time I craved the sight of them, they had abandoned me. *Tania, where are you? Come back to me.*

I stood facing the backsplash covered in chipped linoleum tiles, afraid to turn around. "Some kind of cruel joke." I wiped my face with a towel. "Or, are you simply out of your mind?"

"Hear me out," Ty said, adding "please" in a low voice.

Just then, running out and leaving everything behind crossed my mind. But I couldn't abandon Jack. Even if I grabbed him out of his bed now and ran, where would I go? To Max's apartment? The thought of looking into my father's eyes seemed more daunting at that moment than swimming the entire Pacific Ocean.

I returned to the living room. Ty began to pace again.

"Everything's ruined," I said, dropping onto the couch, pressing my head against the worn fabric. "My life is one giant mess." Despondency was aggravating the pressure behind my temples. Then Ty's voice swam toward me.

"When I was really young, his ravings were all background noise. I didn't give them much thought. My head was in hockey and baseball cards—you know, kid stuff." He came up to the window again and pushed his forehead into the glass, his nose squashed up against the panel, making his voice sound strange. "But as the years went by, I started to listen. I remember the moment it occurred to me that we had never met a Jew, ever.

I started to ask him questions. He couldn't answer. He always resorted to blanket statements of hatred."

"People always blame others for their disappointments," I said.

It was all so pathetic. For a moment, the temptation to roll on the floor in a hysterical fit almost overtook me, but the energy to push off the couch dissipated.

"When I was fifteen, I got a summer job at a small haberdashery store in downtown Bismarck. It was owned by one of the few Jewish families in the area. They had come to America from Russia a few years before my grandfather."

"Did they have horns on their heads?" I asked, entertaining myself with this barb.

Ty grimaced. "The Goldsteins were kind to me, and they certainly weren't satanic. They didn't live for their hatreds. Their focus was elsewhere."

Who cares about the Goldsteins? You're in New York now, ruining my family. Tears welled up in my eyes.

"I vowed then not to sit in my shitty apartment, guzzle vodka, and blame ghosts for my ills." He stepped back toward the couch, standing nearby. "Besides, if my grandfather could spend his whole life despising these people he didn't even know, there must be something about them that evoked such hatred." Ty paused. "Or maybe it was jealousy."

"So you came to find out? Or maybe to see other people's ghosts?"

"No better place than New York to see what his obsession was about. But then, the colors of life here ..." He cleared his throat. "Well, I fell in love."

"So I was your idea of what? I don't get it."

"You were the Goldsteins, but more."

"Max isn't exactly your biggest fan, Ty," I said. "Have you failed to notice?"

"I never cared about that. I'm talking about how your parents bathed you in warmth, made a new life for themselves. And they had great reason to sit around and just bitch about their deal."

"So you simply opted for *different* ghosts," I said, fumbling with the pillows on the couch. "You were sick of the ghosts of Bismarck?"

"You use your ghosts differently."

"Terrific, Ty." I could not help but sound cynical.

"Doreen, look what you do. You weave the unfortunate parts of your life, the horrors of your past, with humor, with compassion," he said. "Somehow, you always make it seem alright, even when it's not."

It added up. Ty let Max's coolness, actually coldness, pass over him like an innocuous rainstorm, never feeling any permanent resentment, tolerating the pellets hitting him. The existence of my ghosts never rattled him, but instead maybe served to energize his spirit.

"That's wonderful for you, but what about the rest of us?" I said, my voice infused with sadness, thinking how Max's distrust of him was now going to ratchet up to a new level. And Seth was going to be proven right—my life was a fraud, a self-delusional fantasy.

Pieces of my insides began to crumble, cascading to the floor, hitting it with thuds. If our union had been a delicate balancing act until now, from here on, it was going to teeter on the precarious edge or possibly fall over.

"Your plan was never to tell me," I said, studying his jawline, intense and tight.

"It never seemed like the right time."

"And you never told your mother you were married either, right?"

"Couldn't find the right time for that."

"So, she doesn't know about Jack."

"No."

Sadness stood upright in my mind like a brick wall, blocking out the sunny frames of Jack and life with Ty as I had known them until this moment. "Did you do *anything* for her during these years?"

"Yes. I sent her money. But she says she never used it, keeping it instead in a savings account for me."

"You'd better call your mother. She's waiting," I said.

Ty hesitated, but when he found me staring at him, unflinching, he approached the phone in the kitchen. He dialed her number. "Hi, Mamo. There's a lot to tell you."

I heard him talking. I watched his dimpled chin move up and down as long-closeted truths spilled out. A lock of hair fell over his eye, but he didn't make a motion to push it back.

I felt sorry for Faith Rockwell, as I pitied myself. How would she live with this reality? Her only child had cut her out of his life and unequivocally aligned himself with her parent's phantom enemies. He had deprived her of the joys of parenthood since he became an adult and of her only grandchild. What would happen if Jack did that to me? Just thinking about it sent chills poking holes in my spinal chord, making me light-headed with fear.

"He's gone?" I heard Ty say. "What about the ceremony?" He listened for a few seconds. "Oh, cremated. Last week." He glanced in my direction. "You should have notified me."

I knew they were talking about the grandfather, and that Faith was crying on the other end of the line, by his facial expression—

pain tangled with discomfort. He was at a loss for words. She now had no one else in this world, I assumed, but Ty.

"Invite her for Thanksgiving," I blurted out. The holiday was the following week.

Ty cupped his hand over the receiver and whispered to me, "She'll say she can't afford that."

"Sure she can. You're sending her the plane ticket."

Chapter 16

F AITH'S SCHEDULED ARRIVAL WAS FOR four evenings later. Ty was at LaGuardia Airport waiting for her flight. I had decided he should pick her up alone.

Since the revelation of my mother-in-law's existence, Ty and I, tongue-tied and confused, had circled each other like Sumo wrestlers. Though uptight, we kept to polite conversation and tended to Jack, in a formal, restrained manner. Frightened of unearthing more emotional land mines, I shoved the topic to my rear lobe until after the highly anticipated face-to-face meeting.

Refusing to divulge the "Faith factor" to anyone, I bit my lip to quell the temptation of confessing to Regina when she called from her trade show in Chicago, and was grateful she was pressed for time. Anyway, she and her husband were going to be with my family for Thanksgiving at Sam's and Bea's; I reasoned she could learn the news along with the rest of the Penguins.

Although the living room had just undergone an uncustomary stint of frenetic cleaning, I straightened it up once again. Jack was newly scrubbed in his pajamas, playing with cars on the coffee table. Replumping the pillows on the couch, I scrutinized the space on my way to the bathroom.

Refreshing my mascara, I puffed blush on my cheeks. As I looked into the bathroom mirror, I saw Ingrid Baumgard's face staring back. *What is Peter's mother doing here?* Her silver hair was pulled back, and her pearl earrings accentuated her pale, stern eyes.

"Doreen, this is what happens when you refuse to be *pliant*," she was mouthing, staring straight at me. She had always loved that word.

Possibly true. But had I been pliant, Max, Sam, and all the Baumgards would be coming over for a turkey dinner in a few days, prepared by *my* Teresa under *my* supervision. I envisioned Max at the dinner, smiling at the lavish spread and the beautiful silver candelabras Peter would have had purchased from the "silver guys" he knew on Forty-seventh Street. Obviously, under that scenario, I wouldn't be waiting for Faith Rockwell right now.

"But this is what I chose," I answered her politely.

"Yes, and you have Jack now, making it impossible to undo this nightmare," the specter of Ingrid said, condescension evident behind her eyes.

In a flash, I pictured myself seated back in Peter's office chair behind his desk, as he exploded about my marriage to Ty, causing me to think, *Which fateful path would have actually been the nightmare?* Staring back at Ingrid, I asked, "What makes you so sure I want to undo anything?"

"Please." Ingrid's mouth opened in obvious disbelief.

I turned and left the bathroom, slamming the door behind me. As I leaned against the wall, trying to get my breathing under control, thoughts of the complex twists in my legacy bubbled up, fogging my mind with words like *destiny, fate, timing, luck. Luck,* that time-honored word. The concept of having it, being able to possess it, somehow capture it, rushed through my brain cells.

Suddenly, I heard the tinkering of a key in the door, obstructing all further ruminations. I was about to meet Faith. After drawing long breaths and smoothing down my hair, I compelled my feet to maneuver me into the living room, where Jack still played with his cars.

In front of me stood Faith P. Rockwell. Her broad face held eyes set far apart, dark bookends to her short, rounded nose. Her grayish blonde hair was frazzled, suggesting years of cheap bleaching. About two or three inches taller than I was, I assessed, Faith was big-boned under her black pants and rubber-soled shoes. Even in that first instant, I felt tiredness oozing out of her, everything about her shouting the same thing: downtrodden. I realized that what Ty had said was apparently true; Faith had not used any of the money he had been sending her, at least not on herself.

"How do you do," I said, stepping forward, extending my right hand, truncating the possibility of having to kiss her or she me.

She nodded as she took my hand in her cold, rough-skinned grasp, reminding me of the alligator skin on Regina's Gucci bag.

"Welcome," I said.

Ty shifted behind Faith, her travel case in his hand. "Flight was perfectly on time." He then pushed her forward. "Mamo, I want you to meet Jack." He motioned to his son to come over. Bending down, his hand on Jack's slim shoulder, Ty said gently, "This is your grandmother."

"A *real* grandma?" Jack said.

We all smiled, welcoming any opportunity to ease the palpable awkwardness hanging between the estranged generations thrown into such proximity. I couldn't help but think of Hala, the grandmother Jack would never know.

"Why don't you sit, make yourself comfortable," I said, unsure what to do or even what to call her.

"How about a drink?" Ty offered.

"How about cookies?" Jack added.

"No thanks," Faith said, her first words. Her voice was raspy, gravelly, like the sound of an object being dragged over pebbles. I noticed she didn't move her head much or look around the room. She stepped over to the couch and sat down, legs uncrossed but close together.

"You know, Jack, it's way past your bedtime. How about saying goodnight. You can play with your grandmother tomorrow," I said, figuring Jack's room would serve as a perfect temporary hideout for me.

"A few more minutes. She just got here," Jack said. "Hey, wanna see my cars?" he asked Faith. I loved little people, the ones under four feet tall; in an instant they were on intimate terms with foreign circumstances and human beings.

Jack grabbed the red bin holding his cars and skipped over to his grandmother. As he lifted each one up to the tip of her nose, describing its details, my eyes found Ty's across the room, precisely over Jack's head. Two golden boys, one large and one small, their chiseled faces aligned, were nodding at the stranger who had just entered our lives. Faith responded to her grandson's entreaties with timidity and meager verbal accoutrement.

As I gazed at the trinity, fascination gripped me. The three possessed a shared DNA, yet it seemed unfathomable to me that the awkward woman was tied by blood to the robust, handsome male specimen sitting beside her. The product of sperm and ovum was not the combination of two parts, but the arbitrary mixture of thousands of ingredients. The complexity of individuality was astonishing. A strapping, open-minded man could be the direct descendant of a broken, introverted woman and her bitter alcoholic father.

For the next two days, the four Rockwells wandered up and down and across Manhattan, showing the sites to the oldest amongst us. Faith continued to be frugal in words but visibly enamored by the skyscrapers, the buzz, and the enormity of the city. She seemed to enjoy the paintings hanging in the Metropolitan Museum, the lights of Times Square, the gelato of Little Italy, the knockoff watches of Chinatown, and the elegant window displays along Fifth and Madison Avenues.

At the end of the second day, with legs aching and minds overrun with facts and figures, we came home to partake of spaghetti. After Jack collapsed, fast asleep in his bed curled up with his latest favorite action figure, I began to clean the kitchen while Ty and Faith settled on the couch. She was leafing through one of the copies of *Foreign Affairs* (I'd continued to subscribe to this magazine). Ty was engrossed in a phone conversation with Brad Barkow about their upcoming secondary offering, tentatively scheduled for late January.

"Okay," Ty said, hanging up the phone, glancing at his mother. "Let's talk a bit about tomorrow."

Faith closed the magazine and perched it on the coffee table. With her back erect and feet firmly planted together, she cocked her head to face her only child. Her expansive flat features somehow reminded me of the icy plains of her native North Dakota, gleaned from my imagination, for I had never actually been there.

"We're having Thanksgiving tomorrow at Sam and Bea's, Doreen's aunt and uncle," Ty said, reaching out to take her hand, enveloping her fingers in his large palm. "Mamo, as you know, Doreen's family is from your father's country."

A glint of light shot through Faith's eyes, like a bright lightning flash in a moonless night. She was about to speak when Ty said, "But, they're concentration camp survivors."

Faith's eyes went cold, fright gripping them as she removed her hand from Ty's. She fastened her hands together in her lap, squeezing until the knuckles whitened. At that instant, I realized Ty had not told her this crucial detail during any of their earlier private conversations. She angled her head toward me, staring for a few seconds before saying, "Which ones?"

"Auschwitz, Bergen-Belsen, and Dachau," Ty answered, as if afraid to let me utter the words myself.

"Auschwitz, near *Dziadek*'s home," she said in a whisper, turning back to Ty. She used the Polish word for grandfather.

Near his grandfather's home. The words blew through me like a Siberian wind. I lifted my face to the ceiling, desperate to see some shadow of my ghosts. *Tania, where are you?* Feeling abandoned, I imagined them with arms around each other, knapsacks on their backs, strolling into the distance, leaving me. I longed for Aaron and Yankel to move around, even smash into fixtures, provide distraction with their high-pitched gaggles.

"I should go home," Faith said. "This can't be right."

"No," Ty said.

"You left Bismarck, obviously not wanting us in your life, Ty. Maybe we should leave it as it was. It's simpler," Faith explained.

"No, going back isn't an option. We now have a chance to rebuild our relationship," Ty said.

"You mean without *Dziadek?*" she asked.

"Yes."

"I loved him, Ty."

"Fine."

"You're not me."

"It was terror, maybe dependence, not love."

"That's your opinion, not mine."

Pandora, in Polish form, had escaped the box, and it was impossible to cram her back inside. We were family, whether we liked the notion or not, indelibly branded with overlapping chromosomal patterns but incongruous histories, forever. Apprehensiveness washed over me. *Family, family,* as Max would say. But, this *was* my family: irreconcilable, conflicted with dangerous tentacles hooked to the same core.

Faith's face turned pinkish as a teardrop traversed her cheek. Snatching the tissues from the kitchen counter, I came and stood near her, extending the box. She looked up through watery eyes, her nose turning blotchy. She slowly pulled a tissue from the container.

"Stay," I said. "I don't know what tomorrow will bring, but we need to start somewhere."

Faith dabbed at the corners of her eyes, when Ty said, "There's a lot to work out. This is all my fault."

"It's nobody's fault," I said.

"Ty's ashamed," Faith murmured, wiping the edges of her nostrils.

"But now we need to go from here. Ty and I have to figure things out too," I said, catching sight of Ty's cheek muscle tightening, "about how we go on." *Or if we go on.*

"You can't hold what I myself detest, against me," Ty snapped.

"But you lied," I said.

There, the words had scampered out. And then, like the emergency lights illuminating an aircraft's aisles, thoughts lit up my brain. *Can I resent Ty for transcending his past? Maybe my resentment lay in my own inability to do just that? Haven't I been lying to myself all this time? Had I in fact been swept away by his dimpled chin, ignoring all the obvious warning signs of future problems?* My questions were melting into one giant tumor of confusion.

"We can't resolve any of this at the moment," I said, knowing my mind was weary. "We need time."

Ty seemed relieved that the situation had not completely imploded. "Let's get some rest for tomorrow."

He always figured any grace period, whatever the duration, was a godsend. This time he was most certainly right.

Chapter 17

THE NEXT DAY, DRESSED IN our holiday best, we entered Sam and Bea's home for the turkey feast. Three blocks farther uptown than Max, the older Lowes lived in an Upper West Side prewar building. The apartment, with high ceilings and ornate wedding-cake moldings, housed an egg cream baby grand piano in the spacious living room positioned under bay windows overlooking Central Park. Reflecting my aunt's predilection for brown, the furnishings and fabrics were in shades owning up to names like mocha, chocolate, caramel, maple, cappuccino, making my mouth water as if I had fallen into a Belgian *bonboniere*.

I glanced over at the French Victorian sideboard, solid walnut with beautiful relief carvings, which my aunt and mother had selected on one of their antique shopping trips. I remembered how the two had burst into our apartment, snowflakes sprinkled on their teased hairdos, jabbering away about their find from the last century, pride pouring out of their mouths, while Max and I had rolled our eyes.

Nearby in the kitchen now, my cousin Sally, Sam and Bea's daughter, was busy preparing a snack for one of her three daughters. Sally had always been a thoughtful older cousin, concerned with my well-being and proud of my accomplishments. Her girls treated their younger male cousin, their only cousin, in a similar fashion.

The middle daughter came flying out of the bedroom corridor as soon as she realized Jack had arrived. Alexa's long hair with pink bow flapped behind her slight ten-year-old frame as she ran to put her arms around Jack and hug him tight, merry giggles coming out of their mouths. They headed off to the large second bedroom, now functioning as a den, ready to play video games. Alexa's father was already parked in the den's Barcalounger watching football.

The long dining table, visible from the front vestibule, was set with Bea's finest set of china and heavy silver flatware. On the taupe damask tablecloth, with matching border, were roses in an ornate silver vase. Dried autumn leaves, collected in the park, were strewn down the center, like an organic table runner.

Since as far back as I could remember, we had celebrated Thanksgiving at my aunt's table. Her cooking was heavenly, her kitchen immaculate, a real "balabusta," as the Penguins called Bea.

Bea greeted us with a smile. Her hair was teased. Large round gold earrings illuminated her friendly creased face. The apron tied around her middle, stained and frayed at the edges, served as testament to her culinary skills. I knew she always thought of her sister-in-law as she greeted me, a tinge of loneliness lacing her hello.

I was about to introduce Faith. I had called Bea earlier in the day informing her of an additional guest. The family was used to my last-minute invitations to friends or schoolmates, always hospitable to a new face during holiday festivities. Before managing to utter a syllable, I was interrupted by the opening of the front door. Regina and Marc, along with my father, entered; they had obviously ridden up in the elevator together.

Since Regina's mother had passed on, my friend had become a regular fixture at my family's traditional holiday meals. As the years stretched on, we added her husband Marc and his children to the roster. The stepchildren were with their mother today, probable explanation for Regina's relaxed demeanor. Under her coat, she was dolled up in a raspberry leopard-patterned sweater with a fur collar and leather skirt. Her hair in an updo with a few curls on her forehead softened her features.

Max nodded to Ty and me as he began to move toward the hall closet to hang his coat. I noticed he was wearing a gray suit, the same one he had worn at Hala's funeral and ever since for formal occasions. He glanced at me and then at Faith for several seconds before saying, "Give me your coats, Regina and Marc," as he proceeded to make space for their outerwear.

We trickled into the dining area, the children dashing out of the den, running zigzags through the elegant rooms. Sam exited the kitchen with a tray of miniature crystal glasses filled with Cherry Heering.

As everyone took a glass, I mustered the courage to say, "Let me introduce Faith." Regina extended her right hand to Faith, her sapphire ring glittering, as Marc moved up behind her. "She is Ty's mother," I added, bracing for the fallout.

Regina withdrew her hand, her face registering shock like a Richter scale.

Sam came close to dropping the tray, tipping it precipitously, but he managed to level it. Sally swung out of the kitchen wiping her hands in a towel, followed by my aunt, her stout, short legs whisking her into the heart of the storm. Max stared at me, eyes unblinking.

"That's certainly a surprise," Edgar, Sally's husband, said from behind us; he was never one to miss a brewing calamity. A large man with a full head of curly hair, he looked as though he'd been napping. "Where's she been hiding?"

"We lost touch for a time," Ty said.

I imagined the wheels of Max's brain cranking away, trying to make sense of the situation, thinking, *This is what my Doreen chose, a midwestern hick, a phony orphan, estranged from his family.*

"Hope we don't find out you also have six siblings somewhere, Ty," Edgar said, smiling. His wife shot him a dirty look, and his grin quickly vanished.

Having recuperated from the initial jolt, Regina met my eyes with a quizzical expression, but I was too numb to help her out. After a few seconds, she hesitantly stepped forward, cleared her throat, and said, "I'm happy that Doreen has a new mother."

The minute the words parted her lips, I knew that Max was going to start to unravel. Out of the corner of my eye, I watched Max's neck muscles stiffen, veins bulging right below the skin surface, his eyes turning murky and furious. I glanced at Regina. I could tell by her reddened cheeks that she realized she had misspoken.

"What kind of person ignores his mother for years?" Max said.

"Things are complicated, Max. There are explanations," Ty said.

"I can't think of any for ignoring a mother. What I would have given to have my parents." Max's eyes found his brother. "Can you imagine still having our mother, our Dorka?" The mention of my namesake caused me to feel as if ants were marching up and down my spine.

"Let's take it slow," Sam said. "Everyone, let's go sit down." He nudged Regina, Sally, and Marc to the chintz couch, upholstered in white chocolate and coffee.

Faith, standing beside Ty, appeared shell-shocked, eyes gazing downward, arms hanging listless at her side. *This can't be easy for the woman, meeting her grandson and me for the first time, absorbing numerous shocks, and now standing here trapped within enemy lines.*

Max shouted at me in Polish, "You have made a terrible mess of everything."

Faith turned to him and said, "She didn't do anything wrong. *To nie jest jej wina.*"

"It's not her fault," Faith answered in her native tongue, which was the same as Max's. All mouths dropped open; heads turned to my mother-in-law.

I've lost control of the situation, assuming I had any to begin with, I realized. Initially, I had thought the Thanksgiving feast would provide containment of the explosion, like a nuclear blast under the ocean waters. The family would learn of Faith's existence and we would all grow familiar with one another while snuggled in the warm holiday milieu. The remaining increments of the backstory, like *Dziadek* and the hatred, would later float ashore on several tepid waves rather than on a gigantic, destructive one.

The room began to swirl around, making my knees wobbly. I needed to sit down, better yet lie down, but I was terrified to move, wishing someone would grab me and carry me to shelter. But it wasn't going to be.

"*Zi iz a proste Polak*," Max hissed at Faith. "You're a simple, low-class Polack."

His derogatory words pierced me like a poison dart, the venomous liquid rushing through my veins toward my heart.

"Yes, my grandfather came from Poland," Ty said.

Now, the whole truth lay splattered before us.

"He died recently," Faith said in a quiet tone, eyes gazing down. She probably wanted to run out of here just as much as I did.

Please, please, as you promised Ty, don't disclose your father's Penguin bigoted beliefs, at least not now.

"So you connected at the funeral?" Bea asked, hopeful of putting some positive spin on the matter.

"No, he was cremated about two weeks ago, but my mother didn't tell me until after," Ty said.

I couldn't believe he had said the word *cremated* with such ordinariness, even nonchalance, in front of my family. It was clear to me, judging by his slumped posture and gray pallor, that Ty believed defeat was inevitable. His capitulation was palpable from across the room.

"Cremated?" Max said. "Cremated?!" His voice rose.

I knew that in his mind, the crematoria of Auschwitz stood billowing smoke; particles of his sister and parents enmeshed in the stench and dust were scattering over the barren fields, while Aaron's body swayed in the wind, the noose cords frozen around his innocent, gaunt neck.

Max stomped toward the hall closet; his fingers grabbed his coat and hat. He opened the front door and stepped out. Sam and Bea ran to the elevator vestibule. We could hear their murmurs for a few moments, as the elevator door clanked open and then shut. My aunt and uncle reentered the apartment, Sam's face ashen and Bea's cheeks blotched with red spots.

"I think we should all be seated and have dinner," Sally said, rising from the couch, addressing Bea. "I'm going to begin serving, Mom."

"I'll help," Regina said as she shot up from the couch.

Ty leaned over to his mother, whispering in her ear. Faith had not moved in all this time, frozen like Lot's wife. His gaze steady, Ty said, "My mother and I are going to leave now. Everyone needs time to think." Tilting his head to Sam, he said, "I'm so sorry we ruined Thanksgiving." He signaled his mother, and she moved toward the exit.

No one, including me, said a word as the door closed behind mother and son. *So this is what we've come to?* Ty was in love with Max's ability to lift himself from the ashes of annihilation to create a new family and adapt in an unfamiliar land. Yet Ty was unable to make Max accept him. In some perverse twist, the descendant of a Penguin hater had propelled his own transformation into a Penguin, albeit an Anglo-Polish version: hardworking, ambitious, family-centric, ascending from the depths of a terrible past. Yet, ironically, Max, to date, preferred Peter and his family— East Side bastions of condescension and snottiness—believing his child would have been better protected by the Baumgard multigenerational Americanized status and their money.

For lack of an alternative plan, I approached the table. The others were also straggling toward the dining area as Sally and Bea brought out platters of roasted potatoes, eggplant and zucchini with tomatoes, squash soufflé, green beans, corn biscuits, a stuffed turkey, and a beef brisket. No one was allowed to bring a dish to Bea's house—she was a solo performer at her feasts.

Regina carried the crystal pitchers with water and lemon slices. The children came rushing in, Jack pulling on Alexa's arm, singing some annoying chant. Sally helped them by serving and cutting. The others started to eat in silence. I knew I would not swallow a morsel, but spooned some potatoes onto my plate anyway.

Regina's husband, Marc, spoke up, complimenting my aunt's spread. Then Edgar asked Marc about the direction of interest rates in the near term. The two conversed about the Clinton economy. Sam was quiet, pale, and focused on his empty plate.

Regina turned to me. "You may not like what I have to say, Doreen, but I think I'm going to say it anyway." She put down her utensils. Her uncharacteristic seriousness was disconcerting, causing me to ache for her smile and throaty laugh, desperate for her to somehow make light of this disaster.

"Can you imagine how much Ty must love you for him to work so hard at hiding his background, his mother, his pain? He's willing to throw it all away to have you," Regina said, wiping her mouth with the napkin. "Hell, my husband doesn't even love me enough to have a baby."

"Hey, this isn't the time or the place," Marc said, annoyance piggybacking on his voice.

"It's never the time or place," Regina said. "What're you willing to sacrifice to be with me?" She glared at Marc. "You say you can't give up your freedom, your golf. You're not sure about fatherhood because you've already been there." She used fingers from both hands to indicate quotation marks for "been there."

This was the first I had heard of this conflict. I had known Regina was set on having a baby, but it had never occurred to me that Marc was averse to the idea. Yellow lights began flashing in my mind, signaling approaching trouble. My breathing felt constricted, and pressure was building in my chest.

"Now, now, no fighting. We've had enough trauma for one day," Bea said. "Let's concentrate on pleasant things, like the peach cobbler and chocolate layer cake for dessert."

"Got to go now," I said, rising from my seat. Suddenly, I couldn't stay another second. "Going home."

"Jack should sleep here—the girls would love a slumber party," Sally volunteered quickly. "Pick him up tomorrow."

"Much appreciated." I felt relieved there would be no need to make pleasant small talk with Jack on the journey home.

Kissing Jack and then Bea good-bye, I took my coat.

"We'll talk tomorrow," Regina called after me.

Outside, the quiet atmosphere was punctuated by an occasional yellow taxi cruising down Columbus Avenue in search of passengers. Most people were still turkeying somewhere. A group of teenagers walked by, laughing and teasing each other. One of the boys had his purple hair moussed-up, reminding me of a peacock. One of the girls, rail-thin with six earrings in her right earlobe, suggested to the others that they go drinking in the Village. The thought meandered through the canals of my mind until it coagulated: *She's right—there's no better place to pass some time than downtown.*

Descending the subway stairs at Eighty-sixth Street and Broadway, I stood at the platform with the teenagers and one other person: a young guy with messed-up hair in a parka thrown over hospital greens, reminding me of Seth. I realized that under different circumstances I might even have visited Seth—he was usually back at his place for football by this hour, after having devoured a meal with his family in Queens.

Getting off the train and climbing to the top of the subway stairs at Christopher Street, I suddenly felt I had come to the right place. Notorious for gay porn, sex accessories, and psychic readers, the street was packed with the emotionally orphaned, like me, who refused to be at home or at the family table laden with big bird carcasses.

Turning right at Greenwich Street, I heard loud music sailing out of an open glass doorway, drawing me into a bar. Beet red walls held rows of black-and-white photographs of models, scantily clad with Marilyn Monroe-inspired hairstyles. I squeezed past the deep crowd near the bar, which was silver and sleek.

The young bartender was shaking a decanter, when he glanced up and nodded. "What drink?"

"Umm," I said, unable to bring any particular cocktail to mind. Alcohol had never been my forte. Bellini martinis were Regina's most recent passion, not mine. I stood there speechless.

"Can't hear you." His face screwed up in a questioning expression.

A voice to my right said, "You'd probably like a Cosmopolitan, Doreen."

"Okay," I said as I turned to look at the man by my side. His pensive eyes rimmed by tortoiseshell glasses were unmistakable. "Alan, what're you doing here? Besides filling in for my ignorance, that is."

"Meeting friends." His smile was enormous, transforming him to almost handsome. "Your drinking habits were always legendary."

"Sad, huh?" I said, taking in his matured features. "Alan Shore, who'd believe I'd meet you here? It's been a long time."

"Since '88," he said.

We had studied for the New York Bar together, having met in the ten-week evening preparatory class. Sitting at Max's apartment or in Central Park on a blanket with New York Bar review books, bottles of water, and bags of cherries, we memorized a myriad of arcane laws and procedures during that summer.

"You were a great study partner. Still practicing law in San Francisco?" I asked. We had lost touch after he moved west.

"Just came back."

"Missed the dirt and cold, I bet."

"Something like that." He smiled again.

The bartender parked a napkin onto the counter. The drink, presumably a Cosmopolitan, followed. I handed him a ten-dollar bill.

"Are you here with people?" he asked.

"My people are elsewhere," I answered.

"What kind of people?"

"Husband, son, mother-in-law, et cetera."

He studied my face a few seconds and then invited me to join him and his friends. Agreeing, I followed him. Alan stopped at a table where five men were crowded. It was littered with martini and beer glasses, plates of olives and nuts. The men were all thirty-something, unmistakably gay, and the loveliest of company for the night.

The hours breezed by in laughter and storytelling. I watched his friends, enamored by the tales of dating humiliation and misdirected romantic efforts by friends; they were cracking jokes and commiserating.

I felt a visceral bond with them. They had lived their younger years with skeletons hung in the closet and had managed, over time, to coexist with them, even thrive in comfortable proximity. I felt inspired, somehow encouraged to begin the process of seeking peace with my own disenfranchisement. I wasn't sure how long this would take or what the final outcome would be, but I reckoned the seeds had been sown.

At four o'clock in the morning, I entered my darkened apartment, tiptoeing to Jack's room. I did not want to lie next to Ty, and my mother-in-law was asleep on the living room pullout couch. Shedding my coat and heels, I crawled into the toddler bed, pulling the blanket over my skirt. Jack's stuffed animals, dark silhouettes, loomed over my head like buzzards. The clock on the nightstand, a Mickey Mouse one, expelled ticktock noises. Rolling over on my side to avoid Mickey's smirk, I crunched the pillows under my cheeks.

Tania swooped down, hitting my back with her knee. She

tugged the blanket and put her left arm around my waist. I felt the end of the bed tilt under my feet, knowing that Aaron had arrived too, expecting he was about to curl up, the noises from his thumb in his mouth soon to follow.

"Welcome back," I whispered, noticing the blue characters in the middle of Tania's left forearm. I didn't turn her arm around, leaving the "A-2112" tattoo to face the new day.

PART III

A LL FOUR PHONES IN MY office were ringing simultaneously. I decided to let them go to voice mail; there was too much work on my desk that required my attention.

Katherine van de Vrande, who had come to work for me, poked her head into my office, and I waved her in. With signature pink pad between her fingers, she seated herself in the chair facing my desk. Her periwinkle blue blouse, ruffles down the front, highlighted her eyes and her auburn hair.

"How goes?" she asked. "I probably shouldn't ask."

"Well, now that you did, I'll tell you—the phones are ringing incessantly; everyone wants details on the offering. This pile of documents is waiting for review, but in the meantime, Dorf wants the leasing agreements done."

JRW Communications, our parent company, was in the midst of another stock offering—in other words, it was selling more of its corporate shares to the public, raising more capital in order to fuel its growth. It was a crazy time for all of us in the company and its subsidiaries, and top performance was required.

For effect, I glanced at Katherine and pointed

at the foot-high pile of documents parked near my desktop computer, the flashing multiline phone, the stack of Federal Communications Commission memos, and the calendar lying open and scribbled with meetings for the week.

Katherine smiled, the kind she used when commiserating. I studied her beautiful complexion; it remained as such despite the wear of her forty-five years. Katherine had come to work for me a year earlier with Lenny's reluctant blessing, after she had grown tired of her commute from Manhattan to the Westchester location of Pellier & Spielman.

She rarely typed anymore, due to the proliferation of computers and to my preference for handling my own word processing. Yet some things remained constant even in the midst of change. Men still ogled Katherine everywhere she turned; her long legs, generous cleavage, and radiant smile, all bundled into one package, were a showstopper. Unfortunately, her brand of sexiness still attracted the scumbags and the cheating married men of the universe. Romance troubles aside, she was an excellent paralegal and all-around dependable assistant.

"I'm almost done with the telemarketing issue." Katherine glanced at her pad. "I've spoken with the FCC, the attorney general's office, looked through our memos on file, and left a message for the DC guys," she said, referring to our firm's regulator specialists with offices in the nation's capital.

"Don't forget—put your memo in bullet-point format."

"Okay." She nodded. "What else?"

"Check with the sales department and see if they've finalized the contract for traffic to Indonesia; then you can start reviewing those agreements."

"Fine." Katherine rose to leave, hesitating. "I was wondering if I could attend the luncheon."

"Why not? Everyone else seems to be."

"Great, thanks." She showed her Chiclet teeth in appreciation.

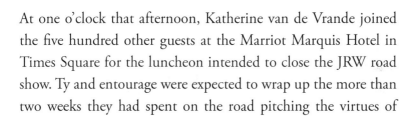

At one o'clock that afternoon, Katherine van de Vrande joined the five hundred other guests at the Marriot Marquis Hotel in Times Square for the luncheon intended to close the JRW road show. Ty and entourage were expected to wrap up the more than two weeks they had spent on the road pitching the virtues of their company.

This stock offering was turning out to be an easy sell. The confluence of new technologies, the vast amounts of capital available, and voracious investor appetite for high-tech stocks constituted a "no-brainer," according to Brad Barkow. The financial markets were wild about telecom stocks in that summer.

Indeed, everyone was at the luncheon. There were telecom analysts, some of iconic stature, in addition to scores of fund managers from across the country and representatives of boutique investment houses, congregated around tables set for lunch. The monogrammed French cuffs slapped each other on the back.

Ty came to the microphone to begin the presentations. I could tell he was tired, even from a distance; it was in his voice. He introduced the next speaker, his Swedish manager. Five European managers of JRW subsidiaries had arrived in New York during the past two weeks for the road show. Some were scheduled to speak at the luncheon.

I glanced around to see the Wall Street megalomaniacs applauding between mouthfuls of grilled portobello mushrooms. JRW Sweden's manager approached the podium, dressed in a gray suit, his whitish-blonde hair plastered down. Flashing computer-generated slides on the screen, he spoke in Swedish-ized English, with tinkles of flatware and china in the background. *Numbers, revenues, network, infrastructure, Internet protocol, inherent costs, management teams.* The words buzzed in my ears.

"Your husband's a Wall Street star," the young man next to me said, leaning in to avoid disturbing the rest of the table.

Swallowing my bite of salad, I turned to him. "Thank you," I said, glancing at his name tag, "Matthew."

"I'm with Millennium Investments and have been following Ty's career since he founded the firm with Wagner and Beekman," the fund manager said.

I nodded and smiled.

"Some career. Your husband has taken Wall Street by storm. Lucky play for him," he added.

"Quite lucky, yes."

"He's worth more than a hundred million."

"On paper." There was no elation in my voice.

Matthew stared at me for a few seconds. He gave me a weak smile, probably attributing my lackluster comment to sheer stupidity. "He'll never have to work again," he said. I detected a rebuking tone, maybe condescending. He then twisted his body to face the speaker, not addressing me again, not even to say good-bye.

That was fine with me. I knew that the Street and those on it judged everyone by their weight in paper goods: stock certificates and option agreements, enamored by the prospect of Porsches, yachts, and summer homes.

By three o'clock, coffee and the dessert of pear tarts had been served, and everyone dispersed to their next meeting, conference call, or stock trade. I was on my way to mine across town.

I jumped on the subway heading for Regina's place, got off, and dashed up Columbus Avenue. I swung right at Seventieth Street, passing the Italian restaurant we favored. The red umbrellas were open over the sidewalk tables. The last time I had been there with Regina and Lulu, it had been winter several years ago, the umbrellas and tables had been in hibernation, and Regina had been on her way to Barcelona in celebration of her one-month anniversary.

Now, Regina, a new mother, was about to be named director of marketing at Puff Cosmetics; she had been invited to the company's board of directors monthly meeting. Her new nanny was slated to start in two weeks. Regina would trust no one, other than Lulu or me, with her newborn. With Lulu on call at the hospital, that left me on call for Regina's baby.

This was the end of her maternity leave. Regina had given birth less than three months before, with Lulu in the operating room standing beside the obstetricians. Despite the arduous delivery and the use of forceps, Regina was ecstatic with the new male in her life. She bestowed on him a mature, masculine, and respectable name: Joseph Pierce Astor. But for now he was too small a person to be called anything but Joey.

I breathed in the air, tipping my head to the brightened skies, inhaling traces of freshly budded leaves—new beginnings. Climbing the two flights of the brownstone, I pondered the recent transitions in my oldest friend's life. Marc had "reconciled" with his first wife and returned to her and their two children, leaving Regina. Between their separation and divorce, Regina had realized she was pregnant despite her having already given up on both her troubled marriage and her uncooperative fertility.

Regina's "obsession" with starting her own family had driven Marc back to his first family, his "more familiar headache," in Marc's version.

What a total jerk, my version.

"Wowee, looking good," I said as Regina opened the door dressed in a cream-colored suit, the long, straight jacket flowing over the skirt.

"Even for a fat new mama?" Regina asked.

"Even more so. Motherhood becomes you."

"Keep saying that." Her throaty laugh spilled out, making the room seem sunnier.

"Where's the most adorable Astor?"

"Over there." She pointed to the coffee table. On it sat a tote bassinet with thick handles. Jutting my face inside, I saw Joey sleeping, wrapped in a blanket with an aqua duck print. His breaths struggled out of his button nose while his fists remained closed. Remembering Madame Sanne, I said in a whisper, "a perfect fait accompli."

"Bottles in the fridge, diapers on the changing table, clothes in top drawer of dresser. He just ate a half hour ago," Regina said.

"I've done this before, you know. Now get out of here. Somebody's going to have to pay for his college."

Regina threw her raincoat over her arm and grabbed her alligator bag. "Thanks," she yelled and was out the front door.

In the immaculate tiny kitchen I searched for some coffee. Regina didn't even know how to boil an egg, but she always stashed coffee in the cabinet to the right of the refrigerator. And she had a stainless-steel espresso machine, the "Cadillac of all makes." She was a believer in caffeinating every facet of life.

In a few moments the strong brew was ready; its flavor teased my tongue as, cup in hand, I perused the compact and functional apartment. Regina had rented it after her marriage fell apart. Her loft bed jutted out over Joey's sparkling new crib. The "main" room, complete with working brick fireplace, sported a sofa with oversized pillows bordered by purple leather fringes. Facing the street, the elongated windows had slatted blinds pulled way up. Bright late afternoon light streamed into the room, dancing off the stuffed animals and toys strewn on the wooden floors.

I lifted the bassinet bag and placed it by my side on the sofa. Settling into the pillows, I studied Joey's mushy head snuggled in a cap of blue. He stirred a bit, flexing his fingers as he made some noises. *Another baby boy, another Jack, another Yankel, another Aaron.*

I thought about Max's sister, Sally, and her son: sweet, fragile, and dependent. I imagined that after a long day at the photography studio where she worked, she would enter her family's apartment, lit by a lonely naked bulb over the kitchen table, stepping toward the bed where Aaron slept, warmed by the nearby oven. She must have blessed her priceless possession.

To others he was no such thing; in the camp, he had been hung like a sack of potatoes. *What makes people perpetuate evil with such nonchalant self-righteousness, destroying someone's whole world in the belief that it's worthless? Why is one mother's child viewed as beautiful and precious, while another's deserves torture and death without the slightest protestation of enlightened society?*

I pictured a little body, hanging limp in front of a barbed wire fence, rows of Auschwitz inmates shuffling by with their tin soup plates, sunken eyes looking down at the trampled dirt. The wind slapped the frail cadaver, making it twirl. As it swung around counterclockwise, I suddenly saw the lifeless face; it was that of my son, Jack.

Tears poured out, stinging my cheeks. It wasn't so much that Jack couldn't grow up healthy and contented as an only child, but the thought of being sentenced to life as the mother of a solitary offspring suddenly chilled me to the core. I was beginning to believe that maybe I was the one who could not grow old feeling contented. I had been beating back this thought for some time. Now, I feared this might consume me. I knew it definitely consumed my ghosts.

My ghosts and I were not on speaking terms. During the last few months, my metaphysical trio had taken the liberty of interrupting my sleep on a constant basis and intruding on my dreams. It took me a while to figure out, but I had finally understood the underlying reason: Jack was approaching the end of third grade. The ghosts were frantic because of the absence of any siblings. The birth of Regina's baby fueled their incendiary behavior.

Recently they had become increasingly insufferable. About a month before, Ty had been in San Jose for meetings. Feeling fatigued after work and then supper, homework, bath, and playtime with Jack, I had climbed into bed hoping to watch a little mindless late-night television and catch a few hours of rest.

As soon as I closed my eyes, Tania joined me; I felt her legs touching my side. I opened my eyes and sat up on one elbow. I saw Aaron flutter down at the end of my bed. For a moment I thought he was about to bring his thumb to his mouth, but instead, he sat staring at me, his large eyes sorrowful; one tear flowed down his pale, smooth face. He began to sniffle, wiping his cheek with the back of his sleeve.

"Stop bothering me," I said. "You know this is out of my hands." I wanted to sound calm and reasonable.

"We must be replaced," Tania said, her tone piqued by indignation. "Time is running out."

"You know very well that I have looked into every fertility treatment, and none of them offer me any answer," I answered.

Investigating the plethora of available treatments, my doctors and I had concluded that none of them could succeed for me. The complications and scarring I had sustained during Jack's birth were irreparable. The ghosts, aware of these findings, insisted their auditory senses had malfunctioned: the words whizzed by their deaf ears.

"We don't care about your explanations," Tania whined. She crossed her arms on her chest.

A shadow passed by the window, disturbing the rows of streetlight streaked across the room. Yankel drifted over and settled himself next to Aaron at the corner of my bed. I noticed that his normally soft, curly hair was matted. He bowed his head while unfolding some tattered pieces of cloth. For the first few moments, I couldn't identify the items Yankel had pulled from the clothes. But then I realized. Heat waves marched through my neck to my forehead, eradicating rational thoughts. Yankel had a rope and potatoes in his hands; his fingers became busy tying the rope around one potato.

"Enough," I shouted at them. I kicked at Yankel, sending him catapulting off the bed. The potato rolled on the floor until it bumped up against the wall. I turned to Tania. "Do you think by torturing me, you will get what you want?"

She stared at me for a moment. "We will be lost forever."

Despair arrested my thoughts. I just craved some respite from this dialogue. I could not bear uttering another word. Pulling the blanket over me, I flicked Aaron off, then pushed Tania away. I gazed at the dresser. Bits of light flickered on its brass handles; I followed their trajectory across the room. Suddenly, Tania swept down in front of me, her hair reflecting moonlight rays.

"Go away," I said, "please."

"No, you are our only hope," she responded as she grabbed at my sleeve.

I could feel my tears ready to burst forth like water from a high-pressure hose. I used every fiber of my being to preclude their spilling out.

Once under control, I turned my attention again to Tania. Her eyes were angry, her fingers still entwined in my nightgown sleeve. I saw Aaron floating near the windowpanes. Then I noticed Yankel was jumping rope. The noose cord was thumping at the floor, the rhythmic sounds unnerving me. Right then, for the first time ever, I felt deep disdain for these creatures.

I tried to dislodge Tania's fingers from my gown. She shoved at me. I pushed back, and we exchanged blows. I felt myself losing my balance. I tried to grab at the bedding, but it was too late. I fell onto the floor. Lying on the carpet, I assessed my situation: soreness in my elbows and the back of my thigh, but nothing seemed broken or sprained. I glanced at the clock on the dresser. Squinting, I saw the time was almost 2:00 AM. Dawn would break in several hours.

I rose slowly from the floor while wrapping the bed coverlet around me. If I wanted to get any sleep that night, I knew there was only one place of refuge. I crossed the darkened hallway and slipped into the upholstered chair in the corner of Jack's room. His face was not visible to me, but I could hear the youthful, even breathing emanating from the bed. I slept for a few hours in the chair that night free of nightmares and intrusive ghosts.

By the time Jack awoke for school, I was drinking coffee in the kitchen, making his lunch, and resolving to avoid all future interactions with my spirits, if possible.

T HE NEXT EVENING, TY AND I were invited to have drinks with Jerrold Wagner and Avery Beekman in celebration of the closing. I was meeting them at the Four Seasons Hotel. After making arrangements for Jack to spend the evening with the family of his playmate Brian, our neighbors, I left my office.

Jerrold had insisted on my participation despite my repeated attempts to get out of it. Realizing that he was trying to show his appreciation for my suffering Ty's constant travels, late hours, and stress (not my working at the subsidiary), I reluctantly accepted. But I felt awkward because I thought Ty should be thanked alone without his spousal sidekick.

I waited for the uptown subway on the platform, which was stuffy, smelling of perspiration and steam. After a short ride, coming out of the subway at Eighth Avenue, I sauntered down Fifty-seventh Street. It had always been my favorite street in Manhattan; it was wide and bright, housing some of the finest stores in the world.

And so much had happened on this street.

I passed the quirky bookstores and art shops nestled around the Arts Student League, where Hala had taken oil painting classes. Crossing over Seventh Avenue, in front of the wide set of doors to Carnegie Hall, I remembered my twelfth birthday, the time Hala had taken me to a piano concert there. I recalled my party dress and patent leather shoes. After the concert we had had tea next door in the Russian Tea Room. I loved its pink and red décor, the ladies wrapped in fur stoles, the noise, the caviar blinis, the excitement.

At the end of the block, I stopped to study a bronze lion guarding the doorway of an antique shop. My jade box had come from this street, purchased by Regina at one of the antique shops perennially going out of business. I had a hunch that the store was still in existence, but I had never asked Regina for the exact name, nor was I about to, determined to leave its origin a mystery.

Further east, I gazed at the mannequins in the windows of Bergdorf Goodman; it was fall preview week. The tweeds and woolen pleated skirts on them seemed paradoxical in the heat, like penguins sunbathing on Laguna Beach. I suddenly pictured Regina's glowing face during the fittings for her bridal gown on a winter's day long ago. Her wedding had been so beautiful, at the Saint Regis Hotel several blocks away.

Thinking of Regina's nuptials, I looked over at Tiffany's, across the intersection. Marc had bought Regina a two-carat diamond engagement ring—now recut by her into stud earrings. At the same place, Ty had bought me a bracelet with tiny sapphires after Jack was born. It had fared better in the long run than Regina's ring, having maintained its original form. I thought I should wear it more often.

As I continued down the street, I came upon the deli where Jack and I had sipped hot chocolate after our Sunday afternoons skating at the Wollman Rink, close by in Central Park. A dot of whipped cream usually sat at the tip of Jack's nose as he drank the foamy treat.

From a distance, I spotted my destination; the flags were flying over the entrance of the skyscraper. The Four Seasons Hotel was a relative newcomer to the street, having cropped up during the latest cycle of the New York City real estate boom. It seemed to embody the city's reincarnation under Mayor Rudolph Giuliani.

The doorman, dressed in a tuxedo jacket and top hat, opened the brass-handled doors as I entered the lobby. A cathedral of opulence and power. The vaulted space was dimly lit, the coolness of the mocha marble floors and walls making me feel calm yet insignificant. I walked up the marble staircase, noticing the huge windows and camel-colored walls enveloping the people in the bar.

From afar I saw the back of Jerrold's head: the oddly shaped sphere bobbing. I could have recognized it in any crowd. I headed for the empty chair between Brad and Ty. Jerrold pushed back his chair and circled the others to greet me. Avery Beekman stood to shake my hand and bowed. As I sat down, I noticed the plates holding nuts, olives, salt sticks, and crackers.

"Well, Doreen, just to bring you into the conversation, we were praising Ty and Brad here on their fabulous success," Jerrold said. The round had closed yesterday in oversubscribed fashion, raising more than the expected hundreds of millions of dollars.

"I got great feedback from Morgan Stanley," Avery said. "The guys trained by me were impressed." Beekman had worked at Morgan Stanley in his youth. Even now at fifty-five years of age, he made it a point to mention that at every opportunity.

I glanced at Brad, who smiled ever so slightly in acknowledgment of the familiar Beekman bravado.

"Ty has become a real leader in the telecom world," Jerrold said.

"Look how far he's taken my initial ideas," Avery added. He

always took credit for the JRW telecom venture. Avery didn't like to be confused by real facts.

I noticed Avery's salt-and-pepper hair, blown out and sprayed. With his puckered expression and lean build, Avery looked like a stereotypical Frenchman. His condescension and snottiness only heightened that perception.

"I think a part of his success he owes to you," Jerrold said to me. "You've been a great support."

"Thank you." That was all I could muster in response.

The waiter approached us, causing a lull in the conversation. Relieved, I ordered a Bellini martini. I knew this was Regina's favorite place to get a first-rate Bellini.

As the others ordered, I glanced around. The stained glass wall behind the bar lightened up the atmosphere. The place buzzed with chatter. Some blondes were dressed in Moschino clothes; there was a smattering of Chanel.

"Brad, let's talk network build-out," Jerrold said, reaching for the cashews.

"The next stage needs to be massive," Avery said, putting his fingers to his tie, stroking at the knot. I checked out the lion print; I figured it was one of the new Hermes spring styles.

"Tommy called me yesterday, after the luncheon," Brad said. "They want to see rapid domestic build-out by the end of the next quarter." Tommy Bolton was the chief telecom analyst at Goldman Sachs, and his word was considered "the gospel" in the telecom world.

"Momentum, my boy," said Avery, his voice an octave lower. "Need to keep it up, Ty."

I glanced at Ty. He had been sitting quietly in his chair, swiveling a toothpick in his mouth during the course of the conversation.

Before he had a chance to answer, the waiter returned with

our drinks. We watched him set down the alcoholic beverages in silence. He placed a martini glass in front of me followed by a silver decanter. He shook it and poured some of the liquid, a pale peach color, into my glass.

Jerrold raised his scotch. "To us."

Brad added, "To luck." He moved his glass, making his drink swirl around, the ice cubes clicking together.

I noticed Ty lift his beer glass for the toast but then place it back on the table without tasting it.

Avery sipped his Campari and set it down. He wiped his fingers on the napkin as he asked, "How's the domestic network coming along, Brad?"

"Good. We're setting up another gateway switch in Florida," Brad said.

"Great for Latin America. Definitely an extremely important market," Avery pointed out.

Brad gave Avery a peculiar look.

"Are you okay with all this, Ty?" Jerrold asked, turning his head. "You've been awfully quiet so far."

"It's fine," Ty said, shifting upright and crossing his legs, "if we want to continue this way."

"What do you mean?" Jerrold asked, looking puzzled.

"I think it may be time to refocus, start to concentrate on profitability," Ty answered.

"Why?" Jerrold asked, clearly surprised.

"We're chasing our tail, and have been for some time now. Raising huge amounts of money, then spending it, then raising it—racing after revenues," Ty said.

"Hell, we're worth millions," Avery said, incredulous. "Why should we change course?"

"It's a vicious cycle. The industry cannot sustain itself for the long run if it doesn't turn profits," Ty said.

"This is the *new economy*, boy," Avery said. I thought I heard a tiny snicker catch onto his last word. "You can't decide to swim upstream all of a sudden." Avery's eyes widened.

"Everyone calm down. What's bothering you, Ty?" Jerrold asked.

"Well, our stock is at a high right now, and we just raised a ton," Ty said. "I think it's time we consider slowing down and growing the business organically."

"Why?" Jerrold asked.

"Not to sound too old-fashioned, but a healthy business needs to be profitable," Ty answered. "Then I would feel more comfortable with our soaring stock price."

I was confused by Ty's statement. What did it matter about the stock price? After all, despite the high stock price, none of the executives of JRW Communications, including Ty, had sold any shares during the heady stock market days. They had refused to undermine the company by appearing to be selling out or anticipating anything, from fiscal quarter to fiscal quarter, other than continued success. At that time, not selling was considered a vote of confidence on Wall Street.

Now Ty wanted his company to validate its reputation as a superachiever and turn a profit.

"Nonsense," Avery said. He moved forward in his seat. "Maybe, boy, you just don't have what it takes …" He stopped, glaring at Ty.

"Avery, please, stop," Jerrold said.

"It may very well be," Ty said, his calm gaze focused on Avery. "But, I believe this game can't go on forever. We aren't profitable, nor are we going to be anytime soon."

"Revenues, boy, not profits. New economy, new paradigm," Avery said, derisively.

"The others are the same," Brad said in a meek tone. He meant all the other telecom players trading on the stock exchange; they lacked profits as well. Our firm was certainly keeping good company in that sense.

There was a pause in the conversation. Jerrold was shaking his head as he picked at the cashews. Avery remained stonelike, unflinching, staring at Ty, who had leaned back in his chair.

I wished I could disappear, somehow evaporate. Maybe glide up to the ceiling and pass through it as Tania had done so many times before. I didn't know what to do with my hands, afraid to move any part of my body in the fear of bringing attention to myself. I left them loose by my sides.

Carefully, I brought my eyes up to look at Ty. He looked pale.

I suddenly wondered if he really was in over his head. If indeed his dream of living a life full of adventure and mirth had escaped him somewhere along the path. He had been so stressed in the past few months. I examined his face, gaunt and tired. His eyes lacked the sparkle they once had. Maybe he really did not have the requisite traits? But to do what? I wasn't sure what Avery's statement meant. But I knew something was amiss.

"It may be time to consider options for the company's general welfare," Avery said.

"Let's not get irrational," Jerrold said. "We've all been under pressure recently."

"The numbers are looking solid for the next few months," Brad said quietly. I knew he was trying to divert the discussion to more positive, less threatening talk.

But it didn't help.

"I'd like to bring some proposals to the next board meeting," Avery said.

"Fresh ideas are always welcome, Avery," Jerrold replied, trying to sound amenable.

"They may be more radical than you think," Avery said, glancing at Ty again.

"We're always ready to entertain new proposals, isn't that right, Ty?" Jerrold asked.

"Absolutely," said Ty.

Absolutely. Absolutely. I was amazed by the coolness of Ty's response. The way that word flowed from his lips with ease. The nonchalance jolted me. As the conversation turned to other business subjects, my mind remained stuck to the preceding topic, like a suction cup to the wall. Did Ty realize what was going on? It took me a few more seconds to realize that Ty had agreed to a time-out, his usual way of defusing explosive situations.

Avery's words whirled around in my head. New proposals to the board. Radical ones. Probably change of management proposals. The words had ridden out of Avery's mouth with shark scales attached. It was clear that the views of Ty and Avery were incompatible.

I felt terrified of the future.

"VERY GOOD, GRANDMA. YOU SEE, he's jumping. That means he went to the next level," Jack said. He brought his hand up to pat Faith on her shoulder.

Jack and his grandmother were playing video games; he was teaching her the Mario game.

"Now what?" she asked as she put down the control pad and took a sip of water from the cup resting on the coffee table. Pushing up her reading glasses, Faith bent over and kissed Jack on top of his head. Jack was lean and thin now, having shed his baby fluffiness. He was developing the masculine good looks of his father: mop of golden hair, dimpled chin, and calm, steady mannerisms, all complementing Max's eyes.

"Okay, follow this. I'll show you a trick you can use whenever Mario gets stuck," Jack said. "You watching?" He checked on his grandmother before proceeding. She straightened up and moved slightly forward on the couch.

It was Faith's fifth day with us; she had come to spend a week in New York.

I thought about the moment when Ty had suggested we needed a dose of Faith. After the Marriot Marquis luncheon, the successful conclusion of JRW Communications' public security offering, and drinks at the Four Seasons with Wagner and Beekman, our schedules returned from hysterical to merely hectic.

One night a few weeks later, Ty and I were having dinner; Jack had finished eating, had left the table, and was doing homework in his room. Ty was mouthing compliments about the chicken dish that I had thrown together. I wasn't listening; prickly feelings were running down my forearms as his words became fuzzier. I knew he was being upbeat and supportive, but a wave of nausea rumbled through my abdomen. I set down my fork.

"Forget the chicken," I said. "You know what we're suffering from?"

"No, but I'm sure you're going to tell me."

"Loneliness."

"Really?" He looked bemused.

"Okay, not you, but I am. We need to be surrounded by more noise and laughter."

"Mini, I hope we're not going to go through this again. You've invited Max a hundred times, to no avail."

"I know."

"Invite Regina over—guaranteed laughs."

"No, that's not what I'm talking about."

Ty put a forkful of chicken into his mouth and chewed for a few seconds. "How about Faith?"

"Faith is not exactly synonymous with noise and laughter."

"No, but she's Jack's only grandmother. Family."

Family, family, as the Penguins said. But I was not in the mood for family advocacy right then. I turned to study Ty's face, but he was focused on cutting his chicken, calmly and methodically. After a decade with him, I knew that he was nudging me in a premeditated direction, one he had been silently mulling over for some time. Proficient in nonchalant advice, subtle prodding, gentle encouragement, Ty, master delegator, allowed those around him to pollinate ideas at their own pace, tending with an occasional spritz of water and dusting of fertilizer. He apparently wanted me to get closer to Faith. In her short weekend visits since she parachuted into our lives almost three years ago, we had maintained cordial relations—pleasant yet superficial.

The doorbell startled me now, bringing me back to reality. I assumed it was Ty returning from his regular Saturday tennis game, having forgotten his keys. I went to the door and opened it, delighted to see Regina, smile stitched on her face, with Joey snuggled in his stroller.

"Lulu is on her way too," Regina said. Her face flush from the trip over, sunglasses on top of her head, she pushed past me with her baby bag and Versace tote.

Jack and Faith put down their control pads and headed over. Jack kissed Regina on the cheek and bent down to peek at the baby. He touched Joey's hand and made a comment about how cute he was. Faith, standing behind Jack, circled around her grandson to welcome Regina.

"Nice to see you again," Regina said to Faith as she swung her tote off her shoulder and onto the coat tree near the front door.

"I thought you weren't feeling well," I said. "Your stomach's been killing you."

"It has, but I felt better and decided to visit. I called Lulu to come with."

Judging by her heels and leopard-print dress, I assumed she must feel better, although her eyes were glassy.

"Came for banana cake. Faith, any left?" she asked. She had nibbled some on Thursday night when both she and Lulu had stopped by, each on her way home from work. Regina seemed to warm to Faith more than I did; maybe abandonment by the male gender and the hardships of single parenthood bound them.

"Sure," Faith said. "I'm just about to lose the game to Jack, my great teacher. Once I do I'll put up some coffee."

"I think I can handle that," I said, heading toward the kitchen, taking out the percolator and a bag of coffee beans from the freezer.

"The cake's not going to do much in the way of reducing this protruding stomach." Regina peered down at the area in question. "But hell, it's delicious."

"You just had a baby," Faith said. "Don't be so hard on yourself."

"That was more than five months ago," Regina said.

The doorbell rang. "Regina, please get that," I said, while rinsing strawberries in the kitchen sink.

Lulu entered, wearing slim pants and a cotton sweater with giant buttons. Saturday was her day off.

"We're finishing Faith's cake," Regina said as she removed Joey's jacket and whisked him out of his stroller and onto a baby blanket she spread on the carpet. After some stirring, he fell asleep on his belly.

Lulu, her blonde hair cascading down her torso, greeted Faith. I watched her fragile features as she inquired as to my mother-in-law's health. I carried sliced banana cake and a bowl of cut strawberries to the coffee table, and then followed with a tray of cups of coffee, cake plates, napkins, and forks.

Regina kicked off her heels and double-checked on Joey before she flung her powder pink manicured toes over the side arm of the chair. "I could use a Bellini martini, but I assume you don't serve those here, so I'll go for a glass of Chardonnay, Doreen," she said as she plumped her hair with her fingers.

I brought an opened wine bottle and wineglasses to the coffee table. Lulu settled next to Faith on the couch, and Jack excused himself to visit with his friend Brian, down the hall. They often played together after school and on weekends.

Faith, Regina, Lulu, and I meandered through talk of the weather, baby food, new Puff products, and Lulu's rental apartment options, as her lease was expiring.

"Okay, you want the latest news now?" Lulu asked, banana cake in her mouth.

"Let's have it," Regina said, refilling her wineglass.

"I'm no longer with Mike."

"Again, you mean," Regina said.

Lulu had been dating moody Mike Epstein, the radiologist, for a second stint, this one having lasted a few months. I suspected the culprit for the relationship revival was loneliness. *Too bad she and Seth had never found each other compelling in a romantic sense*, I thought, but I was not about to bring up that subject again.

"You're competing with my track record," Regina said. "Not a good thing." She sipped some wine and then popped a strawberry into her mouth. It occurred to me that Regina didn't mention her ex-husband anymore, and his visits to Joey had grown less and less frequent until they had ceased entirely.

Lulu looked forlorn, her eyes focused down at her knees.

"I think Regina's joking," I said to her.

"But she's right. No luck with men," Lulu said slowly, as if she were thinking aloud.

"But look how much else you've accomplished," I said. I reiterated how Lulu had put herself through medical school, defying her childhood community and rising through the ranks of a New York teaching hospital, riding on her abilities, although it seemed to remain true that she "couldn't land a decent guy," in the words of Regina.

"It all seems to elude me, somehow," Lulu said, sighing.

"Don't say *all*," I said. "It's absurd to talk like that." I sounded like Hala just then.

Faith had been quiet until now. She was toying with her coffee cup, outlining the rim with her finger. "You have to learn to slay your dragons," she said in her raspy voice.

"How did *you* accomplish that?" Lulu asked, looking up.

"I didn't," Faith said. I knew she meant the abandonment by Ty's father and more so the crucible of her own father. "But you're young enough to succeed, and *you must*. Otherwise"—she hesitated, shaking her frazzled hair—"you end up a ghost."

We were motionless, surprised by her admission, petrified of responding. Lulu cleared her throat and Regina stared at her fingernails. I felt a swell of apprehension building in me. Ghosts seemed to be everywhere.

"And then what happens?" Regina asked.

"You live out your life like an old car stuck in neutral, most of the time deluding yourself into believing that if the pain's dulled—that's enough."

"That's it?" Lulu said.

"You don't belong to or with anyone, especially for eternity," she mused, looking at the ceiling. "Maybe cremation is the only route. It's a scary fate."

Is she speaking about herself or Dziadek? I gazed at Faith, her eyes holding steady, looking right back at me now. "Is that really what *you* would want?" I asked.

"Yes," Faith said in a soft voice. "Probably."

Joey began to move, rubbing his face with his fist. Regina stood and scooped him up. I heated his formula-filled bottle in the microwave while Regina changed his diaper. Somehow, after hearing Faith's stark verbalization, I felt my mood shift, sensed my battery recharging, energizing to consider the possibility of facing down my enemies.

Faith and Lulu, apparently also in an elevated emotional state, bent over Joey, cooing about his curls of dark hair, his mushy thighs.

"This is the most important man in my life—no abandonment issues," Regina said cheerfully.

"At least not for eighteen years," Lulu said.

"Longer duration than any other I've had until now," Regina said, lifting Joey up above her head. A smile spread across his cherubic face, a string of drool hanging at the edge of his mouth.

Soon afterward, Ty returned, perspiring in his tennis outfit, racquet slung over his shoulder. The showers were out of order at the courts, he told us, and he headed for our bathroom. He came back scrubbed and dressed in a casual shirt and jeans, joining us for more chatter.

At eight o'clock we sent out for Chinese food, afraid to interrupt the flow of the evening, steadfastly keeping to our seats. After the food had arrived and I was bringing some broccoli and cashews toward my mouth, I noticed Ty's gaze moving back and forth among "his ladies" as if mesmerized by a Wimbledon tennis match. He was beaming at the convivial atmosphere, absorbing the banter.

The next morning, Ty was fixing pancakes while I scanned the Sunday *Times* and Jack played with his Game Boy, lying on the living room carpet. Faith had just finished showering; she was dressed in a rose-colored top over stretch pants and canvas sneakers. She poured a cup of coffee and pulled out the chair to my right at the table.

The cordless phone rang. I answered it.

"I'm in bad shape," Regina said.

I dropped the newspaper and moved the receiver to my other ear, grabbing a pen. I doodled whenever I felt stressed. "What is it?"

"My pains have been hell all night, and my stomach's distended."

"How bad?"

"Horrible."

"Did you call the doctor?" She had been to see her gynecologist several times in the past three months, complaining of pain.

"You're my only call—can't move or talk too much."

Ty was watching me as he flipped a pancake on the griddle. Faith was sipping her coffee. I noticed she wore no jewelry, not even a ring.

"Hospital, that's what you need," I said, thinking *logistics* while pulling my cardigan around me tighter. "Okay, I'll come over and take you. Don't worry." I hung up.

Dashing to my bedroom closet to find a pair of comfortable shoes, I located my bag and swung through the kitchen to stuff some cookies and apples into it, figuring it was going to be a long day. I was about to head to the front door.

"Hey, how about telling us what's happening," Ty said.

"I think Regina needs to go to the hospital—bad stomach pains," I said, stopping to explain.

"Are you taking her up to Seth?" he asked.

I had totally forgotten that my poker buddy was an emergency room doctor at Presbyterian Hospital. "Actually, I was going to take her to Lulu." Lulu was a staff oncologist at New York Hospital.

"I think you should go to Seth. Lulu can't help as much in emergencies. Anyway, the distance is about equal from Regina's place to either."

"Good point."

"What about Joey?"

"Oh my God," I said. I had hung up in such haste I'd forgotten about Regina's baby; her nanny was off on Sundays. "No nanny."

"I'll go with you and bring the baby back here," Faith said. "Ty and I can manage."

"Doreen, take my cell phone." Ty took it off the counter and pressed it into my palm. "This is why cell phones are useful." We had had this argument many times; Ty thought my abhorrence of the cell phone not only impractical but downright silly. I still was haunted by my first conversation with Faith on Ty's cell phone during my poker game at Seth's.

My mother-in-law and I climbed into a cab; we didn't converse much during the ride. Faith kept her pocketbook centered in her lap, head facing forward. Her reticent calmness was a blessing under the circumstances. I gazed out the window, watching people strolling in the bold late morning sunshine clad in shorts and sunglasses. Outdoor cafés were bustling with the brunch crowd, who were flipping through newspapers and gossiping over mimosas. New York's Sunday summer life in full glory.

The taxi stopped in front of Regina's building. I told the driver to leave the meter running. Faith and I ascended the brownstone steps; Regina had left her door unlocked. We found her lying on the sofa, her face buried in a purple-fringed pillow. Nearby on the floor, Joey was strapped in his infant seat, legs kicking, gurgling. His baby bag was lying open on the floor nearby.

"Okay, Regina, I'm here. We're here, rather. Faith is going to take Joey home, and we have a date at Presbyterian," I said, my tone a little too jolly.

She groaned. I took the baby bag and went to add diapers and baby formula, also shoving in some extra outfits.

"Okay, you're off, "I said to Faith, placing the bag over her shoulder and bending to pick up Joey. "Regina, I'll be right back. Don't move."

After loading my mother-in-law and the baby into the waiting cab and instructing the driver, I ran back to get Regina. She was already seated upright on the sofa, her face a putrid greenish shade.

"Can you make it down to the street?" I asked.

She nodded. Grabbing her tote and my bag, we navigated the two flights like a pair of drunken sailors. We flagged a taxi and struggled into it. Once we were on our way, I paged Seth, notifying him that we were coming.

I looked at Regina's profile; her eyes were focused ahead. She obviously needed some encouragement. "There's nothing wrong—you're young and healthy. It's just some medical glitch, Regina."

"Glitch, nice touch." Her face tightened up.

"You're thinking *narishkeit*," I said, using Max's expression, prodding Regina to smile. "Get that stuff out of your head."

We pulled up under the red-lettered "Emergency Entrance" sign, wedging between two ambulances with their lights flashing; they were unloading patients on stretchers. Amid the frenzied action of the EMS workers, doctors, and nurses, stood Dr. Seth Rabiner, erect and stationary, white coat over his hospital greens, one hand clinging to an empty wheelchair next to him. As soon as I threw the taxi door open, he came toward us.

"So, girls, you decided I needed company today, huh?" Seth said, his face reconfiguring into a forced smile. "Come on, Regina, let's shake up the ER."

Chapter 21

THE WORDS HAMMERED AT MY temples. *Ovarian cancer.*

I turned my gaze to the patient lying in the hospital bed. It was Regina's fourth day after her massive operation; the villainous parts had been yanked out during hours under the knife. Today, she was beginning to recuperate. Her hair was swooped up atop her head with an elastic band, like a pineapple. She had dabbed blush onto her face, lending it an artificial robustness.

"Hey, kid, why so serious?" she asked, exuding joviality over her dull, sterile hospital quarters. "Look at the fabulous flowers."

The room was filled with bouquets of pink, red, and cream flowers, boxes of chocolates, and one bakery box of almond croissants. A large glass vase held yellow daffodils supplied by Ty, brightening the antiseptic atmosphere.

"Really beautiful," I said.

"It's amazing they found this shit," she said, putting her manicured finger on her abdomen. "Otherwise, you know what could've happened." She pulled the paisley hospital sheet closer to her chest.

Yes, I do. But I wasn't about to say.

"I've revised my impression of Seth. Never going to criticize his melancholy shlumpiness again," Regina said, smiling, her teeth suddenly looking larger relative to her face.

"I'll be sure to tell him, as I'm sure you will," I said. "By the way, Faith and Jack are coming up later to pick me up. I promised Jack some time at the Natural History Museum. Joey is with your nanny at her apartment for a few hours. I'll get him later."

Jack had been begging to see the dinosaurs at the museum. The visit would also provide a fortuitous opportunity for me to stop across the street at Max's apartment. I thought it was necessary he hear about Regina in person.

"Then I better make sure I really fix myself up," Regina said, sliding her leg slowly off the bed. "Don't help me." In incremental movements, holding onto the banister on the wall, she maneuvered her way to the bathroom.

I observed her hesitant steps, thinking it was time for Max and me to take similar steps toward fixing up our strained familial paradigm. *Who knows how much time any of us has?* Regina's illness stirred reflections on the elusiveness of life, on our fleeting terrestrial tenure. It made me wonder about family as a dynamic structure. After all, Regina had practically grown up at my house, yet now Max was unaware of her serious, possibly terminal, condition. On the other hand, in ironic fashion, Faith, a virtual stranger to us until recently, had assumed the role of guardian, extending her stay when she learned Regina was going to have surgery. She volunteered to help with Joey, sharing responsibility with Regina's nanny, also giving Jack attention while I ran between office and hospital. With Ty now in Europe for meetings and scheduled to tap down in Australia for twenty-four hours, Faith pointed out there was a dearth of helping hands.

"Here you are, Doreen. What an unexpected surprise," Seth

said, a facetious grin on his face as he entered the room. He was in wrinkled greens, white coat thrown open, with stethoscope wrapped around his neck like a python snake. As usual, he cut a rather shambling figure.

"Funny, Doctor Rabiner," I said. "I'm out of here soon."

"Where is the illustrious patient?"

"In the bathroom getting dolled up."

"So Regina is most certainly getting back to normal. Very good," he said, combing his hair with his fingers.

It occurred to me that during the last few days Seth had seemed cheerier than ever, and I assumed caretaking agreed with him. He had made all the arrangements for Regina's emergency surgery in constant consultation with Lulu. The two had concurred that Regina's surgery should be performed by the world-renowned surgeons at Presbyterian Hospital. If chemotherapy or radiation would be required thereafter, she might undergo those treatments here or at Lulu's hospital across town. *But, first things first.*

"What's going on in the emergency room?" I asked.

"Always rough on Saturdays," he said. "It's the nature of the beast."

Regina came out of the bathroom, her hair brushed out, her made-up eyes catching sight of Seth.

"Looking grand, Regina," he said.

"And much lighter," she said, shuffling toward the bed. "Guess it wasn't the banana cake that caused the stomach. That's good news, at least." She chuckled.

"We're going to talk to the oncology group—see what the future holds for you," he said, referencing her possible treatments. "We'll consult Lulu, naturally."

As if on cue, Lulu entered the room, squeezing Regina's foot a bit as she passed the bed, heading toward the chair beneath the window. She dropped her briefcase on the chair's seat. She was dressed in a lemon-colored suit, short cut jacket over pencil skirt, a sophisticated and unusual look for her.

"Just got out of a conference at Mount Sinai," Lulu said, pulling at her bag in order to check her beeper. "Had to present."

"How did it go?" Seth asked.

"Fine, I guess, but the findings are inconclusive," she said, a tinge of pink spreading over her cheeks as she answered him. She checked her beeper again and returned it to the outside pocket of her bag.

"After you girls have gabbed some, I'd like you to join me with the surgeons," Seth said, looking at Lulu.

She nodded, gathering her hair off her face, twisting it into a chignon. Seth was inching toward the door, when Lulu announced she craved a cup of coffee. Regina chimed in that she could benefit from some cafeteria soup, for almost anything would be better than the regular hospital food. Seth volunteered to get some chicken soup for Regina and to accompany Lulu to the first-floor cafeteria.

"Back in a flash," Lulu said as she departed with Seth. I watched them saunter out, their bodies close together, Seth's head turned down to Lulu, whispering.

"I'm feeling kind of tired," Regina said, repositioning her head on the pillows.

"I've got reading to do, so rest," I said, picking up the *Times* lying on Regina's sliding tray table.

"It's yesterday's," she said in a groggy voice.

"That's fine—haven't looked at it in days. I need to catch up," I said, moving Lulu's briefcase and slipping into the chair.

By the time Faith and Jack arrived, about twenty minutes later, Regina was sound asleep. I brought my finger up to my lips indicating quiet when I heard Jack's footsteps echoing off the waxed linoleum floor and saw him coming toward me.

"Let's go—she's sleeping now," I whispered, gathering my belongings. "Lulu will be back soon; she'll sit with Regina. Besides, we've got dinosaurs to see." I put my hand through Jack's hair, bringing a sparkle to his eyes.

Faith was waiting at the door. Walking toward her, I said, "Ready?"

"Let me just see her," she said.

Faith approached Regina's bed in inaudible steps. Tilting her head down, she came close to the sleeping patient. She gently straightened Regina's sheet, tucking it in around her shoulders, and tiptoed back out.

"She's looking better. Poor kid, so much has happened to her in the last few months." Faith looked pained by her observations.

We walked out in silence, each of us absorbed in our own ruminations. The outdoor sunlight made me squint; I searched for my sunglasses. A drippy saffron haze perforated the edges of the sun, making it resemble the sunny-side-up eggs Hala used to love. I pictured my mother as she took toast and angled it, piercing the eye of the egg, letting the yolk ooze out, salting in between bites. She believed the egg was a perfect food, tasty and nutritious, and that it symbolized the circle of life.

Crossing Broadway to the subway station, we rode the downtown local several stops. There was an outdoor fair of crafts in white tents, hugging the perimeter of the Natural History Museum and its adjacent park. Scores of weekenders were wandering on the cobble-stoned sidewalks, taking in the mosaics, beaded necklaces, children's sweaters, and ceramic bowls. After finding nothing to purchase that satisfied our fancy, we skipped up the stairs of the museum heading straight to the dinosaur exhibit, Jack's favorite.

We strolled through the halls, which contained skeletons of extinct creatures, fossilized bones strung in the form of dinosaurs, recreating their enormous bodies and smaller heads. Although these creatures had not roamed the earth for millions of years, Jack, along with most human beings, was fascinated by them.

I thought of another species soon to vanish: the Penguins. In a few years, none of them would walk among the living, their stories relegated to history books, movies, and the back alcoves of the memories of the few mini-Penguins, their children, who would bother or dare to remember. Hala had already taken her place among the dinosaurs, and time was evaporating for Jack's living grandfather, Max.

I turned past the *Barosaurus* dinosaur, my eyes glimpsing Jack, who was explaining something to Faith. She listened, shaking her head; her feet glided over the museum floor in tandem with her grandson, an expression resembling pride stenciled on her face. It occurred to me that Max's inability to reconcile the existence of Faith had sentenced me to a perpetual state of uneasy limbo, suspended between the Penguins and their haters.

After an examination of *Tyrannosaurus rex,* I suggested we fortify ourselves with a late brunch. In anticipation of my Max visit, droplets of anxiety began collecting inside me and pressing at my fingertips.

We exited the museum, crossing to the café on its southern edge. At Isabella's, seated at an outdoor corner table, corseted by planters with flowers and shaded under umbrellas, we made a conspicuous three-generational trio incongruous amidst the young, mainly single crowd. But I found the noisy atmosphere a welcome backdrop for my trepidations. We ordered cheese omelets, two glasses of Chardonnay, and blueberry pancakes, with a glass of milk for Jack.

"To Regina's recovery," I said, lifting the wineglass, pushing my sunglasses on top of my head.

"She deserves a good life," Faith said, clinking her glass against mine.

Jack brought his milk glass up to join us.

We ate in silence for a while, Jack splashing maple syrup on his pancakes. Faith chewed in a slow and methodical fashion. My eyes scanned Columbus Avenue. In the broad sense, it looked as if nothing had changed since my childhood, with the exception of some wares in storefront windows. My parents had lived on Central Park West since their wedding day, their bedroom overlooking the planetarium side of the museum edifice. Penguins had come and gone to our fifteenth-floor refuge, drinking tea, eating Danishes, playing cards, talking, crying, consoling each other. My friends were welcomed along with the adults and often slept over. I recalled Regina lugging in her knapsack for the weekends. Milk and coffee cake greeted her upon her arrival, and Hala's gentle hands tucked her in at night as well.

"When is Ty getting back?" Faith asked.

"In four days, according to his schedule," I said, glancing at my watch. "Should be on his way to Sydney by now." I played with the food. "He probably left us a message on the machine. We'll check when we get home."

"That's why you should carry a cell phone," Jack said.

"Another piece of unsolicited advice," I teased. "You sound just like your father."

"I think that's a big compliment you just got, young man," Faith said, dabbing her mouth with the napkin, winking at her grandson. The wink reminded me of Ty.

"Hey, there's the flea market," Jack said, distracted in an instant, pointing to the opposite side of Columbus Avenue.

"Every weekend," I said.

"Brian gets Nintendo games there—used ones. Can I take a look?" Jack asked.

"I tell you what, I was planning to say hello to Papa ..." I started.

"Let me take Jack while you visit with your father," Faith interjected.

"Okay, browse the market, and then come up and see your grandfather." It sounded like an excellent plan. "Tell you what—let's have some dessert first. Then we'll split up."

We ordered coffees and some ice cream from the waitress as she cleared our plates.

A few minutes later as Jack scooped a spoonful of the creamy delight into his mouth, Faith cleared her throat several times. "Doreen, remember our discussion the other day when Regina and Lulu were visiting?" Faith asked.

"Over banana cake."

"Well, I've been meaning to tell you, but ... So I may as well just say it." Faith clasped her hands on the table and sighed. "Ty is lucky to have you."

"That's so sweet, Faith. Thanks."

"No, I mean ..." She hesitated. "I mean, besides the other obvious reasons ... lucky that he got to slay his dragons, through you, I mean."

I presumed she was referring to the scourge of their past. "You mean his childhood?"

"Tough early years. It wasn't easy for him. Or for me." She lifted her eyes to the sky above. "He rose above it all."

So, apparently his mother believed as he did, that Ty had

transcended his pre-encoded trajectory, forging a new destiny for himself and possibly for his descendants.

And where does that leave me? Confused, grasping for a clear identity, still trying to reconcile my "unusual" life choices. Why can't I banish my demons into oblivion?

"You're proud of him," I said.

"I think he's broken the cycle."

I looked at this woman, my mother-in-law, sitting across the table, faded and insipid, her identity once a terrifying secret. In a surreptitious manner she had become an integral part of our lives, delivering aid and comfort in unobtrusive ways.

"I'm done," Jack said, pushing my arm. "Look, no more ice cream." His dessert glass was empty. "Grandma, you done?"

"Yes, I am."

"Then let's go." Jack rose to indicate his impatience.

"Okay, go. I'll finish here and head on up to Max's," I said. They were moving away from the table, when I reminded Jack he needed money.

Faith answered, "*I'm* buying Jack video games. After all, we enjoy them together. Besides, it's his birthday next week."

Grasping Jack's hand, Faith and her grandson began to traverse the wide avenue. The street tar was emitting heat, reminiscent of the steam spiraling out of Penguin teacups. A few cars chugged down Columbus Avenue. Jack was jabbering at Faith, tugging at her hand.

After signaling the waitress for the check, I gulped the last of my coffee. Tipping my sunglasses on my nose, I began to prepare myself for the Max visit, practicing some opening remarks in my head. Max was a creature of unrelenting habits, and I knew he would now be finished with his Saturday nap and that he would be reading more of *The New York Times*.

In the distance, I heard screeching sounds. Glancing around, I noticed a fast-moving limousine, a beat-up Lincoln Continental, the kind used in airport car services. It made a sharp left from Seventy-seventh Street onto Columbus Avenue, swerving on the turn. I looked for Faith and Jack, who had not yet reached the opposite curb, and then at the speeding vehicle. Before I could move, let alone scream, I saw Faith turn in the direction of the oncoming car; she clutched Jack's hand up to her chest in an instinctive motion. An instant later, in one fell swoop, Faith flung her grandson toward the curb. The limousine struck her down. The car never stopped, zigzagging between the lanes of the avenue until it disappeared in the distance.

The universe came to a standstill; I was engulfed in a roaring silence. Two people with a dog strolled near my table; they seemed surreal. Faint shouting rippled near my ears until it grew, one note at a time, into a crescendo. My skirt was glued to my chair, my arms shackled to the table. People began running toward the bodies that lay in the street. Sounds of approaching sirens punctured my stupefied mind. Police and ambulances pulled up, blocking traffic on Columbus Avenue. EMS workers pulled equipment out of the innards of the ambulances, while one policeman barked into his car radio.

The young waitress returned with the check, placing it on the table. Realizing there was unusual commotion on the street, she brought her hand up to shade her eyes as she took in the scene. She looked back and forth between the frenzied activity and me.

In a shaky voice, she said, "Hey, isn't that ..." She stopped midsentence and stared at me.

In a sudden movement, I catapulted out of my chair, adrenaline finally overcoming my paralysis. Pushing past the pedestrians ringing Faith's body, I heard a voice say, "She's dead." Peering down, I saw two EMS workers folding up equipment they had been using. Right next to them, Faith was lying in a pool of blood; bruises spotted her neck.

I slammed into someone while groping my way out of that circle, stepping on Faith's bag, its contents strewn on the road. I made my way to Jack. His body lay tossed like a fallen scarecrow's near the curb. One medic kneeling next to him shouted for a stretcher. Two others responded, shoving past me. I circumvented them and then caught sight of Jack's face: eyes shut, mouth open, red blood trickling from his forehead.

I heard the words, "Oh my God, my baby." The voice was shrill and panicked. It was mine.

"Go to Presbyterian Hospital," I yelled at the driver.

I couldn't remember how I had ended up in the ambulance front seat. The paramedics were working on Jack in the body of the vehicle. I opened the window and felt sticky wisps of air lob at my head, while the street scenes whizzed by. I chased away all thoughts, for if my mind engaged in cerebral activity it would explode and shatter.

The red-lettered "Emergency Entrance" sign greeted me, once again. Doctors and orderlies, dressed in white and shades of green, came sprinting out, like leprechauns. One of the medics unloading the stretcher ticked off details. "Hit and run, one dead, this one stabilized on the scene. Young boy, heavy bleeding."

The words became muffled as I ran alongside, trying to grab at Jack amidst the chaos. I managed to plant a kiss on the back of his hand before someone pushed me aside as my baby was wheeled into the operating room, the double doors slamming in my face.

Standing in front of the operating room, helplessness heaped like piles of sand in my stomach, I understood that Jack's future, and thereby mine, was in the hands of strangers. My limbs began to quiver, the tremors growing in intensity. Leaning back, I held onto the wall, attempting to get my breathing, spastic and labored, under control.

"Set him up for an IV in room 3," a familiar voice said.

I turned to see Seth scribbling on a pad of papers. He tore off the top sheet, passing it to a nurse, who wheeled around and squeaked down the hall in her white shoes just as Seth looked up and caught sight of me.

"Doreen?" he said, crunching up his eyebrows.

I couldn't get any words to leave my mouth; the more I tried, the shakier my lips became, while fright slithered from my neck down my muscles to the soles of my feet.

"Get me juice, immediately," Seth shouted, binding my waist with his arms and carrying me to a chair in the lounge area. A male orderly sporting a goatee came up behind Seth with a plastic cup. Seth cajoled the orange liquid into my mouth, one sip at a time.

"Jack," I said after the second sip.

He waited for more information, but to no avail. Finally he said, "Is Jack here?"

I moved my head up and down.

Seth's brow wrinkled, his eyes turning into slits. "The 'hit and run' who just came in?"

Tears trickled down my cheeks. Shaking his head in disbelief, Seth gazed at his clogs and stubbed at the floor. "Doreen, I'm going into the OR. You listening?"

I nodded. "Faith was killed," I told him.

"Oh my God," he said, staring at me.

He stuck the cup in my hand. "Take sips of this every few minutes. Don't move. I'll be out soon to update you on Jack." He rose to leave. "Can you manage?"

"Yes."

His lanky body plowed through the double doors, his white coat snapping behind him. Slumping in the seat, I put the cup between my knees, resting my head on the cushion, hoping to preclude the onset of a migraine. I needed to be alert for Jack, and, eventually, I needed to notify the others: Ty, foremost, and then Max, Regina, Lulu. *How am I going to inform Ty about his only child, let alone tell him his mother is dead?*

I thought of Faith's flat, serene face, her weary hair, her helpful manner, her genuine enjoyment of Jack. Now she lay cold and lifeless under a sheet somewhere in this complex, all alone, once again. The saltiness flooded out onto my cheeks. I let the tears stream down to the edge of my chin and drip off one at a time, like a leaky faucet.

The chaos of the emergency room swirled before my eyes, shapes and colors melting together as if the projectionist had slipped up, screening an out-of-focus film. There were several "rooms," small areas, each containing a hospital bed cordoned off by moveable pink and eggplant curtains, like shower curtains. The staff zipped back and forth between the rooms, the curtain rings chiming each time they slid on the hollow metal rods. The wall speakers bellowed the names of doctors and technicians, nurses and orderlies who were requested in various parts of the emergency room maze. The barrage of names seemed to fall into rhythm with the thumping heart monitors, respirators, and sirens of ambulances pulling up at the entrance, meshing into one giant symphonic performance of the human fight for survival.

"Oh, Doreen."

I heard the words and turned in their direction. Lulu was navigating a wheelchair containing Regina, her knees draped with a thin hospital blanket. I stared at them. It had completely escaped me that only several hours earlier I had left my friends at this very same hospital in order to take in the dinosaurs. Lulu was still wearing her suit skirt and a sleeveless matching top, her jacket obviously left somewhere behind. Regina's hair crowned her fatigued face, harboring dark circled, bloodshot eyes.

Regina put her hand on mine, leaving the other, with IV attached, in a stationary position. As soon as I felt her fingers brush my skin, I burst into sobs, loud and hysterical. Regina joined in, wailing. Lulu stood beside us, somber and quiet, years of medical training evident in her self-control and masked affect.

"Seth called up from the OR," Lulu said. "Christ, how could this happen?"

"You've been here all this time?" I asked Lulu.

"Yep," she said, putting the brake on Regina's wheelchair. Lulu threw her hair back. "Did you notify anyone yet?"

No, I shook my head, unable to verbalize my feelings, for I understood dysfunction had thwarted my calling Ty or identifying Faith's body.

Lulu's eyes were fixed on two nurses walking by with trays of plastic-wrapped operating utensils. "We must find Ty. It's Sunday. How do we do that?"

"Call his cell," Regina piped up.

"He's in Australia," I said. "It may not work. He usually calls us when he can."

"How about his secretary?" Lulu said.

"She's new—don't have her number. Don't even remember her last name," I said, feeling despair inundate my brain.

"What else can we do?" Regina said.

"Look up the CFO—you know, Brad Barkow, on the East Side. Maybe he'll help," I said. The words were tiring me out. I knew it was imperative I talk to Ty, but dealing with his sorrow in addition to mine seemed almost insurmountable.

Lulu stepped away, but not before I said, "If you speak to Ty first, leave out the Faith part, just tell him about Jack in surgery." I hesitated. "Better yet, let me tell him."

I watched Lulu walk toward the nurse's station through the frenetic emergency ward, angling her frame around doctors who were hovering over a patient on a gurney.

"We need to see the penguins," Regina said, clearing her throat.

"We will."

"The Antarctica ones."

"I know what you mean."

"Things seem to be getting pretty screwed up," Regina said, misery building between her words. She was trying to make us both feel better, to somehow make us believe we would have futures that were less than unbearable.

"I told you, only glitches."

We sat in silence for a few minutes. Regina's breathing was slow and winded.

"Speaking of penguins, the ones on the West Side need to be told," I said, looking at my feet.

"When?"

"As soon as I hear Jack's in the clear."

Next thing I knew, Lulu was sprinting down the hall, weaving between patients and accompanying escorts. She stuck her cell phone in my hand. "Ty," she said, out of breath.

"What's up, Mini?" I heard his ebullient voice. "Brad got me out of a meeting. I understand this is Lulu's cell."

"Thanks for calling," I said in inappropriate formality, uncomfortable with the task that lay ahead, realizing Lulu had not divulged any news to Ty.

"*You* called me." Ty's breathing, light but now a bit uneasy, floated through the phone.

"Oh, right," I said. "Jack fell and he needs a few stitches. Seth is overseeing in the operating room."

"Serious?"

"Not too bad." My brain raced for more syllables to string together.

"Should I get home?" Ty asked. Silence greeted his question; I was terrified to elaborate. He clearly comprehended that something was wrong, very wrong. "I'll be there in less than twenty-four hours. Hang on, Doreen."

"Okay." That was the only word I could muster. The phone went dead.

Regina was gazing at me, while Lulu fidgeted with her beeper, strapped to her waist.

"I couldn't tell him the whole truth," I offered as explanation.

"Too cruel to have him travel with that weight on his heart," Lulu said. "You did the right thing."

She disappeared for a time and brought us some coffee. The three of us conversed little. Regina dozed in her wheelchair, while I tried to stay sane by reviewing the tasks and contracts on my desk awaiting my return. Lulu paced back and forth, checking at the nurses' desk from time to time.

After a few hours, the double doors swung open and Seth entered the corridor. His eyes searched the area; locating us, he quickly stepped over. "He's going to be alright," Seth said.

"Be specific," Lulu said.

"More than forty stitches and a blood transfusion, broken ribs, but no brain damage, luckily," Seth said.

"I have to see him," I said.

"Not now. He'll be in intensive care recovery for a while. You can see him once he's in a regular room," Seth said.

"How long?"

"A few hours."

"Go rest, Doreen. Seth will call you," Lulu said, looking to her medical counterpart for support.

Seth nodded. "Go home, Doreen."

"I can't." What would I do in the bleak space devoid of all family members? There wasn't any other place to rest my soul; Regina and Seth would be in Presbyterian Hospital all night, and Lulu was clearly not interested in having me over, since she was due back in her ward across town in just a few hours. Joey was still at his nanny's apartment and would remain there for the night.

"Max's," Regina suggested. "That's where you belong tonight."

"I'll call you there as soon as Jack's out," Seth said.

"I don't think that's such a great idea," I mumbled.

"Go," Lulu said.

Backed into a corner, I procrastinated by shuffling through my bag, combing my hair, and pulling out some chewing gum. "You'll call, no matter what time, you promise?" I asked Seth.

"Yes," Seth answered.

"Go, Doreen," Lulu said.

Then, having exhausted all conceivable ploys, I walked in a slow gait down the corridor to the automatic doors of the entrance, feeling my friends' eyes bore through my back all the way out.

❧

In front of Max's building, I inhaled a few breaths of the humid night air. Standing one block from the scene of the tragedy where Faith and Jack were struck down, I opined, *Nothing seems to have changed, yet everything has changed.*

The night doorman permitted me inside the lobby; he was a more recent hire, unfamiliar with me, so he buzzed Max's apartment and announced my arrival. During the elevator ride, I stifled the urge to cry out, *I wish Hala could be here now.* I was an adult, a parent in my own right with a child in trouble, but I was still a mere kid desperate for a shoulder on which to sob, a guardian to shoo away the horrors and to explain, no matter how unconvincingly, the cruelties of life.

Stepping off the elevator, I found Max waiting, his door wide open, dim light from his apartment illuminating his small silhouette. "It's late," he said. "Something bad must've happened."

Max stepped aside as I crossed the threshold without responding. I parked my bag on the mahogany desk, Hala's favorite. With my back to my father, I said, "We need some tea."

Max closed the door and made his way to the kitchen, his slippered feet shuffling by me. I noticed his frame seemed more skeletal than before, like the dinosaurs I had viewed earlier that day across the street. My eyes scanned the familiar living room, settling for a moment on the candelabras flanking the gold-leafed clock above the fireplace. The drapes framed the full moon and stars glittering through the windows. A faint smell of mildew wafted at my nose.

The teakettle whistled in the kitchen as if beckoning me. I entered the kitchen; the table was set with place mats, two glasses of tea, a sugar bowl, and a small plate of cookies. Max seated himself and waited for me to pull out the other chair.

"Your grandson is in the hospital, recuperating," I said, emphasis on the last word, as I sat down.

"From what?" he asked in a quiet voice.

"He's going to be fine, but he had many stitches and lost

some blood. So, it'll take a couple of days," I said, watching my father through the steam veil rising from my tea glass.

"How did this happen?" Max's face grew pale, the veins pulsing beneath his speckled skin.

"Crossing the street with Faith."

"Faith?"

"His grandmother." I felt the words leave my lips and pierce his face like tiny daggers.

"She was here? I didn't know."

"You didn't *want* to know."

Max clasped his tea glass with trembling hands.

"They were going to the flea market on Columbus Avenue," I continued.

"Right here?"

"Yes, the one Hala liked to browse in." I noticed that the daffodils on the wallpaper were faded now, wilting from the sorrow in the air. "It was a hit and run," I said, afraid to look at my father.

"Hit by a car?" Max gasped.

"Almost. He was thrown out of the way by his grandmother."

Max pushed his chair back. He went to the sink and turned on the water. Still standing upright, his fingers gripping the edge of the counter, his body convulsed as if he were entangled in electric wiring.

"*Oy Gut in himmel*, his ninth birthday." Sobs poured from Max. "Oh God, haven't we suffered enough?" He let out a scream, the kind that could rip the enamel off your teeth, one that I had never heard from him before, not even when Hala passed away. He lifted his clenched fist over his head, shaking it. "You took my parents. You took Sally. You took Aaron. Then Hala. You take and take. Leave us alone already."

I stood up and slid over, putting my arm around my father's shoulder. His shaking intensified; I thought I heard his brittle bones rattle, the pieces barely attached at the joints, like a jigsaw puzzle of a human being.

"This never would have happened if you didn't marry that *shaigets*," Max said. The words exploded through his clenched mouth, searing the flesh on my arms.

It had been quite a long time since he had used that word for Ty. Yet, instead of anger, I felt overrun by numbness.

"You chose a tragic path," Max said.

"Maybe." I released his shoulder. Stepping back toward the kitchen table, I said, "So many years have passed." I lifted the tea glass and took a sip, letting the liquid slide down my parched throat. "Such a long time and you've never been able to see Ty for what he really is."

So much time, and Max refused to acknowledge Ty as the easygoing, yet fiercely ambitious husband of his only child, and Jack's father, and an honorary Penguin by his own choosing.

Max remained in an unyielding position facing the kitchen wall. "You had a chance to make your luck, but you didn't," he said.

Viewing Max's bulging eyes in profile, I asked, "Aaron and Hala, what *kind* of luck was that?"

"We were lucky Hala lived as long as she did; we kept her alive."

"She's gone. I've got a long way to go without her. *You* may call it luck, but *I* don't know what to call it." The doctors had been surprised by how long Hala lived with her illness, but despite the commendable prolonging of her life through diligent care, she still left this earth at the age of fifty-two.

"We were lucky once upon a time," Max said.

"I don't profess to know everything about luck, but I do know one thing: Jack was *not* saved by luck."

"What then?"

"By Faith."

"*Narishkeit.*" Max spewed out the word with hostility.

"Not nonsense. Faith was the only factor in saving your grandchild's life."

"What do you mean?"

"She threw Jack out of the way. She was killed."

"Oh," Max whispered.

My quavering voice reverberated against the walls. "Think what you want about Ty's lineage. His people may have helped ruin our past, but look what just happened—one of them saved our *whole* future."

"What are you saying?" Max looked at me as if I were crazy.

Drops of perspiration dripped from my hair onto my forehead. "Don't you see, Max, our family, tiny as it already was, would have been *eradicated forever* were it not for Faith tossing Jack out of the way." The daffodils appeared to tilt as my words blew against them.

"It would've been totally different without Ty," Max said without making eye contact. "And better."

"And maybe it would've been disastrous." I pushed the chair closer to the table and straightened out the place mats. "Maybe it's time to stop living with old ghosts."

Looking at Max's clenched teeth, I felt that my saying anything more would be a perilous undertaking. Despite our love of Jack, Max and I had failed, over all these years, to converge our contrasting views of family, obligations, and Ty. Max never wavered in his belief that Tyler Rockwell of North Dakota was my luck-deprived, fateful choice.

Yet, despite the events of today and my fears as to tomorrow, I felt certain about my yesterday. I had chosen a path paved with color and humor and more than anything else, the unexpected, and I had set my destiny willingly. Now I refused to regret my choices.

At that moment I seemed to hear a snapping cordage sound, like my umbilical cord, or the noose around Aaron's neck. But the cord was releasing an airborne object, for suddenly, I felt I was in free fall, gliding in the air on a parachute, absorbing the colors of the earth below and the blue sky above and greeting the eagles soaring nearby.

I turned to leave the kitchen. "I'll be waiting in my room for Seth to call. Get some rest as well." My statement echoed Ty's over the years when he blockaded confrontation by suggesting a time-out.

Through the corridor and into the bedroom, my feet carried me by rote to my bed. As soon as I flicked on the bedside lamp, as if sucked into a time machine, I saw my childhood come flooding back: the giggling of friends, Hala's coffee cake with cold milk, Penguin gatherings over tea, Max's wry humor, and tales from a vanished world.

Flicking off my sandals, lifting my feet onto the yellow and blue duvet, I leaned my head against the oak headboard. Scanning my quarters, once my safe haven, I caught sight of the recliner, planted as always in a diagonal position. It had held piles of jeans and sweaters thrown there after school, and frilly dresses slung over its back at the close of parties and family events. I opened the night table drawer to find the deck of playing cards, tattered from poker games with the Penguins, nestled alongside an album of camp pictures glued onto yellowing pages. The reading lamp spotlighted the tabletop, a light film of dust substituting for the jade box that once lounged there.

I pictured Regina, spread out on her stomach, her feet swaying in the air, flicking her hair off of her adolescent face as her hand caressed the inlaid surface. She had just brought me the jade box; the wrapping paper lay crumpled nearby on the carpet. "Doreen, your ghosts will be comfortable in here," she was saying.

I fast-forwarded a few years, realizing that my first step on the road with the boy from Bismarck had coincidentally started in this same room. *The irony of it.* With his back twisted in pain, the investment banker had rested covered with my duvet. Although aloof and quite curt that day, I was drawn to the possibilities that seemed to lie in his unusual chin, choosing to pursue a life with him over "a sure thing" with Peter. To some, it might have seemed like an impulse based on whimsy, but I understood now that it had been a deliberate choice, a defining moment, and a fait accompli. Mine.

Sleep soothed my aching heart, coaxing my eyes to close. I was certain that Tania, Yankel, and Aaron would not be visiting me that night despite their familiarity with the milieu. *After all, even ghosts are afraid for their own survival.*

Chapter 23

J ACK'S CHEST HEAVED UP AND down as he sucked in oxygen, the respirator providing the tempo. He was drifting in and out of consciousness. His skull and much of his face were bandaged; I couldn't help but think of one of his kindergarten papier-mâché projects.

It was late afternoon, the sun baking the skyscrapers and sidewalks of New York. The hospital ward was quiet: doctor rounds long over, afternoon medication having been dispensed, patients were dozing, nurses were rotating for their breaks, the drying floors smelled of disinfectant and wax. I tiptoed to the window, the heat penetrating the glass hitting my slouching shoulders.

Presbyterian Hospital towered over the West Side Highway, which ran under the George Washington Bridge nearby. The hospital's exterior wall, made of rock slabs cemented together, plunged down to the edges of the Hudson River. The complex, reminiscent of a crusader fortress on the exterior, was, on the interior, a modern maze of surgery centers, patient wards, research facilities, and outpatient clinics.

I pondered the facts that now Jack slept wounded on the ninth floor of the main pavilion, and Regina fought for life on its third floor, while Faith lay rigid in the basement of the adjacent building. For some the hospital was a bastion of healing and protection, for others merely a way station between this world and the next.

Out of the corner of my eye, I noticed the digital time at the bottom of Jack's heart monitor; it indicated 4:00 PM. The city granted a few more hours of light until it would begin to prepare for its nocturnal state. It had been about twenty hours ago that I had spoken with Ty in Australia. Time seemed to be moving in a haze of slow motion, as if we were all drifting underwater.

Trying to make some sense of it, I recounted the earlier events of the day. As promised, Seth had telephoned me at Max's apartment, dawn about to break on the metropolis. Jack was out of intensive care and in room 9-112. I had been shocked by the information, for the room number was made up of Jack's imminent age and three digits of Tania's arm-embroidered number. It was a prophetic conundrum, but of what? An omen of recovery or one of looming tragedy?

I had arrived within a half hour to see my child. The next few hours consisted of consultations with doctors, assisting in nursing tasks, and poring over Jack, encouraging his every cell to fight for recovery.

My contemplations were interrupted by footsteps charging down the hall. I recognized the gait. Ty swung into the room, dropping his travel bag with a thud near the bathroom door. Stepping up to the other side of Jack's bed, he leaned over our son.

"Oh my God," I heard Ty whisper while stroking his fingers over Jack's hand, the one free of medical installations. "What's the prognosis, Doreen?" he asked in a voice hung with fatigue. I noticed his eyes hooded by heavy lids, his cotton shirt looking like crumpled wax paper.

"Forty stitches, broken ribs, and a blood transfusion," I said, "but he's on his way to recovery."

Ty rounded the side of the bed and put his arms on my shoulders, pressing his nose into my hair. He gave off the scent of mustiness mingled with exhaustion. I listened to his breathing, strained and hesitant.

"We'll be okay," I said.

He swayed back and forth. "We were lucky, I guess."

"Not luck."

"Call it what you will."

"Faith." I watched him, thinking his mind must be clicking away in puzzlement. "Your mother saved her grandson."

"Where is she? I assumed she was at home," he said. Dread crawled through his words. He released me from his grasp and pushed me backward a bit.

"Sit, Ty," I said, pointing with my fingertips toward the visitor's chair.

"Rather not," he said, his back stiffening and his face growing taut.

"They were crossing Columbus Avenue to the flea market. Video games were on their minds."

"Doreen, get to the point."

"This limo driver came speeding around the corner, like a maniac. Faith realized and threw Jack out of the way."

"What room is she in? Was she badly injured?"

"No." My voice cracked.

"She's at home then, right?" He asked in a hesitant voice.

"No."

His eyes went lackluster, getting red at the rims. My lips twitched as I tried to find the right answer. But before I could, he whispered, "Gone?"

"Yes, I'm sorry."

"Where is she?"

"Morgue, downstairs in the next building."

He quickly retreated toward the door.

"I'm coming with you," I said.

I followed him down the hall and out the front door, barely keeping up with his long-legged strides. In the adjacent building, we took the elevator down two flights to the MC level. Walking through a maze of halls painted in horrid orange, we arrived at glass doors with a sign reading "Morgue."

After we introduced ourselves, the on-call technician escorted us to the back of the sterile area where the walls contained rows of aluminum refrigerator doors; simple wooden benches lined another wall. He opened one of the refrigerator-type doors and pulled out a long shelf. What looked like Faith's limp blonde hair protruded from under the sheetlike gray covering. The technician slowly began to uncover the corpse. I allowed myself one swift glance at my mother-in-law before I turned my head, noticing only her hollow, pallid cheeks, pushed in as if she were sucking on a lemon wedge.

Other than Ty's soft weeping, there was silence in the room. I needed to control my tears, for if I started I knew there would be no end. I kept my eyes focused on the utensils and the box of surgical gloves on the tray table near me. A weird smell tickled my nose.

After a few moments the technician asked, "What arrangements have you made?" He sounded as if he were afraid to wake the corpses with his query.

"I have no idea," Ty said as he slid onto the wooden bench bolted to the wall. He brushed his hair back; his eyes, with large, dark pupils surrounded by red streaks, were staring at Faith's toes. "I guess we need to arrange for burial."

"Did she ever express any of her wishes?" the young technician asked kindly.

"Never occurred to me to discuss that," Ty said, scratching his unshaven chin, probably itching from his long flight, or maybe it was simply from anxiety.

"Strange as it may sound, Faith expressed her wish to me," I said timidly.

"What?" Ty asked, glancing up with a strange expression, as if surprised to find me there at all.

"She was leaning toward cremation."

"Leaning?" Ty repeated.

"Well, it's a long story, but the girls, Lulu and Regina, got to talking with her, and she mentioned that she'd probably prefer cremation, although it wasn't totally clear." I was averse to divulging the rest of Faith's conversation with them.

Ty stood and walked over to his mother's body. He twined his fingers between her exposed limp, stout ones. "Fitting—she chooses to be invisible."

Unobtrusive and meek as always, I thought.

Ty peered down at his mother's face. He brought his fingers up to touch her strands of yellow hair. Droplets of water dripped from his face and bounced off her frazzled crown. I knew Ty was crying but I refused to look directly at him, turning my glance toward the wall.

After several moments, his voice behind me said, "So be it."

Four days later Faith was cremated.

I was at home as I had promised to be when Ty arrived with

the remains. Originally, I had contemplated inviting others, like the Penguins and Lulu, to share in Ty's grief. But almost as soon as I considered that idea I had rejected it. After all, gathering a party with everyone under one roof in commemoration of Faith's life seemed like the perfect recipe for discord and animosity. And I knew how the Penguins felt about cremation.

Earlier that morning, we had decided to split our efforts, ostensibly in the name of efficiency. While Ty was taking care of Faith, I was relegated to taking care of Jack in the hospital. In truth, I was relieved not to have to take part in the cremation. The act, even the mere thought of such, filled me with angst great enough to cripple my functioning. Ty, having undoubtedly sensed this, insisted my presence was needed at the bedside of our son.

According to his team of doctors, Jack was on his way to full recovery. The four practitioners dressed in white lab coats had visited with their young patient during today's early morning rounds. I suspected we received extra-special attentiveness due to the urging of their ER counterpart, Dr. Seth Rabiner. Half of Jack's cranium remained under gauze wrap, but the rest, in black-and-blue form, was now exposed to the atmosphere. His broken ribs, tender and painful, were "healing on course," according to the senior internist.

Now back in the apartment, I changed my position to bring my legs, swollen and hurting, up on the coffee table. Suddenly I heard a squeak emanate from behind the pillows. Frisking the couch, I discovered the culprit—Joey's yellow rubber duck. I smiled, recalling that Joey was now back in the comfort of his home with his recuperating mother. I made a mental note to call Regina later and inform her about the toy.

As I debated preparing some tea and sandwiches for Ty's

arrival, the keys jangled outside our door, making me pull my feet off the table and swing around to greet him. The rugged cowboy was haggard and slightly bent over, weariness blurring his features as he entered the apartment. For an instant, he resembled Faith.

Ty approached the couch in halting steps, keeping his head down while holding a small item in his hands. He slipped onto the couch cushions near me, his eyes focused straight ahead, as if he were studying the floating air molecules in front of him. He cleared his throat and swallowed hard; then he placed the item, a small urn, on the coffee table.

We sat in silence for what seemed like a long time. Ty continued to stare ahead while I examined the urn. It was dull, brown, and simple, like an uninspiring ceramic sugar container. Wretchedness sputtered through me. *Faith deserves a better resting place. Her life, bland and oppressive, need not be duplicated in the nature of her eternal habitat.*

"Maybe we should spread her ashes in Bismarck," Ty suggested in a voice punctured with sadness.

"No, she associated that place with loneliness," I said. I pondered options for Faith's future home: a container decorated by Jack, a Venetian glass perfume bottle, an urn painted with golden daffodils. None of these satisfied me, but one thing was clear. "She belongs with us," I stated.

I felt Ty's shadow pass over me as he moved to the window. As he skewed his forehead toward the glass, the solution crystallized in my mind like the rock candy Hala used to favor. The antidote to Faith's dejected and despondent earthly existence was an afterlife replete with caring, friendship, and appreciation.

Barefooted, I skipped to the bedroom, scooping up Regina's box. I was certain Faith would be content in her new jade abode, in the company of those who owed her eternal gratitude.

C LAUDE THOMAS, THE JRW AMERICA controller, was doodling on his spreadsheets.

He leaned over to his superior, Frank, whispering something that caused the latter's teeth to protrude between his mustache and beard, both now sprinkled with more gray than brown.

"Pass a scone," Claude said, eyeing the tray of croissants and scones from the quasi-French bakery around the corner from our offices.

"*Please* is the operative word," Frank replied with mock indignation.

"Yes, Mom," Claude answered as his fingers tightened around a scone, chocolate flakes bursting through the golden flaky surface.

"Okay," Dick Dorf said, surveying the conference room. "Can we get the kindergarten under control?"

Sporting a plaid blazer and dark polyester shirt, Dorf looked like a used car salesman, but a level up from his earlier, slimier image—all things being relative.

"We have a one-hour window in which to prepare," Frank said, sipping from his cup.

Frank, our CFO, had, as he had many times before, brewed the aromatic dark Turkish coffee in his office and brought the small cups into the conference room. The caffeinated potion was the best part of the management meetings. I gazed into my cup, thinking I was going to miss these. As I looked around, I realized in a sentimental rush that despite years of complaining about them, these characters had somehow slipped into my heart.

It was refreshing to know that my cardiac vessel was still functioning, not just pumping blood through the arteries, but making the soul thick with love and compassion. The outer world had finally reentered my peripheral vision; it had been months since a thought other than about Jack, Regina, or Faith had traveled through my tunneled reality.

Jack, vivacious and spirited again, was back at school and he did most daily activities, with the exception of ice hockey. His scar had healed into a thick, mangled crimson line spanning his forehead, reminiscent of the subway line traversing the seam of Manhattan's West Side. Perky again, Regina had rebounded after surgery. Back at Puff Cosmetics and fussing over Joey, she was calmly awaiting the start of a regimen of chemotherapy. And Faith still rested in the smooth jade box in the company of my rambunctious ghosts. Sometimes late at night, I could hear the spirits whispering, bickering, and laughing, while flying around and through the box, their vocal notes scattering the darkness, looping into clouds in my dreams.

Now I noticed Frank flipping through some documents spread before him on the conference table—the table no longer the swapped one from the receptionist's cousin, but a glass and cherrywood combination acquired from some fancy designer in SoHo.

More recent JRW America hires, the new head of marketing and the network director, flanked Katherine van de Vrande, who had been designated as always to take notes. I suspected that our boss, Dick Dorf, required the company of Katherine's shapely legs more than the scribbles on her trademark pink pad, behavior somewhat reminiscent of my old boss, Lenny Spielman. Regardless, for her the invitation to sit with management was the highest of compliments. I realized that her pad picked up the hue of her silk blouse and the pearls dangling on her chest.

"What time is the conference call?" Dick Dorf asked, turning to Cecilia Robinson, an immaculately coiffed ash blonde fluent in the ways of corporate America and now in charge of our marketing. She was in constant dismay from the actions of our renegade tier-two firm.

"Eleven thirty. Video link is set up through the system," she said, pointing at the television monitor in the corner.

"It's finally going to work?" Claude asked, snickering.

There had been several failed attempts during the last year, so if the effort was successful now, it would be the first time all twenty-two JRW Communications operating entities, spanning the globe eastward from Los Angeles to Sydney, would participate in a simultaneous conference. Three thousand plus employees in one meeting.

"Steve, your update on the network build-out, please," Dick Dorf said, redirecting the discussion to our new network director as he settled his wiry body in his chair.

Steve distributed a stack of photostatted papers. The diagram: colored lines slashing the U.S. map. The yellow line stretched from Los Angeles to Chicago and then down to Dallas; the green one jutted from New York to Charleston and then headed further south to Tampa.

"Where do these hook up?" Cecilia asked, obviously confused by the nonintersecting lines.

"The piece between New York and Chicago is waiting to be constructed," Steve answered.

"The leasing agreement we're working on, right?" I asked, despite the fact that I already knew the answer was affirmative. Katherine and I had been wading through these documents for the past two months.

Moreover, I understood that the network, no matter how expansive, served no legitimate business purpose, for we passed most of the phone traffic in bulk over the lines of other telecom companies, not through our own network. The reason was clear as the Empire State Building on a cloudless day: it was considerably cheaper that way.

But, in fairness it must be said that this bizarre situation wasn't entirely of our own making. During the past several years, Wall Street analysts had vehemently pushed all the telecommunications firms, not just ours, to build out network regardless of utility and profitability considerations. Now, in the autumn of 1999, the NASDAQ remained in a certified state of hysteria.

Ty, of an unquiet mind, continued to believe astronomical sums were being expended on satiating the Street's voracious appetite. Hordes of investors clamored to partake in the *gold rush* roaring toward the close of the century. Frequently, I noticed the dark half moons under his eyes expressing apprehension, his ebullience growing increasingly lackluster each day. Despite the overall success so far of his telecom venture, Ty was troubled by a sense that cracks were appearing under the surface. The façade still pretty much shimmered—an active stock market, the company's shares trading at a respectable although not their highest price, and Ty a millionaire several times over, on paper. But, inside he felt ill.

A few days before, I found him sitting in the dark living room; it was three o'clock in the morning.

"You should've woken me," I said.

"Nah, you've got enough issues."

"What's one more issue at this point?" I tried to joke, but neither of us laughed.

"The money's going to dry out."

"Only toilet paper, unless it's actually *in* the bank," I said. A Penguin statement if I ever heard one, a perfect Max adage. "We haven't considered moving; how seriously do you think I take the whole money thing?"

We still occupied the two-bedroom apartment, as we had since Jack's birth. It occurred to me just then that Ty had actually lived in the same modest apartment building since his arrival in New York City in 1985. I knew that eventually we would like to be owners of a piece of Manhattan real estate, but the plan was somewhere far out on our horizon at this point.

"I'm not talking about our personal funds. The industry is going south," Ty said.

"But the market's been pouring millions into the industry."

"Building unnecessary networks of cable and fiber, switches and whatever—you name it—which don't work. And, even if they work, they are unprofitable. The pressure's enormous. It's a fantasy." Ty pushed his hair back. "I need to get out before it comes crashing down."

Suddenly, instead of more words from Ty, Claude's words filtered into the fringes of my consciousness. I tumbled back into the present and turned my attention to Claude. He sounded almost professional, contravening his former shoot-from-the-hip tactics, particularly regarding the collection of bad debt. After Ty and Wagner had acquired Dick Dorf's company, Claude had reluctantly, at least somewhat, tempered his dubious style. I watched the controller speak of our large volume of telecom traffic to Mexico and how he accounted for this. I heard the words *reciprocity, regulations,* and *revenues,* but couldn't concentrate long enough to string them into coherence, because I knew that in less than an hour, this chapter of my life was going to come to an abrupt end.

"Doreen?" Dick Dorf said.

The name sliced into my ponderings.

"Are you alright?" he asked, yanking me into the conference.

All eyes were upon me. I saw Katherine's troubled expression; I forced an upturn at the edges of my lips in reassurance. *She will soon be stunned, but for now she deserves to be put at ease.* "Fine," I answered, sliding my hands together into a tight knot.

Dick Dorf asked me to summarize the recent developments on the legal front. Complying, I reviewed the deals and documents flowing through our legal pipeline, attempting to sound as normal as possible.

"Doreen, tell the folks about the extra options." Dorf's nasal voice assaulted my senses.

"As you all know, the board of our parent company has approved the issuance of additional options to both new and veteran employees," I said. "You'll each be receiving a memo clarifying the details in the next few days."

Dick Dorf expanded on the issue, speaking with bombast and arrogance. Judging by the contented faces, no one minded his abrasiveness that particular morning.

We broke for a few minutes. While the technicians checked the video equipment in anticipation of the conference, most of the attendees dashed to check e-mail or voice mail or use the lavatories. Steve, the new network director, remained at the far side of the table, communicating on his walkie-talkie with his department, located at our switch site in lower Manhattan. After a few minutes, he walked out of the room.

The only ones left in the room were Katherine and me. We moved our chairs back from the table; she crossed her legs, making her champagne stockings shimmer at the knees.

"I'm waiting for our stock to skyrocket, maybe to sixty. Then I can buy my dream apartment like the one I told you about," Katherine said, her blue eyes sparkling.

"The one right off of Gramercy Park," I said, remembering the one-bedroom with working fireplace and computer niche which had enthralled her. I considered the apartment purchase less outrageous than her wishful-thinking sixty-dollar target for our stock. At present, JRW's share price was hovering at twenty-seven dollars, as it had been doing during the past three months.

"Exactly, perfect place," Katherine said, sweeping her hair back from her shoulders. "How much longer?" She was obviously referring to everyone's favorite topic, the timing of the exercise of her stock options.

I repositioned myself and straightened out my skirt, stalling for time.

"Really, Doreen, when should I get serious about real estate?"

A dicey topic, indeed, considering my position, professional and marital, within the company. I examined her big, warm eyes, her alabaster skin, her crown of hair. We had worked in tandem for most of the last decade, and she was a staunch supporter and friend, often sweetening the stressful hours with lighthearted humor. She had yet to manage capturing a good man, but I felt somewhat consoled that I had at least assisted her in lassoing a gratifying job.

Truth be told, I could have been satisfied with that accomplishment, but I wasn't. Ty's predictions gnawed at me. Of course, he was of the minority opinion, yet I felt that failure to share his forecast with Katherine might someday be construed as a personal betrayal. On the other hand, as an attorney I knew I had to skirt the minefields of "insider trading" or "the breach of fiduciary duties."

I settled for simplicity, or maybe duplicity, and said, "Are you busy this Saturday?"

Katherine searched my eyes with a curious look. My poker face came in handy; I didn't even blink. She parted her lips, about to say something, when I interjected, "How about another cup of coffee?" She shook her head no, while continuing to stare at me.

"In that case, I'm going to check my e-mail," I continued, rising from my seat and exiting.

I wandered down the halls. The elevated, brightly lit turquoise switch room was still at the center of our American operations, providing telecom services to thousands of customers. The surrounding office space had doubled, with the number of employees growing monthly. The reception area had been spruced up in a new blue color, and a large sculpture, an abstract version of an Indian totem pole, greeted entrants.

Sauntering down the corridor, I stopped at my office, claustrophobic and cluttered with stacks of files, yellow Post-its jutting out at different angles, just like in the P&S days under Lenny Spielman.

A few steps to the right, I caught sight of Katherine's raspberry kingdom. Her IBM computer and pile of pink notepads stood beside several framed pictures of her cats, the raspberry walls reflecting off the picture glass. I remembered the times we used to steal a few minutes, over coffee and almond horns (her favorites), in the afternoons, to talk about world news and about the escapades of Dick Dorf, or her latest boyfriend, or just about movies, hair, or even stockings.

On the other side of Katherine, Claude maintained an office, with his desk set under the windows. He played soccer on a semiprofessional team, and one wall was decorated with his trophies. In the corner, a table with black upholstered chairs had served as the scene for many a conference. Calling card distributors with names like Sunny, Miguel, and Dirty Dan used to zip in and out of Claude's office. Katherine would report hearing a surfeit of cursing in various languages, blasting through their shared wall.

By the time I had completed my nostalgic tour and returned, the conference room had filled up again. The videoconference began on time, absent any technical snags. Chairman Jerrold Wagner opened with a few words. In his bumbling style he read a short paragraph, welcoming the management and representatives of all the JRW subsidiaries dotting the globe. Following Jerrold, Brad Barkow, with his hands gesturing wildly, enumerated recent developments, most notably the capital raised by our company, which had brought the total amount so far to an astounding one billion dollars in just two years.

Then Brad relinquished the spotlight to his boss. Ty cleared his throat. He looked elegant in his suit, tie with gold ducks, and starched shirt. On the exterior, he seemed the perfect embodiment of a French cuff.

His words hummed familiar in my ears, for I had helped him compose his speech. He thanked his employees for their hard work, creativity, and dedication. I held my breath as he then paused for a moment, looking toward Brad and back to the video camera. I thought I saw a glint of ambivalence pass through his eyes.

"With great regret and a heavy heart, as of this morning, I have tendered my resignation as head of this company," Ty said. "But not to worry, we've found a suitable and strong replacement for me, capable of taking this telecom conglomerate to the next level."

I mouthed the words with him. Gasps traversed the room, punching at my temples; most eyes turned to me. My coemployees looked dumbfounded and bewildered. Claude registered what appeared to be shock as he leaned into Frank, saying something in his ear. Steve and Cecilia locked eyes as Dick Dorf walked his fingers through his hair, stretching in his chair. He expelled a loud sigh into the air.

Only Katherine crinkled her fair-skinned brow and then released the frown; she jotted a few words on her pad. She lifted her head and caught my eye; her lips smiled ever so slightly.

I presumed Katherine was one of the few who understood the underlying, unspoken reason for Ty's departure: he feared for the viability of the telecom industry. Obviously taking that to heart, she got serious about real estate. The next Saturday, Katherine cashed in her options and purchased her dream apartment, supplemented by a large mortgage from her bank.

T HE DROPS OF THE CHEMOTHERAPY fluid dripped one at a time, in a ticktock beat. The machine, about the size of a five-pound box of laundry detergent, hissed and belched every few seconds, regulating the flow. I followed the efforts of a droplet from the plastic bag down the transparent tube, as it slid in a circuitous path through the skin on Regina's forearm. The bruised area around the tube connection was a rainbow of colors attesting to her struggle.

In a white haze, I saw the nurse stepping around my chair. She flicked the suspended bag with her thumb and forefinger, mumbling something about the session proceeding well, and then whizzed on to the next station. I watched her white sneakers make contact with the floor. We were on the ninth floor of the Herbert Ross Building at Presbyterian Hospital: the Chemotherapy Center. The most dreaded of floors. In private, sectioned-off rooms the most seriously ill patients received chemo lying in beds, while the others were collectively situated in a spacious area, each patient propped in a Barcalounger, all lined in a row along the windows.

"We're almost done," Regina said, reclining in her chair and smiling under her blonde curls. She was wearing one of her many wigs, her eyebrows penciled in over eyelash-free eyes. "Forever, I mean."

"Really? Amazing," I said. "Is that what Houston said?"

Dr. Walker Houston was Regina's oncologist, one of New York's foremost cancer specialists. After each of her previous chemotherapy sessions, Regina went in for private consultation with him. I had met him on two other accompaniments. The other chemotherapies had been "chaperoned" by her Puff friends, in rotation, while Seth often stopped by and Lulu made guest appearances when she could.

Seth and Lulu, together, had decided that Regina should complete the "whole package" of cancer care at Presbyterian Hospital, Seth's hospital, and not transfer to Lulu's hospital, crosstown, for the toxic cocktails. I wondered if Lulu was, subconsciously, more comfortable with consulting at arm's length, avoiding any medical decisions tainted by emotional components.

"Houston said two more sessions, purely preventative ones. So basically, I'm done," Regina said.

"Las Vegas as usual then," I said, pleased with the thought that Regina would be able to attend the annual cosmetics trade show scheduled for the summer. "I'll be more than happy to babysit Joey. I'm sure Jack will want him sleeping in his room."

"Bellagio, here I come," she said, gleaming. "Can't wait to hit the casino and the jazz bar."

"Which wig will you take?" I asked, as visions of her at the blackjack tables in the plush Hotel Bellagio casino in the auburn pageboy or the chestnut long hairdo made me feel warm with pleasure.

"Maybe I'll pack them all, change for each event," Regina said as she rearranged her hairpiece, pulling it down further, the yellow bangs almost touching her painted brows. "Enough about me. How are *you* doing, Doreen?"

"Fine."

"That's what you always say. Really, how has it been since the *big day?*"

"Well, now I have time for—other things. Look, I'm here with you," I said, calculating that since the *big day* when Ty resigned and I followed a month later, I had transformed into a character seemingly taken out of *The Donna Reed Show*.

Right after the calendars had flipped to the new millennium, I had slipped into the role of full-time housewife and mother, trying to catch my breath after an exhaustive run on the telecom treadmill. It was now April 2000, months since I had stepped into a telecom office, or any office for that matter. "And, I hang out with Jack and get to be with my father," I added.

Regina grimaced. I knew she thought my answer was lame, as if taking care of the men in my family would provide enough personal satisfaction. True, it was a relief to be back on amicable terms with my father and to enjoy time with my child, but it didn't obviate the need for me to participate in the "real professional universe," according to Regina.

"Enough with the Florence Nightingale act. Soon you'll tell me you're working at Max's office or doing some PTA work, as if that would shut me up," she said.

Regina glanced around, catching sight of the woman sitting closest to us, who was knitting a quilt while a chemo solution the color of Kool-Aid streamed into her veins. The woman lifted up her face, and the two acknowledged each other, cohorts in their existential fight.

"Relax. I'm going to start searching. First let me see where Ty ends up," I said, once Regina was facing me again.

"Is he okay?"

"Actually, he's been restless. But looking at the current market, at least he feels he made the right decision."

The dot-com market's slowdown was becoming more and more apparent to those on the Street, to the day traders, and to the financial media, in sync with Ty's prophecy. No matter what the numbers reported by the publicly traded companies were, their stocks were plummeting and funding was drying up. Even though many investors and analysts believed, or wanted to believe, that it was merely a temporary dip in the technology boom, all were nonetheless perturbed by the unfolding negative situation.

"Of course he made the right decision," Regina said. "Penguin luck."

"What?"

"Isn't it obvious, Doreen?"

"Not to me."

"His instincts have been fine-tuned, vicariously."

"Huh?"

"Those around you, we hang on in the hope that some Penguin dust will rub off." Regina sat up, leaning so far forward that I could see the tiny white specks in her irises. "Ty was the first one who got it."

"You're delusional, probably a chemo side effect."

"I used to believe your ghosts were bothersome, depressing. Peter thought they were reprehensible. But Ty was the first to recognize them for what they are. He actually welcomed them." Regina's eyes brightened as she took my hand. "Don't you see what they make you?"

"Insufferable?"

"No, more compassionate, more attuned." Regina's voice was quiet and serious. "They push you forward, as they do Ty."

"Oh really?" I was somewhat skeptical.

"Isn't that why you never locked them up, never got rid of them?" Regina asked. She leaned back, her wig tilting to the side. "Think about it. Be honest." Her voice was getting hoarse, her naked lids blinking. She seemed to be fading away. "I'm tired," she said abruptly.

I wasn't convinced that Regina needed a rest; my suspicion was that she simply wanted me to mull over these ideas—in solitude. Yet, after a few seconds her lids fluttered in sleep and her mouth dropped open, letting breaths of slumber flow in and out. *Okay, on second thought, maybe she truly is tired.*

I settled back in my chair. In the deep crevices of my brain, Regina's observations roamed free of opponents. Some of her words tugged at veracity. Since childhood, my transparent friends *had* heightened my sensitivity to the external world. They challenged me to consider the impact on others as factors in my decisions. They brought to bear the significance of my past before I could take even a tiny step into my future. They hurled existential issues at me, even when I was hopscotching on city sidewalks with other pigtailed girls. My thin shoulders were saddled with the hopes, dreams, and disappointments of all the innocent, truncated lives.

My throat felt clammy, and I sifted in my bag for some of my uncle's candies. As I unwrapped one I found at the bottom, I thought of the consequences of Regina's disease for Joey. *The strangeness of life, of destiny.* No matter what one's provenance, ultimately destiny, uncontrollable and unpredictable, takes over. Slides clicked in my mind: Hala smiling at the camera, Sally hunched over her son Aaron's bed, Max and Sam taking their daughters to the circus, Regina and me escorting our boys to the playground.

My picture lens went dark, due to a jolting sound. I realized that Regina's machine was buzzing, declaring her chemotherapy session over. She stirred awake, rubbing her eyes. The nurse came by and removed the plumbing from her arm, rolling up the tubes. I watched as Regina rearranged her wig and snapped open her Puff mirrored case, checking her face for evidence of sleep and illness.

I remembered the last time after chemotherapy, we had sat at a grungy coffee shop several blocks from the hospital, sipping lemonade. The sun had played upon her synthetic curls, and her eyes caught sight of some teenagers traipsing past our table. She had smiled at them as if she had known them for years before focusing her gaze back on me. I recalled her voice that afternoon, melodic and upbeat, as she spoke of her friends, her man—Joey—and her position at Puff Cosmetics.

"I was dealt a fabulous hand," Regina asserted. "The cancer's simply a glitch. Right, Doreen?"

In all honesty I wasn't sure she was correct. But one thing I did know for sure was that I was awed by her optimism.

Now, Regina got up from her Barcalounger. "Did you think about it? Two letters—P and L."

I couldn't believe she was referring to Penguin luck. "You can't be serious?"

"Most certainly can." Regina put on her sunglasses. "I'm expecting to benefit from it as well." She scooped up her bag. "Hurry, let's go. We've got a special visit to make."

"What about the kids?" I asked.

Regina looked at her watch. "We still have time before our sitters need to go home."

I realized she was right. Accepting her offer, I followed her out into a cab.

The sun illuminated the green grass and the shiny boulders of Central Park. Paying for our tickets, we entered the zoo and navigated across the large square, brick buildings framing it on three sides. We passed the lion seals swimming in the outdoor pool, as we made our way along the pathway.

"Ready?" Regina said.

"Absolutely."

Holding our noses, we entered the Penguin House. Passing the tufted puffins in their frosty habitat, we parked ourselves smack in the center of the space facing the opposite way.

"The greatest," Regina said, gleeful.

I nodded my head in agreement, not taking my eyes off of the tuxedoed creatures in the refrigerated glass exhibit. The little Gentoo penguins were standing, waddling, and flapping on the brilliant white ice. I was mesmerized by the way these gregarious two-legged birds scampered and hopped to and from each other in frantic purpose.

"The most adorable creatures in the world," Regina said as she stepped closer to the glass. "They make you love them."

And pity them, like the other Penguins, I thought. I watched one waddle, white stomach protruding, to the edge of the ice. Hitting the water, the penguin shed his awkwardness and swam right up against the glass in a show of grace and elegance, his body a streamlined torpedo. *Maybe pity is the wrong sentiment.*

"They're perfection itself in the water," Regina said.

"Built for punishment, for survival under extreme conditions," I said, recalling some of the details I had read on the subject.

"Just like the other Penguins." Regina then whispered, "And like you. And me."

We stood in silence for a long time watching the creatures interact with each other, seeming to argue, talk, stroll, and slide around. Their red-lined beaks opened and closed in chatter.

"They're only missing a few glasses of tea," I said.

"And cookies, Doreen, don't forget cookies," Regina said, putting her arm around my shoulder.

"Albanian cookies."

Regina expelled a giggle, causing me to tumble into laughter, the kind that unhinges all the emotional cobwebs.

We left the brick house with smiles on our faces. The sun was beginning to set, reflecting off the slick skin of the seals frolicking in the outdoor pool. The fading spring light played peekaboo through the green leaves. We sat down on an outdoor bench. The zoo was quiet now, most young families already home preparing for dinner or taking baths by this hour.

I heard rustlings and turned to see Regina pull two glasses and a bottle of champagne out of her bag.

"Sorry it's a cheapo kind," Regina said, opening it. She poured the drink into the fluted glasses, passing me one.

Holding mine, I saw the bubbles dancing between my fingers.

"One day we'll see them in the wild," Regina said, referring to our plan to get to Antarctica. "But these are fabulous, for now." She raised her glass. "To the penguins, wherever they may be."

We clicked glasses. "To their continued survival," I toasted.

"Amen." Regina laughed.

Chapter 26

"**R**EGINA'S DEAD."

I heard the two-word phrase, but I couldn't absorb it. I extended my arm and looked at the phone receiver, certain that this was some dreadful mistake. Bringing the phone back to my ear, I said, "What are you talking about?"

There was a sigh on the other end. "I'm sorry. I was asked to make these calls," a woman said, her hard gulp audible. "Regina was in a plane crash." I realized the voice was that of Lizzie, the blonde receptionist who sat behind the giant bubblegum pink desk at Puff Cosmetics.

The news felt like shrapnel exploding inside my skull. I tried to get a handle on the subject. Regina had gone to Las Vegas for the annual cosmetics trade show. Regina had called me every day. Yesterday, she had excitedly informed me that she had been invited out to a Bel Air mansion for a party, something she would never pass up. She was scheduled to join her two Puff-founding bosses on their chartered private jet.

"Oh God," was all I could get out.

"The twin engine went down near Los Angeles, crashing into some fields," Lizzie said. "No survivors. That's all I know for now."

I felt the room begin to whirl, the kitchen sink coming at my head while the couch flew upside down toward the windows. I tried to steady myself against the kitchen counter, feeling for the stool nearby. A flash of nausea incapacitated my movements. Perspiration dripped from my hairline. My fingers lost their grip on the phone and it slithered down, twisting like a menacing eel around my legs.

Untangling myself, I turned to find the receiver once again. I reeled it in toward me, wanting to tell Lizzie she should call, at any hour day or night, with even a snippet of information, no matter how small. But instead, I abandoned the plan and trudged limply to the couch, plunging down.

Regina Astor is dead and not from cancer. What is the world coming to? My thoughts stopped flowing, as if logjammed somewhere in the cerebral tunnel leading to consciousness. I was almost glad about the blockage, fearing that otherwise I would begin screaming and slide into hysteria.

"Ma, what'ya doing?" I turned to see Jack holding Regina's son, Joey, in his arms. "You didn't hear him crying, so I took him out of the crib."

In a sudden flash, I remembered that Joey had been in the next room, napping in a portable crib. We were caring for him while Regina was on her Las Vegas trip; I had volunteered because I had nothing if not free time after retiring from my telecom post.

Jack's arms were tucked around Joey, as if it were natural for him to take care of a toddler. Joey balanced one hand on my son's hair, rubbing his eyes with the other one, sniffling. Joey's dark hair was plastered on one side of his head, making his big-cheeked face look asymmetric and somewhat comical.

"Think he needs changing," my son said, in a suggestive tone.

Forcing myself up from the couch, I pasted a smile on my lips. "Thanks, Jack. Sorry I didn't hear him." Extending both arms, I said I would take care of the diaper situation.

As soon as I felt Joey's squashy body against mine, the tears started to swell. My gaze followed Jack's legs as he headed back to his room; then I made my way in careful steps to my bedroom, where the dresser held diapers, creams, and undershirts ready for service. With no changing table in the house, I laid Joey on my bed, trying to deflect my mounting depression with the task of replacing his diaper. But the effort failed, for Joey's brown eyes with yellow flecks peered at me while he smiled, making despair speed through my nervous system.

Innocent Joey had no mother. He would never get to laugh himself silly with her, or witness her gentle manipulation of the world, or experience again her ferocious love. I seemed to hear a far-off voice saying, "Haven't we suffered enough?" I knew it was my father, Max. Despondency prowled through my heart. *Go away, Max*, I begged.

Picking up Joey—his scent of youth, of freshness, of promise, teasing my nostrils—I carried Regina's child into my son's room, asking him to watch over Joey for a few minutes. Jack reluctantly undertook the task.

Returning to my room, I sat down on the bed. I reached for the telephone to make some of the necessary calls. The dial-pad numbers looked like incomprehensible Chinese characters, and I couldn't bring any of the phone numbers to mind. My eyes shifted to the jade box located near the phone on the night table. My breathing became constricted, my lungs were having difficulty cycling oxygen through their chambers.

"How are you, Faith?" I heard my voice ask the jade box. "Heard what happened?" I brought my face within an inch of the top. "Your friend Regina is gone. Do you understand?" I threw myself backward on the coverlet, near the pillows, all fluffed and smelling of detergent with bleach.

"*What's wrong with this fucking world?*" I shouted.

My words ricocheted off the ceiling and back at me, pounding my head. The profanity made me feel lighter, somehow released. I suddenly understood the effect of a piquant four-letter word on Regina; it was invigorating, liberating, and cathartic.

"We are all out of our fucking minds," I whispered, the air almost completely sucked out of me as my fingers gnawed at the jade box. I lay listening to my breathing and the ticking of the alarm clock. The salty taste of tears dripped into my mouth.

Through the mist of sadness, I suddenly saw Tania near the window, her burlap covering whipping at the pane. My eyes searched for the other two. Aaron was cowering in the corner of the room, between the dresser and the wall. Coiled in a tight ball, he sucked on his thumb, not bringing his eyes to meet mine. I didn't blame him for avoiding me. A noise diverted my attention across the room, where Yankel was lying across a row of my old law books.

In that instant, it was as if a tiny spark had set off a ferocious wildfire in my psyche. I suddenly knew it was time to say good-bye.

While opening the top of the jade box, I motioned with my hand for Yankel to approach. Looking inside, I saw that Faith's ashes were heaped in a pile to one side, as if anticipating company. Yankel floated in my direction, his large eyes reflecting both sorrow and apprehension. I kissed his pale cheek while gently guiding him into place.

Next I caught sight of Tania as she sped off toward the closed bedroom door. "There's no escaping this time," I said, because alas, I understood that I now had ghosts of "my own," not those inherited from the lives of others.

As if reading my mind, Tania froze in her tracks, her hair swaying over her rigid, slight form. She crisscrossed her feet. Facing me, she smiled, then curtsied. She flew to me and wrapped her limbs around my waist. Releasing her grip, I brought her arm up to the light so as to see her forearm. I touched the tattooed A-2112 with my fingers before encouraging her too into the box.

From across the room, Aaron's weeping became louder. Knowing he was devastated, I walked over to the bookshelf, with jade box in hand. I stroked his back, spongy and curved, bringing my hand up to rub his face.

"It's been a long trauma—time for you to rest," I said, trying to alleviate his pain. "Others will carry on."

Removing his thumb from his mouth, he wiped some drops off his hollow cheek.

I brushed the back of his neck, and then prodded him to join the other spirits.

In one swift motion, I detached the golden key from its flip-side nest and locked the jade box, leaving the key in the lock.

Two days later, we stood at Beth El Cemetery lining the perimeter of an open pit, the dirt a hideous gray with truncated roots shooting out in random directions like snakes straining toward the topsoil. The sun was blasting with its rays, August strokes of fire. I felt as if I had been plunged into some kind of hell, my navy suit attracting even more heat, making my chest wet with perspiration.

I noticed most of the others in colors similarly incongruous with the season. Somberly clad Puff executives and employees were spread in loose configuration, interspersed among Regina's personal friends. Lizzie, the Puff receptionist, looking austere in her spiked heels and tight black business suit, eyes bloodshot and tissue hanging limp from her fingers, was standing beside Katherine van de Vrande in a charcoal gray pantsuit and sunglasses. Lulu was in a black dress, her beeper hooked onto her bag.

Except for her two pallbearer distant cousins, Regina had no other family representation. Her child, Joey, was at home with a babysitter. Regina's ex-husband, Marc Sandler, was absent because I had refused to notify him, reasoning that he had contracted into a negligible blip on her radar screen. He had relinquished any claim to Regina's life and to Joey long before. Regina's Aunt Agnes was incapable of making the trip from Sarasota, Parkinson's disease plaguing her frail body.

Jack's golden hair brushed up against my navy jacket, reminding me of his presence. I still felt conflicted about bringing him to the funeral, an event inherently unpleasant and even frightening for a nine-year-old. Nevertheless, he was there because I had concluded he needed to gain finality, so-called "closure," regarding Regina's passing, along with the rest of us.

My itchy eyes, hidden behind sunglasses, swept over the tombstones: the tall and squat, the elaborate and simple. All these lives once lived: day in and day out, eating meals, paying bills, attending school, struggling with heartache and joy. All now silenced, lying one beside the other in neat rows, like Jack's Lego building blocks, in this bucolic location not too distant from New Jersey's shopping malls and diners.

Cautiously I let my eyes drift to the stone closest to the excavated area. It read, "Phyllis Astor." Regina's mother. She had lived longer than Regina had, despite her having succumbed to cancer at the age of forty-nine. It dawned on me that in comparison, my mother held the longevity record; making it to the age of fifty-two suddenly appeared to qualify as a humongous feat.

Maybe Max was right—we've been lucky. I caught a glimpse of my father, slightly hunched over, sandwiched between Sam and Bea, the Penguin septuagenarian triplets. Bea's sprayed hair was thinning in patchy areas, and her face had deep crevices, particularly hugging her upper lip. My heart went out to them; more anguish heaped upon these people, who had lived through one of the greatest periods of human suffering.

There was a commotion. I saw Ty, Seth, and Regina's cousins, the four pallbearers, crouching in preparation to lower my friend to her final destination. The veined hands of the grave diggers grasped the sides of the coffin in order to steer it into the void.

"Stop," I said in a meek voice. But the activity continued without pause. *"Stop, now."* My voice was a few decibels louder.

"What's the matter?" Lulu whispered in my ear, while the other mourners around me began fidgeting in their places.

The multiple sets of eyes stung me through my damp clothes. "Hold on for one moment, please," I said.

The coffin stood frozen in midair. The murmurs of the attendants reverberated in my ears, growing until they sounded like a swill of bees. I hesitated and then stepped around the side of the casket, close to Seth. My fingers clutched the box in my jacket pocket; suddenly, I brought it out into the full light of the summer day. A sun streak flashed off the key protruding from the lock.

Looking down at the pine coffin, I considered, for a moment, opening its lid. But then realizing Regina wouldn't have wanted to be exposed in her simple white sheet garb *sans* makeup, I changed my mind, which brought the hint of a laugh to my lips. I knew I needed to respect Regina's vanity, even now.

Extending my hand, I positioned the jade box on top of the coffin and pressed my lips against the rough pine surface. I thought I heard Regina's familiar laugh. Removing the golden key, I clasped it tightly in my palm, straightened up, and nodded at Ty.

As I stepped away, the men resumed their activity. Closing my eyes to the sound of shovels scooping dirt, filling the open wound of Regina's eternal quarters, I whispered, "Good-bye, dearest ones. Take care of each other."

T HE BLADE SLICED THROUGH THE whiteness in a circular pattern. The sharp edge and its twin swung in tandem over the shiny surface. My eyes swept up from the skates to the number *3* emblazoned on the back of the jersey under the word *Rockwell*.

Jack was playing ice hockey, his team having made it to the semifinals at the Chelsea Piers sports complex. It was Sunday morning, and they were up against the powerhouses of Manhattan amateur ice hockey from the Upper East Side. Ty had been to most of Jack's other games, coming to practice often as well. But, for this particular game, Jack had invited his mother. As captain of his team, he had wanted me to see the new outfits donated by a father of one of his teammates and experience a game firsthand.

Later that afternoon we were going to celebrate at Max's apartment, regardless of the actual outcome of the hockey meet. My father had announced he was planning to honor the event with Hala's Rosenthal china. The blue and gold set had sat in the wasteland of the closet since the earthly departure of my mother.

The gathering was to serve as more than just a commemoration of Jack's athletic achievement. Indeed, it was to mark our belief that we were finally, hopefully, on the road to recovery. After all, it was February of 2002, and we had weathered enormous personal and collective tragedies.

For one thing, the telecommunications tsunami had come crashing down on the bullish stock markets at the start of the twenty-first century, leaving destruction of trillions of dollars in its wake. Although Ty had been correct in his predictions, he felt far from vindicated, suffering from anxiety, dark half moons hung like permanent museum exhibitions under his eyes. Then, just when I thought I saw a glimmer of promise that he might find his footing again, came September 11th.

On that day, Brad Barkow, Ty's former CFO, perished on the ninety-seventh floor of the World Trade Center's North Tower. For weeks, when Ty wasn't at the Ground Zero volunteer tents attending to firefighters and construction workers, he was sitting ashen-faced in front of the television.

I understood the pain and unspoken guilt Ty felt about Brad's fate. Several months after Ty had resigned, Brad, no longer content at JRW Communications without his boss, had moved to a lateral position with an investment house "scraping the sky high above Wall Street." His new firm lost more than three hundred employees on that day in 2001.

Ty wasn't the only family member left devastated in the aftermath of the terror. Max had also been wordless in his misery, while Sam repeatedly whimpered the words "September first." I knew he was referring to September 1, 1939, the day the Nazis had stormed into Poland, ushering in the horrors that annihilated their entire universe as they knew it then. The catastrophic day in New York had rekindled the trauma of their youth. They cried long and hard for themselves and their adopted land.

Those terrorist acts seemed to have unhinged the bolts once fastening Max's paradigms of fate and luck; it was evident something fundamental in his core had shifted. He was somehow more amenable to accepting the effects of uncontrollable inequities, like an old gnarled tree acquiescing to the forces of wind and rain. Maybe it was all in an effort to avoid snapping. Or maybe, it was simply accepting the long-denied premise that luck was not made, but merely *perceived*. Perhaps, if one believed as such, then, by definition, one *was* lucky.

I heard the beeps of the ringing phone. My fingers diving into my bag, I located the Nokia instrument and pressed the *talk* button, bringing it up to my ear.

"Mini, where's the snowsuit?" Ty's voice crackled through the receiver.

"In the top drawer, left one, of the dresser," I answered. Joey's dresser, compact and in cobalt blue, sat adjacent to Jack's computer table. The two boys now shared a room. "Make sure you take an extra hat, the multicolored one, as well."

"Okay, got it. I'm going to run some errands and then we'll meet you at Max's," Ty said in a rushed tone, before we bid each other good-bye.

After redepositing the cell phone, I thought about the upcoming luncheon. Ty and Joey were meeting us at my father's Upper West Side apartment for the celebration of new beginnings. As a family we had expanded to envelop Joey, a fresh configuration bringing bittersweet joy to my heart and a smile to Max's craggy face. The patriarch now had a virile team by his side. I guessed he had come to terms with the fact that this was the closest he would ever get to more descendants. I was certain Max reasoned that Joey was of the same faith and his mother had been like a second child to him and to Hala.

In Joey, Jack would have a lifelong companion, alternatively annoying and comforting, while Ty had "his boys" with whom to share his sports and playfulness. And, I had my enlarged household composed of lovable men, although the youngest had admittedly pledged the fraternity under heart-wrenching circumstances. It could never be a perfect fait accompli, for I missed Regina every day of my life and my heart bled for Joey's loss as well.

Recently, Ty had been taking incremental steps on the path of professional rejuvenation, reminiscent of the first green patches of grass sprouting at the close of winter. The handsome onetime banker, with more gray strands now appearing in his hair, was beginning to get involved in new business projects and was slotted to coach ice hockey next year. He was even contemplating penning a book on the telecom industry's flameout.

As for me, teaching a prelaw course at a local community college, I felt grateful for the flexible hours and, more so, for the opportunity to interact with optimistic and impressionable minds. Hopefully, that would serve as remedy for my mental weariness. Gale winds still intermittently pounded at my battered soul. Perhaps the exuberance of the students would somehow cause a rainbow to unfurl in the heavens to soothe my eyes.

I envisioned Max's luncheon table set with crystal glasses and the Rosenthal china, Sam and Aunt Bea beaming at my sons, while the antique clock chimed on the fireplace mantle. My father would be serving Cherry Heering while I assisted in dishing out grilled chicken and potatoes. Lulu, blonde hair in a French braid, would be chatting with my uncle, Sam, while her husband would be conversing with Ty.

Lulu was coming with her *husband*, Seth Rabiner. The thought still struck me as unfathomable. Every time I pondered the development, I reached for the phone wanting desperately to hear Regina rejoice in the news. Seth and Lulu had become romantically involved while caring for the patients, Regina and Jack. All my matchmaking attempts throughout our younger years had failed to bear fruit, but, in the end, unassisted by meddling friends, it had happened.

In hindsight, I felt foolish that I had missed the telltale signs. It should have been obvious by the way my two doctor friends interacted in the hospital, but my mind then had been occupied with existential issues. The kiss I witnessed between Seth and Lulu in my kitchen during the gathering at our apartment after Regina's funeral caught me off-guard, actually dumbfounded.

Now they were living in Seth's apartment, spruced up with some feminine accents. Seth's crumpled façade seemed somehow enlivened by a cheerier, glossier veneer. Lulu finally had a partner undaunted by her seriousness and her background. They were expecting a baby girl in May. Her name was to be Gina for Regina.

Tears came to my eyes as a vision looped through my neural organ. Regina' lips framed her white teeth in a smile. She was seated beside Faith and Hala, the three in the midst of a poker game with bubblegum pink chips stacked in front and frosted Bellini martinis at each elbow.

"My namesake. How fucking fabulous is that, girls?" Regina's throaty laugh filled the air.

Couldn't have phrased it better myself, I thought.

For a seemingly long time, I watched the scene as if it were a movie. My eyes absorbed the movements—Regina with her crimson lips jabbering away as she dealt the cards. After Faith mouthed something, Regina looked at her, her smile singing as always. Hala grinned as she swept up her hand of cards. They all looked radiant, content, blissful. For an instant I envied them, hungering to join them. But then I realized my place was here, on earth. For now.

Averting my eyes, I played with my necklace, rubbing the tiny, jagged key dangling at its end. It had rested against my chest since the day of Regina's funeral, serving as a reminder, as my amulet.

The winter sun illuminated the large rink and adjacent rows of benches dotted with spectators, mainly parents and siblings of the hockey contenders. Watching the adolescents again as they whisked over the frozen surface, I located number 3 hunched forward as he skated, stick positioned for striking at the little black puck. His blades furrowed the ice while wind whipped at his new uniform. As he turned, his feet crisscrossing each other in graceful dance, his young torso rotated in my direction. I had to admit the new black-and-white outfits were fashionable, crisp-looking, and lent an air of professionalism to the previously ragtag team.

The words imprinted on their fronts were the most spectacular. The jerseys read, "Downtown Penguins." The words delighted me. The loveliest penguins in the world, unburdened by the demons of history, soaring through life on flipperlike wings, buoyed by freedom from hatred, oppression, and prejudice.

I reflected on the altered state of my own penguin world. For one thing, with the passage of years I had grown more appreciative of my Penguin pedigree, more readily attributing some of my nuanced insightfulness to it.

And, in line with Faith's prophetic words, I had mustered the courage to replace my demons. Alas, the term of Tania, Yankel, and Aaron had expired. I had ghosts of my own now. The coming years, however many they might be, would be spent with Regina,

Faith, and Hala alongside, *my legacy spirits.* I was more than sure they were capable of doing the job from here.

The shriek of the referee's whistle jolted me out of my reverie. Looking up I saw players, two from each team, in a headlocked position, fists pounding at each other, sticks swinging wildly, chopping the air around them. Other players skated up to try to disengage the fighters, but instead they all ended up in a heap with arms flailing and helmets falling off and skidding on the ice. The shrill whistles continued until the referees in striped uniforms managed to claw the players apart.

I was about to turn my eyes away. But suddenly the warring players parted, revealing Jack as one of them. Tucking his helmet under his arm, Jack skated a few feet around one of the referees to retrieve his stick. As he raised his head he scanned the bleachers, and finding me, he winked. The Rockwell trademark. The fast one-eyed maneuver that bound them—one of the links in their genetic chain.

Once appalling and puzzling, the hereditary connection of the three generations of Rockwells now filled me with wonderment. Faith and Ty, descendants of a bitter Penguin hater, could indeed be nurturing, compassionate, and beautiful. The riddle brought me to yet another one: the genetics of the Lowes. After all, the solitary descendant of two New York Penguins married a North Dakotan *shaigets* and produced a magnificent, well-adjusted young man who straddled his paradoxical heredity with ease.

Again, I reminded myself that genetics was complex and creative, producing unpredictable results, sometimes fantastic ones. A whimsical process splashing color, vibrant and diverse, upon the world *like ten thousand daffodils tossing their heads in sprightly dance.*

More of Wordsworth's poetic words popped into my mind. I whispered the last verse of "Daffodils,"

> *For oft, when on my couch I lie*
> *In vacant or in pensive mood,*
> *They flash upon that inward eye*
> *Which is the bliss of solitude;*
> *And then my heart with pleasure fills,*
> *And dances with the daffodils.*

I OWE MY DEEP APPRECIATION AND gratitude to all those people who over the years encouraged me to put my storytelling in writing, and:

*   to Sally Arteseros for editing
*   to Ray Jacobs for cheerleading
*   to Dr. Mark for being my "fairy godmother"
*   to Mary Yost for encouragement
*   to my husband and sons for inspiration and pride and good material
*   to my friends who were my early readers and critics
*   to those who were forced into Auschwitz and miraculously came out again; and then managed, against all odds, to live full lives of laughter and success despite the tremendous sorrow.

Acknowledgments